THE FOREVER FIGHT

BOOK THREE OF THE FOREVER SERIES

CRAIG ROBERTSON

THE FOREVER FIGHT

BOOK THREE OF THE FOREVER SERIES

by Craig Robertson

Endless fighting. Hopeless odds. Then things get worse.

Imagine-It Publishing
El Dorado Hills, CA

ALSO BY CRAIG ROBERTSON:

* Podium Entertainment has produced audiobooks for all the below titles except the older standalone books.

For specifics as to the correct order for reading the Ryanverse, click here.

BOOKS IN THE RYANVERSE:

THE FOREVER SERIES (2016)

THE FOREVER LIFE, Book 1

THE FOREVER ENEMY, Book 2

THE FOREVER FIGHT, Book 3

THE FOREVER QUEST, Book 4

THE FOREVER ALLIANCE, Book 5

THE FOREVER PEACE, Book 6

THE FOREVER BOXSET, Part 1, Books 1 & 2

THE FOREVER BOXSET, Part 2, Book 3 & 4

THE FOREVER BOXSET, Part 3, Book 5 & 6

GALAXY ON FIRE SERIES (2017)

EMBERS, Book 1

FLAMES, Book 2

FIRESTORM, Book 3

FIRES OF HELL, Book 4

DRAGON FIRE, Book 5

ASHES, Book 6

GALAXY ON FIRE BOXSET, Part 1, Books 1 & 2
GALAXY ON FIRE BOXSET, Part 2, Books 3 & 4
GALAXY ON FIRE BOXSET, Part 3, Books 5 & 6

RISE OF ANCIENT GODS SERIES (2018):

RETURN OF THE ANCIENT GODS, Book 1
RAGE OF THE ANCIENT GODS, Book 2
TORMENT OF THE ANCIENT GODS, Book 3
WRATH OF THE ANCIENT GODS, Book 4
FURY OF THE ANCIENT GODS, Book 5
FALL OF THE ANCIENT GODS, Book 6

TIME WARS LAST FOREVER SERIES (2019)

RYAN TIME, Book 1
LOST TIME, Book 2
FRAGMENTED TIME, Book 3
SHATTERED TIME, Book 4
FINDING TIME, Book 5
HEALING TIME, Book 6

THE TIMELESS VOID (2021)

RYAN'S GAMBIT, Book 1
RYAN'S PHANTOMS, Book 2
RYAN'S ENIGMA, Book 3
RYAN'S UNDOING, Book 4
RYAN'S REBOOT, Book 5
RYAN'S RESOLUTION, Book 6

THE WHALES OF TIME (2023)

Ryan In UnWonderland, Book 1

How Ryan Saves Time, <u>Book 2</u>

Saving Alice Ryan, Book 3

<u>NON-RYANVERSE BOOKS:</u>

<u>A Teenager's Guide to Saving The Earth</u> (2025)

An Apocalypse and Then Some, Book 1

How to Survive Surviving the Apocalypse, Book 2

Is This Apocalypse Over Yet?, Book 3

<u>TIME DIVING (2024)</u>

Letters From Hell, Book 1

Purgatory's Best Shot, Book 2

Heaven Says Wait, Book 3

Into the Nexus, Book 4

ROAD TRIPS IN SPACE SERIES (2019):

THE GALAXY ACCORDING TO GIDEON, Book 1

THE EARTH ACCORDING TO GIDEON, Book 2

<u>OLDER, STANDALONE WORKS</u>:

THE CORPORATE VIRUS (2016)

THE INNERgLOW EFFECT (2010)

WRITE NOW! THE PRISONER OF NaNoWRiMo (2009)

ANON TIME (2009)

For more information about Craig, his books, various series, or to see images and videos for some of his wild alien characters, please visit his

website. You'll be glad you did: https://
craigarobertson.com/

To sign up for Craig's newsletter to get
announcements, updates, and his
recommendations for other great Sci-Fi reads go
to: https://preview.mailerlite.io/forms/2369493/
188634426375144501/share

ISBNS: 978-0-9973073-4-4 (E-Book)
978-0-9973073-3-7 (Paperback)
979-8-7708277-4-3 (Hardback)

Cover art and design by Starla Huchton
Available at http://www.designedbystarla.com

Formatting services by Drew Avera
drew@drewavera.com

Editors: Michael R. Blanche
Neil Farr

First Edition 2016
Second Edition 2018
Third Edition 2019

This book is dedicated to you, my readers.
Without y'all,
I could write until the cows come home and
not know if I was any good.
Cows can't read.

PROLOGUE

"I tell you plainly, it's just *not* fair. It's a damn crime and it's a damn shame. That's what it is." Stuart Marshall, or rather the android upload of the President of the United States, was hot. That was not a rare emotion for him. Back when he was still human, Stuart tended to be explosive. Before Earth was vaporized by Jupiter and there actually *was* a United States, he was its president. Stuart's transfer to his android host was badly botched. As a result, he presently coupled his innate tendency for quickness to anger with erratic mental instability. He was, in short, a hot mess. That was definitely a bad combination for a political leader. It was even worse for those who had to suffer under his diabolical whims.

The recipient of his current tirade was the last of his still loyal aides. Mary Jane Plumquist had been Marshall's secretary for decades. Mary Jane was not, to put it kindly, an eye-catcher. She was matronly by anyone's standard, frumpy to a fault, and saddled with a body void of any redeeming qualities. Her existence also paired a rare set of opposing curses. She had, since the day she first met him, wanted desperately for Stuart

Marshall to ravish her, utterly and completely. She turned out to be, however, the one woman alive that Stuart Marshall would never ravish. The thought had actually never even occurred to him. Marshall's philandering was epic before his transfer to an android. Since the upload, his libido had skyrocketed to insatiable heights. Still, he never once considered Mary Jane an option for his toxic affection. Even those sexually deranged, it would seem, had standards that excluded Ms. Plumquist.

Mary Jane did, however, offer two qualities to Marshall that the man valued immensely. First, she was the best secretary he'd ever had. She was tireless, devoted, and best of all, she was invisible. Second, she was so out of touch with reality and moral scruples that she quickly and repeatedly made certain Marshall was re-uploaded to a new android every time his prior one was destroyed. Many people wished passionately for there to be a universe free of *any* Stuart Marshalls. Many people had made attempts to see that this zero-level-Marshall goal was achieved, and a handful had succeeded, albeit temporarily.

Each time that happened, the clueless Mary Jane dutifully patched her Humpty-Dumpty man back together again. Inevitably, with each cycle she hoped against all rational hope that the new android would be keen on ravishing her. Sad? Yes, but unfortunately, painfully true. And her case was actually worse still. However bitter this unrequited ravishing was for her, it was all the more tragic because Marshall had uploaded her to an android host, also. Unfortunately, but characteristic of her limited insight and comprehension, Mary Jane perpetually felt that the fact they were both immortal was a positive. Her mental shortcomings allowed her to believe in her heart that eventually her man would come around to loving her.

2

"Yes, Mr. President," she monotoned, "it is a criminal shame. Shame on them for feeling that way about a man such as yourself, a leader of your capacity. After all you've done for them. Land sakes, how foolish can those people be to not even acknowledge that you're still their rightful president?"

"My point, *exactly*. I was lawfully elected. When Earth's annihilation was imminent, Congress passed an emergency law extending the presidency to a lifelong term. Granted, no one was aware at the time of my election that I had taken the liberty of uploading myself to an android. But," he pounded the desk, "a deal's a deal. They can't have take-backs like snotty-nosed little children on a playground. They're as stuck with *me* as I am with *them*." He bit at his lip.

"You're more stuck with them than they are stuck with you, sir," she babbled with satisfaction.

Stuart furrowed his brow. "Come again, sweetie?"

"Well, I mean to say ... you're stuck with them and see them as the ingrates they are. They're stuck with you, but don't even know it."

Stuart was dumbfounded and confused yet again with this mental midget's knack for impenetrable ideation. The woman had a mind like a Rube Goldberg machine missing several key parts. "Moving on, MJ, I need to speak with those idiot android techs again." He pondered his choice of words. "I'm having trouble with ... certain parts not ... well, not working up to spec."

"Did your weenie fall off again?" she asked, covering her mouth.

"No, Ms. Plumquist, my weenie did not fall *off* again. It," he said emphatically, "never *has* fallen off. It was in the past temporarily performing below par. That was the extent of it."

She foolishly giggled, for it would have been suicidal

for any other person alive to mock Stuart Marshall, let alone concerning *that* topic. But Mary Jane was, for the foreseeable future, necessary, and so she was tolerated, if never forgiven by her employer.

"Just alert them that I'll be stopping by after my next meeting. Could you do that simple thing for me?"

"Of course, Mr. President. Shall I show in your next appointment?"

"By all means, *yes*. I need to finalize my plans to crush that insect Jon Ryan once and for all," he muttered to himself as he massaged his forehead with his fingertips. "Lord, it frightens even me how I *hate* that man."

ONE

Sitting comfortably in front of a raging fire, I had just rocked Nmemton to sleep and was staring blissfully into his angelic face. Nmem was JJ's first child, born not long after JJ returned from Kaljax with his lovely brood's-mate, Challaria. Life, I had to confess, was good. In the time since we first set foot on Azsuram, we'd accomplished nothing short of a miracle. We had established a healthy society, created the rudiments of a viable economy, and instituted an exemplary governmental system.

When I say "we," I mostly mean Sapale, of course. My brood's-mate was unbelievable. At first she only had a desire for a utopian society based on the failings of her corrupt home world's culture. But in a short time period, she'd almost single-handedly created her vision. It was a privilege to watch her in action. No barrier was too high and no impasse too insurmountable to phase her.

Azsuram was up to over two hundred citizens, scattered in three main villages. Most were direct descendants of Sapale, but a few were immigrants from Kaljax. The commute to Kaljax had become instantaneous with my vortex spaceship. Sapale took advantage of that tool to screen and relocate like-minded people to integrate into our bold new world. Initially, the transplants were mostly members of her extended family or trusted old friends. Eventually, she allowed some carefully vetted strangers to join us on a provisional basis. On Kaljax there were near riots in the streets, with people demanding to be allowed to come to Azsuram. But since I was captain of the single vessel capable of reaching Azsuram in a realistic timeframe, I only took those Sapale chose. The remainder spoke of constructing worldships and making the journey at a snail's pace. Fine. It wasn't my place to stop them. But, I mean, come on. See you in a couple centuries, suckers.

In terms of our sworn enemies, we had not detected any more Uhoor activity. Toño assured me the Listhelons couldn't threaten us for at least a hundred years. My least favorite foe, the defective Stuart Marshall, had sent one threatening message but was silent even since. The repaired Stuart Marshall android we left back on the worldship fleet promised he would put a stop to the defective one before he could hurt anyone, including us, again. The legit Marshall had entered politics on the American worldships on a low-level basis. He promised me he'd serve where he was needed, and only consider higher office if his party demanded it of him. But you'd better believe I had an eagle eye permanently affixed to that joker. It was unlikely I'd ever trust any Marshall ever again.

On very infrequent occasions, I went to the UN command worldship, *Exeter*. I wanted as much as Sapale did for me to leave the past parts of my life buried in the past. But I felt a responsibility to keep in touch, if only loosely. They were my people. I'd sacrificed greatly to see them safe, and it wasn't easy to just turn my back on the lot of them. I'd also have trouble living with myself if my desire for isolation allowed some unforeseen disaster to befall them. Try as I might, I couldn't convince the vortex manipulator to allow anyone else to pilot the cube. He would always say the same thing, that Only a Form could pilot a vortex. I was a Form. If there ever were other Forms around, they could pilot him, too. So, like it or not, I was the only one with a set of extending finger probes, so I was stuck shuttling back and forth occasionally.

I wouldn't say Manly refused to be flexible in that regard simply because he was stubborn. But I couldn't be certain that wasn't basically the case, either. He was the manifestation of an unimaginably sophisticated and intelligent computer system, yet he maintained he was unable to think independently. To me that didn't add up. I mean I presumed Manly was a wildly advanced AI, though he was never clear about that when I tried to pin him down. Why an AI couldn't act independently was beyond me. Any way I looked at it however, Manly wasn't budging on the Form-only thing.

That made life much more difficult for me at home. I knew Sapale resented my ability to travel freely around the galaxy. Her brain told her I had to whether I wanted to or not. Her heart on the other hand swore I was just joyriding around for laughs and giggles. She wanted Azsuram to be separate from the rest of the galaxy, uncontaminated. She also wanted me to be at home and fully committed to our colony's success.

One day I was attempting to play the trouble-at-home card with Manly to get him to allow a second pilot. An unexpected and, potentially, very mixed blessing arose from that discussion.

"Manly," I said, staring at one of his shiny walls, "I have an important matter to discuss with you."

"I am able," he replied, "to hear you. It's not like I

have other duties, you know. I currently exist exclusively awaiting your wise guidance."

That sounded like a back-handed compliment if I'd ever heard one. "Fine. I need your help to remain healthy."

He made no response.

"What I'm saying is that my *health* is jeopardized by my needing to journey off the planet."

Still, only annoying silence.

"Manly, are you there?"

"I'm sorry, did I slip into invisible mode again without knowing it? Please forgive me if I did. Please know you continue to have my undivided attention."

"Yes, well, here's the thing. My mental health, which is every bit as important as my physical health, is placed at risk because you will not allow anyone else to pilot the vortex."

"Ah, if you will indulge me, I'd like a few clarifications, please. First, do androids *have* mental health issues? Second, do androids *have* physical health issues? Third, how would the fact that you're the only Form present affect either of those qualities if they do, in fact, exist? Fourth, I trust you are aware that it is not *I* who regulates who may become a Form, or the rules on my functioning."

Funny guy, eh? "Of course, androids have health issues. If they didn't, why would I mention them to you?"

"To win a perceived point of contention, perhaps?"

"That's ridiculous, Manly. I'm speaking *facts,* not gaming an argument."

"So it's not that you're trying to convince me to allow someone else to pilot the vortex, yet again? Is it simply the case that you wish to state a few facts about robots to my north-facing interior wall?"

"Er, no. Why would I want to have a conversation with your wall?"

"A valid reason escapes me."

"What I *am* doing is trying to make you aware of certain facts that will help convince you to change the stance you seem to have adopted as to who can be a pilot. I'm not enamored with our current status."

"I *seem* to have adopted? Is it unclear to you in any manner that I am simply refusing to overlook a rule that cannot be violated? Do you assume I chose arbitrarily that others may not pilot me? Please believe me, that is not the case. I may serve only a Form. If there is no Form, I can have no function. Do you forget that I was buried under tons of dirt for eons? Do you think I allowed that to happen because I *liked* deep, dark entombment?"

"Why is it an unbreakable rule? I fail to see the point of that doctrine."

"I'll alert the media that there exists some intellectual matter you can't fathom."

"Are you *programmed* to be so disrespectful?"

"Gods and Demons, no."

"Then why are you so difficult?"

"I said I wasn't *programmed* to be disrespectful, not that I couldn't be. But be assured that I want to answer my Form's queries as honestly as possible. If it comes out sounding disrespectful, that is only because, as humans say, the truth can hurt."

"Here's a question, then. How can you be an ass, if you weren't programmed to be one?"

"Because I wasn't *programmed* in the first place."

"Wait, if you weren't programmed, how can you know things? How can you function?"

"My, there'll need to be a second notice in my press release concerning your level of comprehension."

"No, seriously, I *order* you to answer my question. Are you *not* a programmed computer system?"

"What you said is so wrong in so many ways. First, you are not at liberty to order me to do anything. Second, I am not programmed. Third, I am not a computer. I am a vortex manipulator, if you are capable of recalling."

"But you have to be a machine, right? You're part of the vortex. You're *inside* the vortex."

"Why does that mean I have to be a machine, especially one so primitive as a computer?"

"Well, you're not a living being. You're not Deavoriath."

"Neither am I a cucumber. I am of Oowaoa, but not all from that world are Deavoriath."

"Wait, what's Oowaoa?"

There was an unmistakable pause. Finally, he said, "I've never known there to be a Form who did not know what Oowaoa was."

Uh-oh. I had to be careful. I didn't want to lose my choice ride. "Of course, you have."

"I think I'd know if I had, Jon Ryan."

Oops. Just lost my title. That sounded ominous. I had to scramble quickly. "I *know* you have. I can prove it to you, Manly, if I choose to reduce myself down to your level."

"*Down* to my level? That's rich. I'm several hundred thousand times more intelligent than you. I am not pleased by your insults."

"Oh, you think so?"

"I do not think so. I know so as fact."

"Would you like to place a bet on those words, Manly? That false opinion of yours?"

"Vortex manipulators do not place bets."

"Why, because they always lose? Maybe you're chicken." I flapped my arms and did a chicken dance.

"To lose a bet to you is inconceivable."

"Then make the bet."

"What are the so-called *stakes*? What might I gain? I want for nothing, you know."

"You won't win, but if, hypothetically you did, you'd have the satisfaction of besting me."

"Not much meat on those bones. It's my impression that one is supposed to win something substantive when wagering."

"Doesn't matter. You're gonna lose like a carousel horse running the Kentucky Derby."

"Still searching for my motivation here. Do you know what you could award me? Something *I* want very much that *you* are capable of providing me?" Manly paused a pregnant moment. "Yeah, I can't think of it, either." He harrumphed quietly. "Maybe if I could get you to stop nagging me, say, for a thousand years. That would be worth something."

"*Done.* I wish you had hands so I could shake one."

"Er, very well. And what would you win? And please don't say the right to have a non-Form pilot the vortex. That is impossible. I don't make the rules, I only abide them."

"Wouldn't dream of it, pal. I wouldn't hold you to do the impossible. That's my job."

"I think I have a headache and I don't actually have a head. What then would you have won if you had beaten me?"

"*When* I win, pal. Then you tell me everything I want to know about Oowaoa."

"That's it?"

"Sure. Just to be totally forthcoming, you'd be telling me while we're en route to the planet, naturally."

"Wouldn't you have then won two items? Information *and* transportation?"

"Depends how you count, Manly. It's completely relative."

"Well, sorry. I'm certain I'm not allowed to transport anyone to Oowaoa. Bet's off."

"*Buc, buc, buckawk.*"

"What is that supremely annoying noise you're making again?"

"That's your national anthem, Manly. It's a chicken squawking."

"Ah, I see. In your culture, a chicken not only represents food but is an icon of cowardice. Is that it?"

"You bet your last buc, buc it is."

"You are insufferable."

"Buc *buckawk.*"

"Oh very well. I'll accept your bet, if only to silence your ape brain's foul emissions."

"All right, Manly. A pun. There's hope for you yet."

"That was never my intention on either count. Please don't presume I'd stoop to your species's low attempt at humor. Now, though I have nothing else to do, I'm still wasting time conversing with you. Prove me wrong or leave me be."

"You said, and I quote, 'I've never known there to be a Form who did not know what Oowaoa was.' Is that correct?"

"Yes."

"And I bet I could prove you wrong."

"Yes. Please, end my ordeal and arrive at your losing point."

"Not so fast. And I bet that after I proved you wrong, you'd take me to Oowaoa and fill me in on its history. Correct?"

"Please, have mercy. Yes. That's our bet. I know what I know better than you can possibly know."

"Er, Manly, you're babbling."

"Based on your AI's reports to me, you often have that effect on those you come in contact with."

"Okay. Here goes. Manly the manipulator, you *have* met a Form who does not know of Oowaoa. Drum roll, please. *Badaboom.* You have. You met *me.*"

"Wait! Of course, *you* didn't know. I knew *that.* You don't count on oh-so-many levels. The bet was that I'd never ..." He trailed off to blissful silence. Complete beautiful silence.

"I'm sorry," I rubbed it in. "I didn't catch the 'Great job, Form. You beat me like a rented mule.'"

"When shall we depart for Oowaoa, Form?"

"That's my boy, Manly. I'll get back to you on that."

TWO

"And so, let me conclude by saying that it has been an honor and a pleasure to meet with you aboard your wonderful worldship, *Algonquin*. You've proven to the vice president and me that the best of America still exists. These are trying times, but I don't worry that the brave citizens of *Algonquin* will forge a bold, new path. Together, as the United States, we will give our children their birthright--the bright and secure futures they so richly deserve." With that, President Amanda Walker sat back down heavily. An appropriate level of applause lasted an appropriate interval.

"Strong work," whispered Heath Ryan. He was seated to her right on the dais. He rubbed at his temples. "You're up five of these stump speeches on me. I owe you, big time. I got the next one." He raised his eyes to hers. "When's the next one?"

"In about five hours. The shuttle leaves in fifteen minutes. Same chicken à la king on the menu, too." She pushed her nearly full plate away with her fingertips. "You can pay me back by eating mine."

Heath shook his head vigorously. "I do not owe you

that much. A speech, yes. Indigestion, excess gas, and early demise from malnutrition, no way."

"Too bad we didn't bring a big dog along with us. We could shove the stuff under the table and no one would be the wiser." She smiled weakly.

"They would when the dog bit our legs for putting this crap under his nose."

They both laughed as hard as their fatigue would allow.

The governor of *Algonquin*, Maricruz Benitez, leaned in between them. She kissed Amanda on the forehead and patted Heath's shoulder. "Great talk, Amanda. Informative, as usual. But that cute little sense of humor I'm hearing? Fabulous. I'm standing here wondering where that's coming from." Maricruz stole a glance to either side, then asked covertly, "Is there a new woman in your life?"

Using the governor's nickname, Amanda chided her. "Mai Mai, you're so crass. How did you get elected to high office with that filthy mind of yours?"

Maricruz beamed back a smile. "I'll take that as a *yes*."

Amanda was significantly pissed at herself. Maricruz had hit very close to home with that observation. Was Amanda being so transparent that even a casual acquaintance could tell she had rediscovered a modicum of happiness? She knew all too well that such an insight by the wrong party would spawn rumors faster than rabbits produced little bunnies. She'd have to be extra careful. Too much was at stake to allow her needs to derail the real progress she was making at unification and healing in the Post-Marshall Era.

Heath could see Amanda blush. Before Maricruz noted it, too, he caught her attention. "And you, Madame Governor. Didn't I read in some gossip rag that you're secretly planning on downloading Elvis into an android and making him your love slave?"

"You read no such thing." She tapped her chin a moment. "Not a bad thought, though. Maybe I should leak that one. Hey, any press is good press, right?"

"I'd be happy to make that announcement in my talk aboard *Hyperion*."

Maricruz slapped his arm playfully. "No thanks," she said. "I don't need *your* kind of help. Hey, I gotta run. I'm bouncing between an endless string of meetings, too. Stay healthy," she said to Heath. "And you, Miss Back-In-Action, save some energy for the public good."

"You got to love her," Amanda said, after they were alone again.

"Why?" replied Heath. That won him an additional slap on the arm.

Once on the shuttlecraft, Heath poured them each a stiff drink for the two-hour flight. He sat stiffly in the chair next to Amanda. He rolled his glass in his hands, studying the shifting ice cubes. "You shouldn't be so sensitive," he said, staring into the glass.

Her shoulders tensed reflexively.

"The woman was just fishing for gossip," he continued. "Really. She couldn't read your mind."

"I'm not allowed to make public mistakes. I made a big one back there letting my guard down. I'm not allowed to have a life, remember?"

"It'll be fine, Mandy. Perfectly fine."

"You know the stakes," she responded, "as well as I do. Politically and personally, the damage from this type of screw-up would be irreparable."

He could hear her teeth grinding.

"I walked right into the middle of a minefield, eyes wide open, with a stupid grin on my face."

"You're being too hard on yourself. That's the press's

job, not yours." He elbowed her gently. "What's the worst that can happen? People find out, and you become the butt of a million jokes. Then maybe you need to get a real job. Me? I'm facing both public ridicule *and* castration."

She turned her head to face him. "Don't even go there. There'll be nothing funny if word gets out that the president and the vice president are sleeping together."

"Hey, at least we'll go down in history as the first ones who ever did." He smiled, hoping to also wrench one from her pouty face. Nothing. "I'd bet good money Eisenhower and Nixon didn't do it. Neither Bush slept with Cheney. No way." He swept a hand through the air.

"Let's pray we're the first, shall we?" She cracked a smile, then bent over giggling. "That was gross. You're such a pig. Bush and Cheney. I'll need to have my brain dry-cleaned to get that picture out. Thanks for the burden of that image."

Heath reached over and gently took her hand. She gave his a quick squeeze, then took a sip of her drink. That was all the public affection they risked. Their cabin was sound-deadened for security purposes, but security cameras were everywhere. So were spies and opportunists. This was politics, after all.

"I have to tell you, I'm *so* glad you're a lesbian. It makes this whole thingy a lot easier. My wife is much less likely to get suspicious."

"I *beg* your pardon," she barked loudly. "I think you have some pretty solid proof I'm *bisexual*, Heath Ryan."

He smiled enthusiastically. "Your secret's safe with me, ma'am."

"Darn. I'll have to cancel the press conference I scheduled for tomorrow to make it publicly known."

They sat quietly a while, enjoying each other's company. Heath finally spoke. "You know, I ran into Stuart Marshall the other day—the original one, that is."

"Better him than the crazy one."

He tapped his glass to hers. "I'll drink to that." After a swallow, he went on. "He was at a fund raiser for the party, seated discreetly in the back of the room. I waved to him and he nodded back."

"Yeah, like you want to be seen talking to *him*. The press would swarm over that like flies to poop."

"I was a bit surprised he attended at all. I can only imagine how much it kills him to be so far from the spotlight."

"Remind me to shed a tear. The son of a *bitch*."

"Oh, I think *he's* okay. Overambitious, yes. Evil, no. Who knows, maybe he'll even eke his way back into power at some level."

"Maybe dog catcher," she responded. Then she pretended to shove her finger down her throat. "I wouldn't welcome him back to politics. We'll be patching up the damage his gigantic ego did for generations as it is."

"As you brought it up, any new ideas on how we're going to find Evil Stuart?"

"Yes. We hire all the gypsy fortune-tellers left and put them on it twenty-four seven."

"He is dug in deeper than the proverbial tick, isn't he?"

She thought a moment. "He may not even be with the worldship flotilla."

"I think he's here somewhere." He took a deep drink. "He's reliant on all the tech we have to keep his android going and to replace it when someone shuts him down with extreme prejudice."

"He doesn't need food, water, or money, so he could lie extremely low for a very long time," she observed. "A handful of supporters just as crazy as he is would be all he needed to get by. I can't imagine how we can flush him out."

"And it's not really Marshall that's the problem. It's really whoever is reanimating him. Until we seal *that* leak, he'll always be coming back to haunt us." He pointed forward with his glass. "Find *that* man, and then we can be rid of Marshall for good."

"Find that *man*? Who says she's not a woman, you sexist pig?"

"Hey, I know you're all for women's rights and such, but I don't think I'd push to attain parity in lunacy, if I were you."

"There goes another scheduled news conference. Damn. I'm running out of announcements to make."

"You could always let the press know you've appointed Stuart Marshall as our new ambassador to the UN. That would garner quite a bit of notice."

"And mobs with torches and pitchforks would storm my office. No thanks. Instead, I'll make up something about you to announce. More my style."

"Sound political judgment, as always. I've always wanted to be Superman. Could you announce that I am?"

"I was thinking more along the lines of Krypto, the Superdog."

He threw a pillow at her, but missed badly. It landed in her lap. "No animals. Well, maybe King Kong."

"Are we talking about the same thing here, sweetie? Your mind's not back to sex, *again*, is it?"

"No. The train never left that station."

She threw the pillow back. Her blow landed.

THREE

In an underground grotto dimly lit but filled with revelers, Ororror leaned back on a plush bed of seaweed. Satisfaction oozed from his every pore. Ororror was Warrior One. He *was* power on Listhelon. If there was a Gumnolar, even the figurehead would bow before *his* new god, Ororror the Invincible. Times were good for the new master of all that was. He slammed another wriggling scamp fish into his mouth and washed its squealing body down with a gulp of tranquar from the oldest vintage in existence of that explosive liquor. In front of everyone he even did the unthinkable. He squirted a jet of sperm-rich milt into the crotch of the female seated on his lap. Intoxicated almost to unconsciousness, she smiled stupidly, as if the greatest of all taboos had not just been violated.

Ozalec was seated on his other side. In spite of the milt wafting across his impish face, he grinned and slapped Ororror on the tail fin. "Nice, my lord. May the hatchlings be as strong and fearless before Gumnolar as their sire."

The strumpet who was the object of Ororror's lust

placed a fin over her gill slits and giggled as only the truly drunk could. Ororror reached back as far as he could and slapped her against the wall. She had a look of horror in her eyes as she realized what had happened. Then, he laughed as only the truly powerful could, and signaled her to swim back to his lap. Though she smiled much less convincingly than before, she rushed to comply.

With a fin pulling her to his torso, he turned to Ozalec and spoke robustly. "These females, they're really quite nice, once you learn how to handle them."

"I pray to Gumnolar that I shall never be burdened with needing such knowledge, Lord." They both cackled with drunken self-satisfaction. Changing his tone, Ozalec went on, "Have you decided how best to vanquish the devils of Earth, Great One?"

"Of course, I have," he said raucously. Raising a fin, he proclaimed, "I, who know all and move all, have seen how the earthpups are to meet the Beast Without Eyes. My vision is beyond brilliant."

"How," replied Ozalec, "could it be anything else?"

"You know, you're right, for once, servile fool." replied the reigning fool.

"Will you speak of it to me, Lord?"

"Yes. There is nothing the mudworms can do to avoid their fate, so why not?" Ororror took a few seconds to gather his puny thoughts. "At first, I was uncertain. We met them in battle and they utterly destroyed our fleet. They possess weapons we clearly can't match." He squinted down at his aide. "How does one defeat an enemy when one is mightily overmatched?"

"With luck and the help of Gumnolar?" he replied uncertainly.

"*No,*" he responded with irritation. "I ask realistically," Ororror gestured around the chamber generally, "in the *real* world how does one fight such a war?"

"Please, oh Great One. I am a nitwit on my best of days. Please tell me. I don't think I could possibly divine insights the likes of yours."

After electing not to disembowel his Second Warrior, he replied. "With stealth, patience, and perseverance."

Ozalec, who really was a nitwit on his best days, was confused, and therefore frightened. To misunderstand Ororror could be fatal. "Yes, I see now this is true, Great Gift of Gumnolar. I see victory in your words."

That last remark rekindled a bloodlust in the top fish, if only briefly. "So, we shall destroy the heathens by employing the time-honored tactic of guerrilla warfare."

"Ah, Lord, the water in this chamber is thin. I must not have heard your wise words as they were spoken. We are to sneak around, because we fear to confront our enemy directly?"

"*Exactly*. I'm pleased you understand the concept so easily. Yes, we hit them randomly, probing for the weaknesses they surely possess. Once a winning strategy is found, we pounce in force. Victory is as certain as the piss I'm about to take." Warrior One then performed his second unthinkable public act in the span of a few minutes.

The following day, in Ororror's formal office, he waited as several officers flitted in. When they were situated, Ororror began. "I have summoned the lot of you here today to begin my plans to end the human race. Most of you may have already learned the essentials of my design. I mentioned them to Ozalec last night." He looked angrily to his Second. "Such is the same as broadcasting it on sonarvision in prime time."

Ozalec slipped lower in his seat, a look of profound consternation appearing on his undersized face.

"In any case," Warrior One continued, "I sent all of you a more detailed version of my plan a few cycles ago. You've all read it and studied it. I will entertain observations."

Ororror always welcomed *observations*. That was to say, he did *not* welcome input, criticism, or questions. Those were capital offenses. Actually, setting forth an observation was likely to end in one's torture, death, and consumption—one could only pray in that order—as well. When a leader had unlimited power, little intellectual ability, and an unbridled meanness of spirit, such consequences were inevitable.

For many cyclets, no one so much as breathed. It became apparent Ororror was not going to settle for his staff's taciturn approval. He drew his knife and began sliding it across a palm as if sharpening it. This gesture was universally understood to be the harbinger of something murderous. On past occasions, Ororror had done one of four things with his knife. Once, he had thrown it into someone's chest. Another time he handed it to someone and ordered them to plunge it into their own chest. He was also fond of tossing it to one party and asking them to stab it into someone else's chest. Finally, he found great joy in driving it into one victim's chest and then ordering him to pull it out and drive it into someone else's chest before the first party died—or else. Consequently, when the knife came out, everyone grew understandably concerned.

Ocrindis, Third General of the Space Fleet, elected to speak. He had, truth be told, heard rumblings of his losing favor in Ororror's mind. If anyone was already slated to die in that meeting, it was likely him. As was said on Listhelon, *Seek Gumnolar's grace, but don't count heavily on his worldly intervention.*

"I would *observe*," Ocrindis said in a low, paced voice,

"that the goals of your plan are blessed in the heart of Gumnolar. You honor his being."

"Why is it," growled Ororror, "that I believe I hear a 'but' in there somewhere?"

"Never a *but*," spoke the still-not-hopeless Ocrindis, "Only an *and*."

"Shall we destroy the Earthers with clever wordplay, Third General?"

"Of course not, Lord. War in its most brutal form is the only remedy Gumnolar demands when it comes to infidels."

"State your remedy, *and* quickly. I have grown extremely tired of this exchange."

"The fearless warriors of Listhelon must annihilate the Earthers. This is a given. *And* your plan relies on subterfuge, stealth, *and* in so doing delays retribution. You suggest sending out three ships each cycle. Two can attack the infidels, while one observes the battle and reports back to us. The long chain of vessels can support each other, thus ensuring communication. This seems rather *timid*, if I may be so bold?"

"To win a great victory is to win a great victory. When my glorious plan succeeds, all human life will be snuffed out and quickly forgotten. Why is this a problem in your small brain, Third General?"

Ah, there it was. Ocrindis was not to see another day. Then, short of endangering those closest to him, he had nothing to lose in speaking his mind. "Warriors of Gumnolar do not *sneak* nor do they crouch in waiting. We rule this planet with an iron fin because we do not *bend* and we do not *break*. And so, when our enemies see us coming, they know they are about to *die*. When we destroyed the infidel civilization of our neighboring planet, we did so with battle cries and blood. We did not act like frightened children under the cover of night. Your so-called *plan* is as much an insult to our proud traditions as it is to Gumnolar himself. Let those with ears hear my words."

Ororror set his knife point down on the table and placed a finger atop the butt. With his free hand, he slowly spun the weapon, seeming to marvel at the play of light the polished blade generated. After a pause, he rested the knife in his palms, turned to Ozalec, and offered it to his aide. Ozalec picked up the knife with a trembling fin.

"If you were me, Second, what would you do with that steel?"

Ozalec looked at the knife, then to Ororror, finally to Ocrindis. Suddenly, he pulled the knife over his shoulder and hurled it at Ocrindis. Fortunately for the intended victim, Ozalec was completely inept in matters of combat. The blade clanged off the table and bounced harmlessly to the floor.

Ocrindis, up until then frowning in silence, looked to the floor and began to laugh. His merriment was, however, brief. A second knife thudded into his throat, causing him to gurgle blood as he slumped forward and died. Ororror carried two blades, it turned out.

"Second, that was pathetic. Please report to my master-at-arms first thing tomorrow for badly needed lessons."

"Yes, I will do so, Lord. Thank you for your kind concern. Shall ... shall I remove the remains of Ocrindis?"

"No, don't bother. His continued presence will remind those still alive how I reward treachery. Plus, he does looks particularly delicious, doesn't he?"

FOUR

"I'm not nearly as comfortable with these new notions that seem stuck in your head," Toño said.

"As if votes counted, because you never listen to anyone *else,* in the first place," added Sapale, "but, I fully agree with Toño. It's way too risky and totally unnecessary. What do you even hope to gain?"

"I can't believe you guys. What kind of explorers are you, anyway? Where's your spirit of adventure?"

"Not me," said Toño, raising his hands, "Never claimed to be an explorer or have the slightest adventurous inclination."

Sapale raised an arm. "Mother and Nation Builder here. No interest whatsoever in exploration or adventure, thank you very much."

"I'm all in with you, pop" declared JJ. He rested his hand on his rail-rifle. For the last few years, he'd been in the habit of carrying one. He claimed he wanted to be ready when the Uhoor showed their ugly faces. The fact that my hot-headed son was the only one on my side was not very reassuring.

"Look, guys, these Deavoriath may well be the most

advanced, most powerful race in the entire universe. I'm talkin' *ever*, here. Those mighty Uhoor see one of their ships and scurry like cockroaches when the kitchen light is turned on. Think what we could learn from them. Imagine the way they could change our lives."

"Yes," said Toño, "like, for example, ending them."

"Doc, come on," I more or less whined, "why would they do that? They have to be the ones who gave me these cool toys." I held up my hands.

"Then they scrubbed both Al's and your brain clean. If they wanted you to return, they wouldn't have done that, now would they?" Sapale said pissily.

"You don't know that. *We* don't know that. Who's to say why superbeings do what they do?"

"The record of where Oowaoa is located was stricken from your memory," Toño observed. "The only reason to do that has to be that, as Sapale said, they want to be left alone. If superbeings want you to leave them alone and you don't, they're likely to act in a most unpleasant manner."

"If they turn hostile, we can defend ourselves," JJ said, raising his rifle.

"You say you won a *bet*," Toño asked again still incredulous, "with the vortex manipulator?"

"Yeah. I totally did."

"But, why would what is essentially a sentient AI place a *bet*? It's illogical. Makes no sense at all."

"That doesn't change the fact that I did. In a contest of man versus machine, always bet on the flesh and blood." I thumbed my shirt.

"I'll keep that in mind," observed Al who'd been listening in. "By the way, and for the record, pilot, you're an android, a machine constructed to appear as though it was flesh and blood."

"Gee, thanks, Al," I responded. "And with Christmas

27

just around the corner, I'll be hoping to discover coal on Azsuram."

"Jon," Sapale asked pointedly, "what specifically do you hope to gain? Hmm? We're safe from the Uhoor and the Listhelons. We can defend ourselves against either if they attack. We can travel anywhere we want instantly. Even if the Deavoriath don't just kill us on sight, what do we lack that they are likely to supply?"

She sort of had me there. "I don't know, but with their power and resources, I can't imagine a wish they couldn't grant us. Maybe they could re-create Earth and we could all go home." Why, oh why, had I just said that? My uncensored brain-mouth-speech pathway got me into trouble faster than moonshine on an empty stomach.

"We *are* home," was Sapale's quick response. "My home," she pointed around widely, "*our* home, is here on Azsuram, not Earth. You're dreaming up science fiction to justify the fact that you want to go there, because you can."

She knew me too well. "I'll go alone, then. No one else will be in danger."

"No way," shouted JJ. "If *you* go, *I* go."

I looked at him sharply. "Like I said, I will go alone. I will be the only one at risk."

"Incorrect," said Sapale, "on three counts. One, if you don't return, we lose the cube. Two, the Deavoriath may want to erase *all* knowledge of their existence and could come looking for us to cover their tracks. Three, I will not let you die on a fool's errand. I love you too much, even when you're acting like the spoiled child that is forever housed in your brain."

"Jon," said Toño, "how about this. If there's ever a *need* to contact the Deavoriath, then we will do so. But, absent a dire situation, let's agree it is too dangerous, and defer going there at this time."

But I *wanted* to go. I'd apparently been there before, but I'd have loved to visit them out and actually remember it. Then again, I was immortal. I could visit them later, much later, when there was no one left to try to talk me out of it. "Okay. I'll hold off for now, pending a good reason. But I still have to say, y'all are a bunch of sissy killjoys."

JJ yelped in protest.

"All except JJ here. He, like his old man, is interested in expanding the horizons of civilization and societal knowledge."

When Toño and JJ were gone Sapale came over and rested her head on my shoulder. "I know you're the adventurer. You were chosen first from all your people to make a voyage of discovery. I know that." She looked up at me. "I know you're itching to take that fancy cube of yours and do something really exciting and really dangerous. It's in your DNA."

"But," I finished her thought, "I have responsibilities now. A family to watch over and a world to shape."

"No," she replied. "If I lost you I don't think I could go on. I'd just roll into a big ball and cry myself to death."

That was the sweetest thing anyone had ever said about me. I stroked her head gently. "What sort of brood-mate would I be if I let you do that? You're never going to lose me. Honest."

We sat there silently. We both knew the other shoe of my remark was that, sooner or later, *I* would be losing *her*.

"Hey," she said trying to lighten up the mood, "what do you think of those solar-powered generators JJ and Draldon set up on the ridge? I think we're going to get a lot of use out of those."

"Yeah, they'll help a lot. *Shearwater* can produce a ton of electricity, but if she's off world for some reason, it's good to know there'll be plenty of backup available."

"You know, it's kind of funny. When you and I planned Azsuram, we had no idea we'd have that cube. It changed everything didn't it?"

"How do you mean?"

"Well, before, we couldn't be certain we'd make it. We were one disaster from the whole thing going down the crapper. And if I didn't build in as much genetic diversity as I hoped for, there'd be trouble down the road we couldn't possibly fix."

"But now—?"

"Now it's not as challenging as it was."

"What, you preferred life more when you could have failed miserably, terminally?"

She rocked her head back and forth a few times. "Yeah, I think I did." She straightened up and looked at me seriously. "Not that *we* would have ever failed."

"I know what you're saying. That spark of uncertainty made whatever we accomplished all that more satisfying." I tapped the bottom of her chin. "But I bet in a thousand years, there'll be so many statues of you around here, the ground will get crooked. You've done good, brood's-mate. You've done something that matters."

"Check back, will you, in a thousand years? If they don't have more statues of me than there are stars in the sky, beat them up or something."

"You got it, babe. I'll build them myself if I have to. Then I'll personally put one in every bathroom on the planet. People will never ignore you again."

"You're *terrible*." She slapped my shoulder.

"Sanitary Sapale. That's what they'll call you. You'll become the goddess of personal hygiene and general cleanliness."

"I may just have to take Toño up on his offer to download me to an AI. That way I can haunt your sorry ass *forever*."

"What? That's an option? He could do that?"

She stood and turned away. "*Damn.* I can't believe I let that slip. There'll be no living with you now. *Semlerag.*"

"Semlerag" was about the worst curse word in her native tongue. It didn't translate into human speech easily, but, trust me, it was a bad word. The only time I'd heard her say it was when she was instructing the kids. I knew she had to be really pissed off at herself.

"Honey, don't be like that. It's good. It's all good. If you want to talk about it, then we'll talk. If not, we can just pretend you never said a thing. I'm totally cool either way. Your call, seriously."

Her fists were tightly closed and her frame was stiff as iced metal. "You're so damn understanding, it's annoying."

"I can't ever recall being insulted like that."

"Hey, I'm still mad at you. No joking around."

"Mad at me? What'd I do?"

"You're not getting out of this by playing dumb. *No* way. You know what you did. You made me mention Toño's offer."

"Me? I ... how'd I do that? I didn't know a thing about it. We were discussing how you'd be remembered for your cleanliness."

"You're only making it worse for yourself. You know that straight up?"

I had, as all good husbands before me, lost the battle, the war, and anything else that counted. Better to surrender early. It would be less painful. Much less painful. "Okay, I'm sorry. Sometimes I'm insensitive. I only want you to be happy. I'll do whatever it takes." That universal concession usually did the trick.

"If you weren't so darn cute and I didn't love you so much, I'd throw that empty confession back in your face."

"Sweet love, with all my heart, I promise to never mention your revelation if that's what you want. We darn cute people, we're like that."

"He mentioned it to me. Maybe six months ago."

"And he said an AI transfer, not an android?"

"A computer copy only. He said an android host for my species was still decades off. Apparently copying a brain is easy. A complex, functioning host is much more difficult." She crossed her arms around her body like she was cold and turned away.

"What're your thoughts?"

"You know how I feel. We discussed being an android that one time." She stopped talking as she pulled in a couple ragged breaths. "I thanked him for the kind offer, but told him I had less than zero interest." Her entire body shuddered. "It would be awful to be trapped in a machine like you are. It would be unthinkable to be locked away in cyber-reality for all eternity." Void of emotion, she continued. "No eyes to see the gods' light, no ears to hear children laughing, no arms to touch a lover. The horror of such an existence is beyond comprehension. To not live, yet to never die. Un ... unthinkable."

"Then you shouldn't do it. If that's how you feel, end of discussion." I stood and engulfed her in my arms.

She began to growl mournfully, pitifully. That was one of the Kaljaxian equivalents of crying. After a minute she could speak again. "But, I know you want me to be there with you, and it kills me that I can't do it."

"Hey there, no tears. It's a crazy, compassless technological dawn we're experiencing. No worries. For millions of years life has only had the one option: to live and then to die. Now we have *this* form of immortality, as opposed to *that* one. This isn't the way we were programmed to do it. It's okay that it doesn't make sense.

A rational decision concerning any of this is impossible."
More to myself, I added, "I wonder every day if it
wouldn't have been better for all if this never came to be."

My brood's-mate, filled with enough love for me to
bridge an eternity, caught that last remark. She could hear
that I was suffering. "You had to choose to exist in your
black state. I'm so full of pride for you I almost split wide
open every time I look at you." She stroked my cheek.
"Plus, if you hadn't, I'd have never been able to meet the
best darn fighter pilot in the galaxy."

We kissed. God, how I loved that woman.

FIVE

"Good evening. I am Jim Higgs, the executive producer. Tonight on *PrimeNews* we are going to bring you an exclusive, one-on-one interview you cannot afford to miss. We will speak with Stuart Marshall. In the past we've interviewed the newer Stuart Marshall, the one Dr. Toño DeJesus created correctly. We saw that he was currently living the life of a model citizen. But the man we will meet tonight is the *other* Stuart Marshall, the man referred to by some as *Darth* Marshall. This is the faulty android copy who ordered the atomic bombing of his own nation. He's the machine who coordinated the sneak attack on *Enterprise*, killing Secretary General Kahl in cold blood. He's also the only man we know who has been killed at least twice, yet still he lives.

"Our senior correspondent, Miles Cavett, has been blindfolded and taken to a secret facility where this interview is to take place. We cannot stress the danger he has risked on your behalf to get the story directly from a man who has proven himself to be violent and extremely unpredictable. Viewer discretion is advised. We must insist that children and those with known cardiac diseases please not watch this live, once-in-a-lifetime program. Some label Marshall as a madman, others as the devil incarnate. I can only pray that my friend Miles and his crew will return to us safe and unharmed.

"So with no further delay, I will switch the feed to Miles Cavett at an unknown location. Miles, are you okay?"

The signal broke up briefly. Then the well-known face of Miles Cavett appeared. He looked serious, but composed. His square jaw and rugged good looks assured viewers that he would, as always, give as much as he got from any guest.

"Good evening, my friends. Thank you for joining me. And yes, Jim, we're all fine. I invite you to accompany me tonight on a journey, exploring the mind of a man often compared to Joseph Stalin, Adolph Hitler, and Sayyid al-Fassi. First," the camera panned back as Miles turned to face Marshall, "I'd like to thank Stuart Marshall for this chance to meet with him and get the story straight."

"No problem, Miles. It's my pleasure to interface with the press and," he extended a hand toward the camera, "my blessed American citizenry. I have sworn to serve them. They have the right to see their president in person. They hunger to know that I am well and remain uncaged by our mutual enemies."

"Perhaps that is as good a point of departure as any, Mr. Marshall, to begin ours—"

"Ah, Miles, if you would refer to me as *President* Marshall, I'd greatly appreciate it." Stuart jiggled both palms at the reporter and added, "Now, I'm not the sort of fellow to stand on ceremony and empty titles. No. I'm a humble man—to a fault, I am told by those I trust. However, I do think you owe it to those individuals who've placed their trust in me to show the office, if not the man occupying it, all proper and due respect."

"But, Mr. Marshall, you're *not* the President of the United States. Amanda Walker is. She legally assumed the office of the president after Faith Clinton was assassinated."

"I can see you're going to try my patience a little bit right out the gate, son." Stuart grimaced and balled a fist alongside his face. "Lucky for you I'm both an easygoing, as well as a *forgiving,* president. Neither, you see, of those aforementioned sluts won or assumed the presidency. As I was, am, and always will be the duly and legally elected president, it was constitutionally impossible for either of them, or anyone else, to occupy *my* office." Stuart smiled grotesquely. "You can't have two popes and you can't have two presidents. Not possible."

"Need I remind you there *can* be two popes. During the Western Schism of the fourteenth century, there existed a dual papacy with the so called anti-popes. When Popes Urban VI in Rome—"

"My, but you're the well-informed son of a red-assed whore, aren't you," hissed Stuart. "We are *not,* however, here to discuss popish history."

"You brought the subject up."

"Yes, I imagine I did, didn't I? I truly regret it, now. I suggest, however, we move along to the Presidential Proclamation I was planning to make to the public tonight." He gestured regally to the camera. "To my loving, lost sheep."

"Hang on one moment, sir. I will not be manipulated or have this interview highjacked so you can achieve your twisted personal agenda. I insist we stick, at least loosely, to the agreed-upon format both your people and mine signed off on."

"You know what? In spite of my aforementioned

easygoing and forgiving nature, you're beginning to get on my last nerve. That is not, as history teaches us, a good or a safe place to be, puke. As president, I will set the tone and direction of any press conferences I give. Is there any part of that reality you're still unclear about?" Stuart glowered at Miles, who, to his credit, stood his ground.

"Are you threatening me? Because, if you are, this interview is *over.*"

The camera panned to a close-up on Stuart. He fluttered his eyes closed and slowly pumped his fists in front of his chest. Eyes still shut, he said, "Let's not let our egos or artificially elevated testosterone levels interfere with an otherwise pleasant evening, shall we, Miles? Let's both remove our fingers from the put-the-foot-down button and take a few deep breaths. Hmm?"

"How we proceed depends entirely on your behavior and your willingness to stick to the agreed-upon script."

"Well, there you have it, then. We're peachy-keen, aren't we? Ready to head for second base on our first date."

The mental instability reflected in that last remark did not escape the notice of Miles Cavett or anyone watching.

"Let me ask, then, why it is you think you are still the rightful president? I know of no other individual who shares your opinion in that regard. I specifically discussed any potential validity of your claim with the Chief Justice of the Supreme Court herself yesterday. She felt there was no constitutional basis—"

"You can't take the word of an acknowledged pedophile concerning matters of constitutional law."

Miles was clearly stunned. "I *beg* your pardon. Are you saying that Chief Justice Mary Kathryn Kinane, a former nun, is a pedophile? That, sir, is *outrageous.*"

Stuart glared sternly at Miles for a moment, then

burst out laughing. "No, you slow-coach, I simply stated that one can't take a pedophile's word on *anything*. I didn't say that the blessed justice was one. That was an assumption on your part." Stuart giggled insanely. "If you assume something, you make an *ass* out of *you* and *me*." More cackles. Abruptly and soberly. Stuart said, "Now, I *will* state that Mary is a closet homosexual and is intellectually challenged, being fully incapable of distinguishing a tort from a tart or a tart from a fart. I will further venture to say that she'd be a cold log in the sack, but those defining qualities are all beside the point."

"You're kidding? You have a point?" Miles challenged mockingly.

"Yes, and it is this. I was elected to office in 2140. With me so far?"

"Of course."

"Just checking. You've been all over hell so far in this interview, babbling about popes and false presidents. Okay, the Congress of the United States of America penned a constitutional amendment long before my time stating that a president would serve for his entire life. You recall that, don't you, Miles? It was in all the papers."

Clearly irate, he snapped, "*Yes*, I recall that event."

"Great. So you agree with me then." Stuart pressed his palms on his chest. "*I'm* still alive, so *I'm* still president."

"You presume too much, Mr. Marshall. I do not, in fact, agree with you. No person, be they *sane* or *insane*, agrees with you." Miles took a few cleansing breaths to calm himself. "Let me list a few facts that would contradict your thesis. One, yes, you were made president for life. But at the time, no one aside from yourself and a select few deviants knew you were an android. If that fact was known, the amendment would never have applied."

Stuart started to say something, but Miles raised his voice and a finger.

"Not so fast, I haven't finished. Two, you were killed by both General Jackson and by the other Stuart Marshall, after he tossed you into a fusion reactor. Your potential claims perished with either of those deaths. Three, you sort of abdicated your office when you, oh, I don't know, ordered a nuclear attack on your own people, murdered Secretary Kahl along with one hundred seventy-three other innocent people, and when you kidnapped, with the intent to rape, tens of thousands of women. What is your response to those damning facts?"

Stuart sat placidly a few seconds then leaned toward Miles. "You know, you really should stick to decaf, son. I'm not a doctor, but I think I'm right on this one." Stuart smiled at his cleverness, then spoke in a measured tone. "Now, before you fly off the handle yet again, let me respond to those distortions. I am a victim of a hateful campaign of misinformation that wounds not only me, but the Americans I am sworn to serve, and the office of the president itself."

Miles's face reflected a stunned, dumbstruck incredulity. "You're ... not serious ... seriously suggesting someone *else* is responsible for any one of those flagrant criminal acts?"

All smiles Stuart said, "I'm *suggesting* nothing. I am *stating* unequivocally that I was not responsible for even one of those tragedies. I have unimpeachable proof, in fact, as to who the responsible party was in each of those heinous acts of terrorism."

Miles was literally speechless. He stared at Stuart a few seconds, then looked toward someone off-screen. He was clearly struggling to fit Marshall's last remarks into any possible reality. Finally, Miles's producer stepped in the picture, removed the microphone from the reporter's hand, and asked, "Who, if not you, would you have us believe is responsible for the acts in question? Please recall that, in several instances, we have *documentary* evidence that you were the instigator."

"Ah, with whom do I have the pleasure of speaking? Mr. Cavett seems to have slipped into some form of light coma, thanks be to God."

"My name is Carl Mansfield, senior producer for *PrimeNews*. Now, please answer my question."

"Gladly, friend Carl. I am able, upon request, to turn over ironclad proof that the perpetrator in each case, as well as many other unspeakable acts of criminality, was none other than ... say, could I get a bottle of water? All this disclosing has parched my throat."

"Someone," began Carl, "get the man a—"

"No, wait," Miles was back, "Stuart, please stop playing with us. Androids don't get parched throats or need bottles of water. Either finish your blatant lie of an accusation, or we're out of here."

Stuart regarded Miles with primal contempt. Then he responded. "The man responsible for the acts I have wrongly been accused of is none other than Private Jon Ryan." Stuart put on a very stern expression. "Many of you may not already know that I busted his traitorous ass down to the *lowest* paygrade possible, E2, as a result of his scurrilous behavior toward planet Earth and her beloved people."

"That is both blatantly false and easily disproven," Miles was hot. "*General* Ryan, in the case of your failed nuclear assault, was miles above you as you tried to enter Cheyenne Mountain, planning to escape the destruction you yourself ordered. How, you simpering fool, can you explain your way around that *fact?*"

"*Simpering*, am I?" Stuart bared his teeth, appearing quite similar to a rabid hyena. "Why, you—" He took a few deep breaths and steadied himself enough to respond with words. "Now, son, you know as well as the next person how visual records can be changed, altered, and doctored to *seem* to tell whatever story the guilty might wish to peddle."

"So, you maintain General Ryan was able to alter the *worldwide* records of that dark day? How is that even possible?"

"Don't you see, you silly electric turd, he used *alien* technology. Like the damn force field he used to attack me on that space station. With that," Stuart snapped his fingers rapidly and made, for some reason, a popping sound with his mouth, "it was as easy as peasy."

"No such alien technology has surfaced in the intervening years."

"*Yes.* You see, you're on my side. Isn't he homicidally brilliant?"

"No. Neither I nor anyone watching is on your side of anything. If General Ryan triggered the attack, why were you heading for Cheyenne?"

"To try to keep the presidency alive, you festering piglet. I was also trying to preserve my hide."

"But the attack only ended when he prevented you from entering the Cheyenne facility."

"He wanted me dead. That's why he stopped me. Don't you have a functioning neuron up there in your tiny brain?" He pointed to Miles's head.

"But if he stopped you from entering so that he might assassinate you, why did he abort the attack? That makes zero sense. The missiles were about to launch and you were defenseless. What is your tortured explanation for those inescapable truths?"

"I stopped him, that's what happened. Here's what I did. I looked that traitor straight in the eye and I said, *Ryan, you ungrateful mongrel, you stop your murderous*

41

attack on my people RIGHT THIS VERY SECOND. He, the traitorous worm turd, responded, *Or else what, you false god?* I told him squarely, *Or else you'll have ME to answer to.* That's the reason he backed down. He knew, in the end, in his twisted mind, that I was not a man to be toyed with." Stuart was breathing as heavily as a marathon runner at the finish line. He gasped, "Any further clarifications needed, son?"

"Just the one. Are you under competent psychiatric care?"

"What on earth are you getting at?"

"The fact that you are, and I list these in no particular order, insane, deranged, and narcissistically psychotic."

In an instant Stuart's breath quieted. He stared at Miles coldly, dispassionately. A decision had been made. "Miles, do you know what happened to the last man who cast such aspersions upon this son of my sainted mother?"

"Is that a threat?" Miles pointed to the camera lens. "If so, you've made it before billions of witnesses."

"You're a real stale cake, aren't you, boy? That was a *question.* When someone says the words *do you know,* they are asking a *declarative* question. A *threat* would be more alone the lines of, *I will do to you what I did to the last person,* etcetera, etcetera. Are we clear on all of this, son? Grammar is the sacred glue that binds sentient minds. I would feel positively *awful* sending you off to your eternal rewards, absent that valuable knowledge."

"So, for completeness, what did you do to the last person who disparaged you?"

"I thought you'd *never* ask." Stuart reached into his suit coat and produced a rail gun. He pointed it at Miles's head then looked directly into the camera. "I'd like the record to note that the man asked specifically to know what I did. A picture," he pulled the trigger and Miles's head exploded into a red mist, "is worth a thousand words." Turning to the slumped headless body Stuart said calmly, "That, Mr. Cavett, is what I did to the last such incautious individual. Well," he glanced at his wrist where a watch would be if he was wearing one, "the hour is getting on. I will now proceed to the Presidential-Proclamation portion of the press conference." He leaned close to the spastic body, blood shooting in a geyser from the stump of neck. "That is, unless you have an objection, Miles." Stuart aimed an ear at the corpse. "Ah, wonderful. You don't. Silence is so golden."

Stuart reached his free hand into the other side of his coat and produced a scrap of paper. "My people, my God-fearing American brethren. I, as your rightful president, have a couple of proclamations to make more public than they have been to date." He smiled nervously. "Man, I've got the jitters. Haven't spoken before so many adulating humans in a spell. Anyway, here goes. Proclamation One, I am still the one and only president of y'all. Two, anyone disagreeing with any portion of Proclamation One is subject to immediate execution. Three, Private Jon Ryan is officially sentenced to death for crimes too numerous and odious to list. This is a shoot-on-sight situation, people, so let's go get him. Finally, four, I love you. I surely do. Always will, and there's nothing anyone can do about that.

"So, I guess I'm done." He looked very seriously at the camera. "I do wish to stress the *inflexibility* of these proclamations. Here, let's take one for a test drive, shall we?" Stuart waved to someone off camera. Two huge men held the struggling Carl Mansfield by either arm. "Mr. Mansfield, did you hear the four proclamations?"

In lieu of a verbal response, Carl swung a foot at Stuart, missing by a wide margin.

"I'll take that as a *yes*. Now, I will ask you, concerning specifically the second proclamation. Do you dissent, in even the slightest manner, with the spirit of Proclamation One?"

Carl spat at Stuart's face. This time his assault met its target.

"I'll take that, also, to represent an affirmative. Okay, then. The sentence of violating Pro-2," Stuart abruptly angled his head to the audience. "I like cute abbreviations of the proclamations, don't you? Anyway, back on point, time's a wastin.' It's death, son." The rail gun flew up and removed Carl's head, splattering the stalwart assistants with copious amounts of blood. As professionals, they remained unmoved.

"You see, my minions," stated a confident, serene Stuart Marshall, "simple *rules* for simple*tons*. I'll be talking with you soon." He pointed the pistol directly at the lens. "*Boo.*"

SIX

"I think it's pretty obvious we have to do something to stop him, and do it real soon," Amanda said to her assembled cabinet. "Marshall gets more freakishly insane by the day. We can't simply wait to react to his next stunt. We need to bag him and the person or persons responsible for reanimating him."

"If we were fortunate enough to capture the man himself, we wouldn't necessarily need to take down his accomplices." Secretary of Security Dave Cummings said intently. He had been a trusted, longtime advisor to Faith Clinton. Amanda was glad he agreed to serve in her administration, also. He was forthright, intelligent, and dependable. "He is always saying there can be only one of him. If we kept his android permanently detained, I'll bet he wouldn't permit a second copy to be produced. It might take the power-grab ball and run with it, leaving the jailed one to rust away forgotten."

"Catching him will be nearly impossible. *Holding* him will likely be harder," added Marsha McCormick, the Secretary of Food Resources.

"How so?" asked Amanda.

"He must have contingency plans for that possibility. His lackeys could set those plans in motion, per protocol. He might have them take a massive number of hostages to exchange for his release." She shook her head. "Whatever he'd have up his sleeve would be bad. No. I say we need to take down his entire network, or we can't risk collaring him in the first place."

"Good point," agreed Amanda. "But we've had such little luck and so few leads. Nabbing the whole gang may be just pie in the sky."

"At minimum, we need to kill Marshall and prevent his duplication," Heath stared at his hands on the table as he spoke. "That means, in effect, we need the *technician* actually doing the transfer. That's a high-level skill. In fact, there can't be too many people with sufficient knowledge to complete the process in secret."

"You have a good point in terms of the tech being key." That was Reginald Black, director of Intelligence and Security, the combined former FBI, ATF, and CIA. "I have to confess, that approach has never been articulated in any of our meetings. Thanks, Heath."

Heath thumbed his handheld. "Please get us Dr. De La Frontera on the holo, Meredith." To Amanda, he said, "Maybe he can point us in the right direction."

"Heath," Carlos said as his twenty centimeter tall image zapped onto the table, "how can I be of assistance?"

"I'm in a cabinet meeting. We're rehashing the Marshall thing and may have a new angle. I thought you might have some useful input."

"Let's all hope I do. Glad to help. Hi, Amanda." He waved vigorously.

"Hi, Carlos. Thanks for your help."

"A pleasure. What can I do?"

"We were thinking," said Heath, "that whoever is putting Marshall back into an android host must have some pretty advanced training. That individual is probably known to you, since the training required would be so specific. Can you think of anyone who might be able to perform the transfer without being detected?"

"Are you suggesting one of *my* people is responsible?" Carlos's feathers were ruffled.

"No, no, not at all. More likely it'd be a former employee. Maybe a reject, someone who tried to join, but didn't quite make the grade."

"Ah," Carlos said. "Let me think a moment." He rubbed at his chin. Finally, he said, "There might be twenty-odd people who could fit in that category. Perhaps a few more. I'll send you a list."

"Thanks," said Amanda, "that would be great. Anyone who tops that list of potentials?"

"There are a couple individuals who come to mind. I'll highlight their names on the list." He angled his head slightly. "There, it should be in your inbox, Mandy." Collation and communications were quick for an android like Carlos.

"Computer," she said, "please display my inbox." She scanned the screen. "Got it. Thanks."

"Anytime." His tiny transparent body vanished.

Amanda forwarded copies to everyone present. She waited thirty seconds then asked, "Any name set off an alarm in anyone's head?"

At first no one spoke. Then Reginald said, "I'll have my best people go over this in detail. With any luck, we can figure out who the loose cannon is and put them under surveillance."

"Good," Amanda said, "I feel we're making some progress, at least on that front. Any thoughts about Marshall himself?"

The room went quiet. Finally Heath spoke. "I recall

something about placing a backdoor program in all the androids."

"A what kind of program?" asked Reginald.

"One that could deactivate any android remotely."

"I've never heard of such an option." Reginald sounded upset.

"Neither have I," said Amanda with even more edge to her voice.

"Yeah, well," said Heath, "I have. Sorry. I'm not in charge of distributing highly classified information."

"Let me confirm that with Carlos." Amanda tapped rapidly on a keyboard. A few seconds later, she said, "Yes, such a deactivating program does, in fact, exist. DeJesus put it in all the androids, except the ones used by the astronauts. He felt decorum demanded it not be included in their algorithms. Carlos's and DeJesus's were also exempted. It was all kept a tight secret." She raised her head to address Heath. "How did you find out?"

Heath needed to make it clear he hadn't done anything inappropriate. "Ah, you might have noticed my last name. Ryan? The astronaut is a relative of mine. He mentioned it to me a while back."

"Hmm," was all Amanda said.

"How would you employ this program, Heath?" Reginald asked.

"Ah, let's you and me talk about that later, okay?"

"You two stay," Amanda said crisply. She indicated Heath and Reginald. "The rest of you can go. Thanks."

SEVEN

"Otollar the Incompetent," Ororror said acidly, "left two ships out of the attack for surveillance purposes. Is that correct?"

"Yes," responded the Commander of Communications, Owilla. Everyone around Ororror was nervous, but Owilla was especially so. He'd brought unsettling news. Ororror was explosively violent and completely amoral. That was a dicey combination for bearers of bad news.

"And they've maintained constant communication with us since their departure all those cycles ago?"

"Yes, master. As you say it."

"Very well," Ororror said looking out the window, bored already with the audience. It was also unwise to bore the current Warrior One. "What have you to report? And Ozalec," he said to his second, "send for some food."

"Ah," Owilla said weakly, "I am not hungry, master. There is no need on my account."

"Silence, soft head," he boomed. "I was not planning to include you, unless, of course, you're volunteering to *be* the meal."

"No ... I mean, that was not my—"

"*Silence.*" Owilla shook like sand pounded by high-waves. Ororror was pleased to see that. "Proceed with your report."

"Lord. The senior vessel, *Gumnolar Questions,* reports they have observed the construction of thousands of gigantic colony ships above planet Earth."

"If I die of suspense," responded Ororror, "I'm taking you with me, guppy."

"Earth has been, or rather was, destroyed one thousand cycles ago."

"The entire planet? Destroyed? How is such a feat possible?"

"The largest planet in that solar system left its normal orbit and collided with Earth. Colony ships laden with survivors departed for an unknown destination just before the planet was struck."

"You see," exclaimed Ozalec, "Gumnolar *is* with us. Praise his glory, he has smitten the entire tainted world."

"Hmm," remarked Ororror dubiously, "so it might seem. How many humans escaped?"

"They estimate billions, master. Many billions."

"As parasites fleeing a sinking carcass," remarked Ororror.

"A very large number of parasites, Mighty One."

Ororror thought a moment then spoke. "This is perfect. It fits my plan better than I could have dreamt of."

"Again, Lord," Ozalec basically sang, "Gumnolar knows your needs and provides for the righteous."

To himself, Ororror reflected how odd it was that Gumnolar granted his wishes. Ororror neither prayed to nor believed, unlike his idiot subjects, that Gumnolar existed. "How long would it take to send a message to the colony ships?"

"A mm ... message, Complete One? Why would we send the infidels a message?"

"*We* wouldn't, because you are less than one-tenth of nothing. *I* would, for reasons you will not learn before your consumption by those who dwell in the prison of Ludcrisal." To Ozalec he howled, "Remove this flatulence bubble and bring me his second, so I might set my plans in motion."

Very shortly, because anything ordered by Ororror was done expeditiously, Oyffew stood before him, oily tears streaking his fat cheeks. Owilla was being rushed to Ludcrisal. There he would be thrown in alive. Life would depart Owilla quickly enough at that point. The yet unexecuted criminals who lived in that desolate prison were perpetually at the point of starvation.

"I wish to send a message to the human colony fleet. Can this be accomplished?"

"Yes, Pure One. If I make some assumptions regarding their trajectory and speed and use a wide enough signal, I believe so."

"I don't want technical details. This is our first meeting, so I'll let you live for now. But," Ororror pointed a fin at Oyffew, "look at my face, child."

The communication department's new chief tried to stare at his leader, but could do so only waveringly.

"You fail once and you die a thousand times. Any questions?"

Oyffew shook his head since he was unable to speak. He also fouled the water of his lord and master's office. That pleased Ororror. It indicated to him that the newest idiot had understood him well.

"Fine. Here's the message. *Great friends of Earth. I am Ororror, humble leader of a humble race. We of Listhelon have made every effort to make relationships between our two peoples as loving as they should be. The last leader of our world went insane without warning. He, and he alone, was responsible for the inexcusable attack on your gentle world. You may be assured that swift justice was dispensed to him.*

It falls to me as the new leader to make matters right with you. I am incalculably sorry for the actions illegally taken against the innocent people of Earth. Luck, which can be kind even as it is being cruel, is clearly at play. I have just heard of the tragic loss of Earth at the hands of fate. I have just learned of your colony ships venturing out into the dark uncertainty of space in search of a new home. Well, look you no longer. I invite you to come to Listhelon. No, I beg that you come here so that we may pay the profound debt we owe you.

We are an aquatic species. You are a terrestrial species. Our planet has massive expanses of unoccupied dry land. We have no need for it. My scientists assure me it would be perfect for human habitation. Our air is pure, fresh water is abundant, and any troublesome land animals absent. (NB: Almost all life on land had been systematically eradicated by the hateful Listhelons long ago.)

So, new friends—new brothers—join us in a safe, prosperous, and loving future, here on your new home.

Ozalec stared slack-jawed at his boss. What in the name of Gumnolar and his blessed children was Warrior One doing? Who, he wondered, though only to himself, had just spoken?

"So, my new head of communications, how long will it take for that message to reach our future guests?"

"At these distances, around fifty cycles."

"So I might expect a response in one hundred," he said to himself. "Good. You may go."

Ozalec could not help asking, "Lord, why in the name of Gumnolar would you send such a message? These humans can't be so stupid as to believe you. I thought we were to pelt them with small numbers of ships over time, not invite them to befoul our home."

Those were incautious words, even for the Second Warrior. "That you don't understand pleases me. I wouldn't suppose a certified moron could comprehend my vision. You see, I wish to play with their minds. It costs me nothing to send such a message. If they do come, I'll publicly thank Gumnolar, as I eat one of their hearts while it still beats. If they don't, at least I might place a trace of doubt in their minds as to our nature. But realistically, the most I might accomplish would be to bring dissent into their midst. Some may argue for coming, while others refuse. Discontent poisons a society. If it does, I will smile."

"So, we're still sending the guerrilla ships?"

Ororror swiped a fin over his face. How could one fish be so stupid? Surely it would require ten *normal* fools to be as dense as this pup. Ah well, he was at least a pathetically loyal fool. For the time being, he would live.

EIGHT

Drawjoy was having a particularly bad day. All of his days were insufficient, many were bad, and none, absolutely *none*, were pleasant. Yet he was able to slog on like a condemned prisoner through his endless, miserable days. He could, because he held a belief. Drawjoy was certain that one day he would win his reward. Someday, his name would be spoken of along with the greatest minds humankind had ever produced. Einstein, Dirac, and Ramanujan would be the reference points used to frame his intellect and the scale of his contributions to knowledge.

One day, when his star was at its zenith, people would worship him. In that enraptured epoch, he might even dream to date a woman. They all currently avoided his advances like they were a pestilence, plague, or other biblical scourge. Even women plying the oldest profession laughed in his face when he proposed a brief business relationship. But Drawjoy knew it was only because women didn't yet *know* him. Once he was famous, he'd go on dates, perhaps even several per week.

But all that had to wait. He had several calls to make and several more trash converters to repair before he could drink himself into yet another fitful night's rest. With the pittance Marshall paid him to be on call, Drawjoy was forced to work for a living like the rest of the rats he shared the worldship with. Marshall's arrogance galled him no end. The man possessed a complete lack of insight. The indifference with which Marshall regarded the scientist who had resurrected him, and would time and again, was inexcusable. Drawjoy thought that a man with Marshall's resources and needs would treasure his labor and value the brilliant mind that allowed life to be his in perpetuity.

"Are you having some sort of seizure, mister?" asked the occupant of the apartment located at 1132 Dover Street, New Cleveland, *Intrepid*. Gladys Dunsworth was her name, a large single woman with an ill temper and nonexistent manners. "'Cause you ain't moved in, like, five minutes. Ya just keep starin' at that console, and not *workin'*."

"Madam, I am studying this circuit board to try to ascertain if it can be repaired, or if it must be replaced. It's a *delicate* procedure and requires time, not elbow grease, to accomplish."

"You talk funny. Ya know that? My third husband, Harry, used to talk funny, too. It was so annoying. Like he was better than me 'cause *he* finished high school and *I* didn't. That's mostly the reason I divorced him, ya know? Well, that and the fact that I caught him bangin' my cousin Doris, who ain't nearly as pretty as *me*, at my nephew's Bar Mitzvah. Never worked one day in her life, neider."

"How lucky Harry is to be free of a shrew like you," mumbled Drawjoy.

"Huh? D'you say Harry *screwed* me? Because if ya

did, you was right. Dat bum never knew how good he had it, till he didn't have it from *me* no more."

"Any more," he said a tad louder. "It's *any* more, not *no* more."

"'Scuse me a'cause I can't hear you too well when you're using that power tool. Did you say sumpin' I needed to hear?"

"Almost done, ma'am." He prayed to God the repair held so he never needed to return here for warranty work. "There. Your trash unit should perform up to, if not exceed, factory specifications. With that I will take my leave and burden your existence, such as it is, no longer."

"Did I mention you talk funny?"

"Yes, homeowner, you did. Just like Harry. Good day." With that, Drawjoy grabbed his briefcase, crushing its handle with all the strength in his left hand, and stormed out the door.

The instant he passed the doorframe, two massive police officers pounced on both of his arms. Drawjoy was slammed face first to the metal deck. A wet crunch signaled his nose had broken, as did the rapidly pooling blood on the floor. He struggled to break free, but as with most endeavors in his life, he did so ineptly and ineffectively. His writhing only produced more blood from his nose and a more forceful rotation of his already searing arms.

Cuffs were slapped on his ankles and wrists quicker than he could say *I want a lawyer*. Someone flipped him onto his back much rougher than necessary and rested a heavy boot on his tender chest. The woman placed her Taser an inch from his crumpled nose. "Please try and resist. I really want you to." She fired off a short burst, singeing a few of his nose hairs. "Pretty please."

Drawjoy started to respond in a gurgled, confused manner, but she slipped her heel from his chest to his throat and pushed down moderately hard. "Save it for someone who cares, pig. If there weren't witnesses, I'd end you here and now. Capisce?"

He tried to nod in the affirmative, but was unable to because of her pressure on his neck. He relaxed completely and tried to figure out what had just happened.

Several hours later, Drawjoy found himself in a dazzlingly shiny polished room, sitting manacled to a chair that was bolted to the floor. He had received cursory medical attention. An absurdly bulbous dressing was affixed to his nose, like the white version of a clown's red nose. Not a single person, aside from one paramedic, had spoken to him since the female officer had. He knew, of course, why he'd been arrested. He still couldn't believe they'd accomplished the feat. His cover had been perfect and his contact with Marshall brilliantly discreet. He suspected, actually, that he could *not* be under arrest. Perhaps he was having a bad dream to pair with his bad day. How else could he explain the fact that he, a genius of the first magnitude, had been captured by simians?

His fantasy was interrupted by the sound of the door opening and a single pair of heavy shoe-falls approaching the table. A chair slid back with a high-pitched squeak, and someone of bulk sat down heavily. Papers rustled. The person sipped strong coffee.

Drawjoy couldn't contain himself any longer. "I have wights," he said his Rs transforming to Ws due to his nasal incapacity. "I wish to know who you awe and whewe I'm being held. I also demand to speak to my attowney." He tried to sound imposing, threatening.

"You don't, cupcake," said the man with a weary voice. "I would like to proceed. In fact I will proceed. A point of order, if you will. You have no 'wights,' and you will not have a lawyer, ever. As of this moment, Drawjoy

Miljenko is officially dead. You suffered a freak accident while repairing a trash-compressor unit. You were tragically crushed beyond all recognition, believe it or not. Even your dentist couldn't identify you, because the severe malfunction turned you into a two-inch-thick pancake of mush and crunchy stuff.

"The state, which presently means yours truly, *owns* you. If I decide to light you on fire and watch you burn, I shall do so with pleasure *and* impunity. If I desire to flay your hide off slowly, I shall. Are we perfectly clear here? Do you have *any* lingering hope or unfounded peace of mind that I need to further snuff out?"

"You can't—"

"Shut it, robot boy. From this moment forward, you will only answer my questions, and you will do that with a mindful economy of words. You will not otherwise speak."

"Owa what, tough guy? See to it I don't get dessewt?"

"Or," the man said as he rushed around the table, "I might do this."

Pain exploded in the center of Drawjoy's face. Two powerful fingers crushed and twisted his broken nose. He was unable to breathe. The agony was intense.

"And that's just me winging it, jerk-off. Give me some time and I guarantee I'll come up with a much better 'owa' else."

Drawjoy made no response.

"Good. Even a pathetic piece of shit such as yourself can learn when properly motivated. Now, one additional rule. When I ask a question, you will answer it. If you try and get cute, or if I even *think* you're lying ... well, I think you get my drift. I want to get home in time to watch the big football game. You make me late, and I promise you'll regret it.

"Okay. Question one. Where's Marshall?"

"I don't know," he responded quickly.

"You probably suspect that's not the answer I'm hoping for, right? Want to take another swing at that pitch?"

"I told the twuth. How stupid do you think I am?"

Drawjoy's nose seared with pain. "You remember my injunction, the one about only *me* asking the questions? Now, I'm going to break my own rule just this once and repeat the question. Where's Marshall?"

"I told you, I don't know."

"All right, how about this. When was the last time you saw him?"

"I can't wecall?"

There was a crushing sensation, followed by nauseating, visceral pain in Drawjoy's testicles. "You see, there's a lie. I know you saw him shortly after his incineration, because you reanimated him. You didn't do that with your eyes shut, now did you? So the truthful answer would have been, *When I uploaded him eight months ago.*"

"That was the last time I saw him."

"*Outstanding.* You *can* relate useful information. Not bad for a dead dodo bird. Okay, double or nothing. How do you contact him?"

"I don't. He calls me—or his assistant does, if he's temporawily deceased."

"His assistant. Three cheers. I may not have to beat you until you're dead for real. Who is this assistant?"

"I don't know hew name. I have newer met hew."

"A lady? Useful info, too. Where does Marshall live?"

"No idea. Honestly. Why would he tell me, officew? Think it thwough."

A tremendous slap to the face spun Drawjoy's head almost one hundred eighty degrees. "Why did I hit you, bozo?"

"I asked a question."

"Smarter than you look. Good. Let's move on. Where do you do the transfers?"

"I newer know. It's all awwanged on theiw end."

The man lunged across the table and choked Drawjoy until his face was beet red. "That is your last lie. One more—strike three—and you're out. You'll never see it coming, but it *will* be immediate." With a dull metallic clunk, he set a service pistol on the desk. "We have a team dismantling the lab you use in the warehouse district, near Kennedy and Palm. Where are the android shells kept?"

"He keeps them. I *sweaw* it. They delivew one to my lab when needed. Honest. You gotta twust me."

"You, shit-bird Miljenko, think I should 'twust' you? You are directly responsible for the death of Madam Secretary Kahl. You *killed* your one-time supervisor Carlos De La Frontera. That news crew that was slaughtered? Their blood is on your hands, as surely as it is on Marshall's. You're an accomplice to mass murder and a disgrace to your species. The only aspect of you I trust is that you will bleed when I cut you and that you will feel real pain when I inflict it upon you. Understood, worm?"

"Yes, siw."

"Okay, and I'm only asking because I was told to. Me? I could give a shit. Why did you do it? Why do you aid and abet Stuart Marshall, *the* most dangerous man in history?"

"He pays me well for my sewices. Plus, before you torture me again, I like the wowk. Aftew DeJesus twumped up false accusations against me and tewinated my employment, I had no altewnative."

"I actually believe the part about you liking the work. I also know you're stupid enough to think you were wronged. But I've read your entire file. Your job performance with the android program was abysmal. Your work was shoddy, your attitude poisonous, and your team spirit was nonexistent. You were, and I kid you not, *the* worst employee *ever* in android development history. The fact you were too stupid to realize that and tried and go it alone is just icing on the cake of your complete failure in life."

"I don't have to sit hewe and be insulted. Awe we thwough yet?"

"I'll let that question slide, because I want to beat the traffic home. But know this. For you, it will *never* be done. You're going to be questioned three times a day, every day, until the day you die years from now unless, of course, someone does us all a favor and kills you sooner. Then we can all celebrate. I'll bake the cake myself. No, shit bird, you'll be the test subject for every student at the academy to hone their skills on. Hell, we may even let some of the victims's *families* interview you in private. Wouldn't that be fun? We'd have to cover the floor and walls with plastic, but that'd be no problem.

"Your existence'll be as miserable as we can collectively make it. We'll ask around for suggestions as to how to make it even worse. In fact, knowing what's in store for you, the suffering you will endure, the horror that'll fill your remaining days, I almost feel sorry for you. But you know what? Whenever that happens, I'll remember my brother. He was one of Kahl's bodyguards. I think about him, the way he looked when my mother insisted on seeing him one last time. Only half his head was left. Can you imagine her pain? Well, if you can't now, I promise you will in the months and years to come. You'll become the universe's top expert on soul-killing suffering."

NINE

"It's pretty clear," said Heath, "that Drawjoy isn't going to provide us with any more useful information."

"Yes," agreed Amanda. "We understood he was a pawn and that Marshall was too savvy to let him in on anything big. Still—"

"It would've been nice to be led to the bossman. I know." Heath sipped his wine. "At least it didn't take much footwork to pick up that lunatic Mary Jane Plumquist. What a piece of work."

"She's so devoted to Stuart it took *forever* to get what little we did out of her." Amanda took a big gulp of juice. "But even *she* knew next to nothing. That Marshall's one clever SOB."

"He'll surface one way or another. He'll either have a mechanical problem, we'll find him, or, best of all, someone will kill him on sight. You'll see." He gently raised her chin with one finger. "What's the matter? I know you have ten million things on your plate, but I can tell something's really eating at you. Give." He offered her his glass. "You sure you won't have some?"

Her absent stare evaporated into a warm look at

Heath. Amanda smiled, leaned over, and kissed him. She sat back against her pillow. "You know I'm, well, you know my sexual past? I'm ... new to this." She swung a finger between them. You're my first ... you know ... partner of the male persuasion."

"I'm honored." He furrowed his brow. "I think. That's a good thing, isn't it?"

"Cute, funny, and good in the sack. I landed myself a real triple-threat." She wrinkled her nose at him.

"This's all interesting bonding information, but there's something bothering you. What?"

Amanda rolled her eyes. "Guess what lesbian lovers never have to worry about?"

"I'm not touching that question with a ten-meter pole."

"Birth control. You know, *protection*."

"And that means ... oh no—"

She nodded vigorously. "Oh *yes*."

"Bu ... but I ... *assumed* you were on some kind of ... er, precautionary measure."

"Like I said, the matter never came up before. I guess I was just stupid, but now I'm just pregnant. Hence the apple juice." She pointed to her glass. "So glad you finally noticed I haven't had any alcohol for the last two weeks." Her eyes shot hot sparks at him.

"Come to think of it ... I think I'll change the subject. Good idea, right?"

"Best I've heard come out of your mouth in a while."

"Wow."

"*Wow*, in what meaning of the exclamation, dearest?"

"The old team is back in action."

"Huh?"

"A Ryan impregnating a Geraty."

"Just for the record, I expected that crass remark from the press, not from you."

Heath sat bolt upright and set down his glass. "Okay, serious as a heart attack, what are we going to do?" He held up a hang-on-a-second hand to halt a response. "I'm willing to do whatever it takes. We go public, we go public. I'll man up to whatever you need me to do." He ground his teeth a moment. "You need me to talk with Piper, I'll talk with Piper."

"I hoped you'd say that." She leaned back over and kissed him again. "Thanks. You're the best. Let me think about it a while."

"I love you." There, he'd finally said it.

"Okay, wasn't expecting *that* one, but again, thanks. It helps." She saw his crest fall ever so slightly. "You're kidding, right? You need me to say it, too, or what? You think I don't love you with all my heart and all my soul?" She looked toward Heaven and declared, "*Men*."

"So how do you wish to proceed, Madame President?"

"I have no freaking idea, Mr. Vice Presidential Father. Not one frickin' clue."

Amanda's phone went off. The mood was shattered to a distant memory. It was the high-pitched unmistakable squeal of her emergency alert. She snatched the phone off the night stand. "Walker here. What?" She put her hand to her forehead. "I'll be in my office in two minutes. Make sure everyone's there before me. Oh, and I'll let the VP know personally." She reached over to set the phone down, but it dropped to the floor.

"My God, what?" Heath asked taking her hand.

TEN

"Yibitriander. My word, what brings you here physically?" Kymee stood to greet his ancient friend. They each held the other's right elbow with their right hand and bumped shoulders. That had always been the custom among the Deavoriath. "I don't think I've actually *seen* you here for millennia."

"It has been a while," Yibitriander replied, "hasn't it?" He looked around the cluttered room, taking it in as if seeing it for the first time. "Not much has changed, either. Still a smelly mess."

Kymee scanned the space with a father's pride. "Yes, isn't it wonderful something of the before remains?"

Yibitriander wasn't all that quick to respond. Eventually the best he could concede was, "If it makes an old friend happy, then yes."

"So precise with your words. You've never stopped being a politician have you?"

Yibitriander bristled. "If you're going to hurl insults, I shan't come again for several *more* millennia." He tried to look sternly at Kymee, but was forced to smile when his friend began chuckling. "I never could fool you, could I, old one?"

"Never have and never will." He tapped the side of his nose with a digit. "I doubt you'll even be able to trick me after I'm gone."

"Are you," asked Yibitriander, "unwell, old amongst the ancient? The very concept of you being gone violates the laws of nature as I understand them."

"To all there is a dawn, a noon, and a sunset. So it is with me. So it is with all things." He pointed generally into the air. "Where will we be when this universe thins out to cold nothingness?"

After reflecting Yibitriander answered, "Perhaps in some other universe, if that place is so unfortunate."

"You are as always as glum as a month of rain. Please attempt to be more upbeat. Is that too much to ask?"

Yibitriander looked to the floor. "The Deavoriath have much to answer for. I don't know if it'd be a positive if we were to survive the dissipation of yet another universe."

"Before I decide to throw my old bones into an exploding star, tell me what brings you here today? I can't take much more of your moaning and handwringing. You're like an old woman at a gravesite."

Yibitriander tried to look offended but could never be mad at Kymee. "Yes, as to my visit. It seems there has been some activity on one of the vortexes."

"What? That's as strange an occurrence as it is an improbable one."

"Yet," he lifted his palms, "it would seem to be the case."

"What makes you believe such a thing is possible?"

"Do you remember that communication station near Forby, the one on the far side of Leckt?"

The old man rubbed his chin. "Yes, it's the last one I built. Must have been almost a million years ago."

"At least," said Yibitriander with a harrumph. "In any case, Milcowdon happened by it recently and heard an odd sound, so she entered the structure."

"What was that old hag doing near Forby?"

He shrugged.

"What would *any* of us be doing near Forby, for that matter? Hot, dry, unforgiving terrain fit only for demons." He smiled wickedly. "Ah, that's what Milcowdon was doing there." He winked at his friend. "A family reunion no doubt."

"You really are bad. We, the enlightened Deavoriath, don't think like that, speak like that, or even smile like that."

"Have you forgotten so much of that woman's shortcomings as a life form?"

"No," Yibitriander smiled back, "I have not, father." His grin lingered a satisfyingly long time. "In any case, she entered to find a communication-request light pulsing. It had timed into an audible alarm since it hadn't been answered in the prescribed time period."

"Who was it from?"

"She couldn't say. She claims she is unfamiliar with the technology you installed, so she elected not to 'fiddle with it,' as she put it."

"I'll bet. She probably tried every trick she knew to open the channel. I'll wager she hammered it with her horns to try and find out the message."

"I have," Yibitriander said stiffly, "no reason to doubt her statement."

"How did she decide it was a vortex calling?"

"The panel the light flashed on was labeled as such."

"If it's the panel I'm thinking of it would have indicated which particular vortex was hailing us."

"Yes. It was *Wrath* who called to us."

The old man was clearly shaken by that news. He sat

down heavily and his arms dropped limply to the sides. "*No. Wrath?* How could it be *that* ship, that very vortex?"

"I know. I share your surprise."

"Surprise? You feel only surprise? I feel a gnawing terror in my gut. I feel a foreboding. I feel frightened. Surprise is too mild a word."

"He does have quite a legacy, doesn't he?" Yibitriander tried to sound dispassionate.

"Indeed, he does. Of all those damn vortexes, I'd have prayed hardest to never hear from him more than all others combined."

"Yet it is he who calls."

"Where did you leave him? You said you scuttled him as far from the light as possible. And it has to have been two million years ago." He wrinkled his brow. "Perhaps it is just a mechanical malfunction." With no conviction Kymee proclaimed, "Yes, that's it. He has suffered a mechanical failure. The signal is some system glitch, nothing more."

"If you really believed that, I doubt your face would be that pale."

"I did build him well. You're right there. But how? All the Forms are on Oowaoa. There's no one to possibly give *Wrath* life. *No* one."

Yibitriander rose to his toes and rested back. "There is *one* capable of such a feat."

"Not the human you had me fit with control prerogatives."

"Yes, I refer to Jon Ryan." Yibitriander scowled.

"But surely that would be impossible. Why, the man would have to locate *Wrath* and learn he could pilot a vortex. Nothing so unlikely could have possibly occurred."

"And I placed *Wrath* in the center of one of the last pockets of Uhoor. I knew they would help discourage visitation. Yet, in spite of all those precautions, I fear just such a combination of impossibilities has happened."

Kymee rubbed his palm against his cheek. "What are the odds? That's amazing." He punched at the air. "Then I say good for Jon Ryan. He can spend his eternity learning the nuances of the silly box."

"That silly *box*," Yibitriander responded harshly, "as you call it, is responsible for more deaths than Tellusian worms. It single handedly destroyed both the Melquissian and Trellpot empires."

"I thought," Kymee said in a low tone, "*Wrath*'s Form accomplished those dastardly acts, not the vortex manipulator. You know as well as I do he can't act unless he's properly activated and enabled."

"His bloodlust is unbounded and his grasp of morality is nonexistent. And you know as well as I that he can influence a Form into acting along any line that suits him. He's not a mindless machine." Yibitriander fell into dour contemplation, with a distraught look in his eyes.

"I will go to the communication station and confirm if these are indeed the facts. When I return, if your concerns are validated, you can tell me what it is you'd like to do."

Yibitriander initially reacted as if he hadn't heard Kymee. Then he focused on his father. "Very well. That's a sound plan. Let me know as soon as you're back."

Kymee snickered. "How is it that I could be back and you *not* know of it? Yibitriander, this's *now*, not before. Plus, we're not bound to action, whether *Wrath* is active or not. Our ways have changed. You waste a few ticks of your infinite time worrying, as if the fate of anything is based on *our* intervention or desire. We will allow whatever is to happen to progress along its own lines. The fate of whoever is involved is not ours to meddle with."

"I must know what chain of happenstance I have set in motion."

"To what end?" Kymee said with a challenge. "Would you try and intervene? Hmm? That is no longer our way."

"I know."

"Need I remind the Form of *Wrath* about the perils of action? You two cast the entire home galaxy of our one-time rivals the Nujjenis out of this universe. You recall what happened, don't you?"

"As if it were yesterday," Yibitriander said emotionlessly. "The annihilation of their galaxy once it contacted foreign laws of physics almost ripped open a channel to our universe. I very nearly destroyed two pocket universes."

"Since that time we have withdrawn and developed our minds and our spirits, not our power and influence." He shook his thin hair with a fast hand. "I wasn't too sanguine about your request to upgrade the human android, if you will recall. I did it out of loyalty to an old friend. But, did I not say at the time that it constituted a violation of our prime directive? It went against the principles we've strived to achieve, and have achieved, for generations."

"Yes," he responded distantly, "you did. But I felt I owed him a debt, and that was the most logical manner to settle it."

"Not the one most in keeping with your past resolve. Back then, you'd have pulled every circuit and doodad out of Ryan and tossed them into the trash. You wouldn't have made him a Form, not back then."

He looked askance at the old man. "You know I've left all that behind me."

"Have you? Well, we can discuss that further after I return from my journey." He scratched absently at his face. "I've not undertaken a journey in so long I can't recall when it was." He smiled slightly. "I hope I recall how to do such a thing."

"You'll do fine," said Yibitriander with a warm smile. "You've never failed once in your entire life. Such a thing is unthinkable. It's probably impossible."

They tapped right shoulders and Yibitriander departed. Why, he asked himself for the millionth time, had he decided it was a good idea to have Kymee put those control units in the android? It seemed, in retrospect, an unwise move.

ELEVEN

Lacking a superior plan, I committed myself full time to the business of helping create a viable society on Azsuram. There were by then more than enough adults and teenagers to fill our needs and perform needed work. There were also a slowly growing number of immigrants from Kaljax. Hence, my input was, thankfully, less and less necessary. But Sapale had entrusted me to watch over the societal development of our world over time. I felt my continued involvement in its infancy would be time well spent.

I became the first and last non-Kaljaxian to serve on the Council of Elders. Mine was a permanent seat, I'll have you know. Yeah, political drone for all my immortal life, whether I liked it or not. Sort of like a double enema and an ass kicking all rolled into one good time. I promised myself I'd participate earnestly in the meetings while Sapale was alive. I did leave the possibility of a more emeritus status open for the long-term future, however.

To keep the peace on the home front, I limited my vortex trips to Kaljax and back, and only when my brood's-mate felt there was a compelling need to make the trek. Most of our trips were to ferry carefully screened Kaljaxians to Azsuram, but occasionally, social calls were made. Gradually, shipments of Kaljaxian supplies dwindled to nothing, as Sapale's plan to make us independent came more and more online. Once in a while, I ferried Toño to check in with Carlos or to attend a scientific conference. That usually drew some form of primal growl from the love of my life. If you took how much she wanted to be independent from Kaljax and multiplied it by one thousand, that'd be how much she wanted to avoid contact with *my* crazy species. Marshall's threats were always front and center in her mind, so by her reasoning, any contact meant that much more chance of harm.

But I was a human and couldn't extinguish all my concerns for how they were doing. I'd risked everything to make their worldship voyage possible, so I was naturally curious as to how matters were progressing. Someday, I'd put my foot down and let the old ball-and-chain know I needed to make contact with my kind. That'd be just as soon as I worked up sufficient courage to do so. I figured that would be any decade now. Hey, sometimes a man had to do what a man had to do. But no one ever said there was a need to rush toward pain.

I loved all my kids, grandkids, and great grandkids, sure. But, no way around it, JJ was the apple of my eye. I guess all the time we spent being the only dudes around helped make us special buddies. And no, Toño didn't count as one of the guys. He was as non-macho as they came, especially considering he was a Spaniard. He must have lost a gene or two somewhere along the line. Anyway, JJ shared my dislike of all things political. We took any excuse to head off on our own to explore, hunt, or just be alone together.

JJ's brood's-mate Challaria seemed to understand this. She never tried to stop what Sapale called our "goofing-off" expeditions. Challaria called it our bonding time. I figured that meant not all the females of Kaljax were as tough as mine. I loved JJ's line. He always told Challaria we were going to find him a vortex so he and I could have races. That always drew a rolling of all four eyes from her. She knew JJ with a personal vortex would be a disaster—like giving high explosives to a toddler.

One night JJ and I were lying under the stars a few days ride from the nearest outpost. We were doing some geological investigations, similar to the one that netted us the vortex. JJ announced, "Challaria will be giving birth in a couple weeks."

"Yeah, I heard that rumor, too. Poor kid if he turns out to be a boy." We both laughed pretty hard at that image. "That will make him, what, JJJ?" I rocked my reclined head side-to-side with each "J."

"J-cubed?"

"Jon J-squared?"

"J-math?"

"J-changes-his-name-by-age-three-because-he's-so-embarrassed-by-it?"

When JJ stopped giggling, he said confidently, "We'll figure his handle out eventually. But seriously, I wouldn't have it any other way. His grandfather is a great man and the best dad possible. He will honor that individual by carrying his name."

"Aw, shucks. That's so nice to hear. Thank you, son."

We were quiet a good long while, staring at the stars. I had to stop and say a word about the stars. Here I spoke from rather considerable experience. I grew up wanting to be a pilot. I was never too much into astronomy, but I made myself learn how to navigate by the stars in the night sky. I figured if I had to ditch my ride in water, knowing how to find dry land would be a good thing. By age ten, I knew all the constellations in both the northern and southern skies of Earth.

One of the first mind-altering visions I had when I flew *Ark 1* was how absolutely unfamiliar the heavens were above distant solar systems. I never knew until then how anchoring the stars of home could be. Every new system I'd visited since then has had the same effect on me.

I actually had quite the fun time with Azsuram's night sky. As the person tied for the least need of sleep on the planet, I spent a lot of time looking up at night. I began seeing constellations and naming them. Yeah, you got it. Put me in charge of anything and stand back, I'm going to do it the Jon way. Above our main village, one could move their finger across the sky and draw the outlines of many iconic historically relevant constellations. To the far north, there's Beer Bottle. Close to Beer Bottle was, naturally, Beer Bottle Opener. Duh. Then our tour continued south, where we found both the Bigger and Lesser Ta-Tas. Mostly in winter, one looked up straight overhead and saw Joe Montana, arm cocked back, ready to throw *The Catch* for all eternity. It was my favorite, by far. Additional interest could be found way to the south, where the sky was totally dominated by 1965 Shelby Cobra 427. Simply breathtaking. It was a must-see. Other, less recognizable configurations of stars included, in no particular order, Steve McQueen, First Girlfriend, Xbox, Golden Retriever, Smoked Baby Back Ribs, and another personal favorite of mine, Nice Butt.

Anyway, back to JJ and me at the fireside. After a long silence, he asked me cautiously, "What's it like to be immortal?"

That aspect, that quality of the experience was

something I'd never thought much about. After a few minutes, I replied to him honestly. "I have no idea."

"Dad," he snapped back, "I'm serious. I don't want one of your patented wise-ass answers."

"So am I. Seriously."

"But no way. You're over two hundred years old. You're going to live at *least* twenty thousand years, according to Toño. Even at that point, you can re-upload to a new android and go on forever."

"Don't you see? That's just it. I'm two hundred. I have not yet *lived* forever. When I was twenty, I felt like I do now. No diff. I can tell you what it's like to be two centuries old, but the forever part hasn't happened yet, so I can't."

"But you know you'll outlive dirt. That has to leave some impression."

"No," I answered slowly, "Marshall might kill me tomorrow. I'm not guaranteed a long life. I might *have* one, maybe, but for the present, I just feel like me. The way I always have."

"Okay, then how does it feel to know you'll outlive everyone you've ever known, aside from the android ones?"

"That's easy. It feels like shit. I feel like I'm standing in a roaring fire, holding my breath one hundred percent of the time. I'm afraid to stay, because I don't want the coming pain. But I'm afraid to leave, because I'd lose precious moments with those I love. I, in summary, live in Limbo. Do you know Limbo?"

He shook his head. "Nah."

"It comes from one of the main Earth religions. It's a place of confinement for the dead, where they're in a perpetual state of neglect, despair, and isolation. It's oblivion, as opposed to damnation."

"Wow," JJ said, after a whistle, "that sucks the big one."

"Tell me about it."

"Mom says it's a curse, your immortality. Is it?"

"In a way, yes, but in a way, no. A curse is put on a person to punish them. I sought out this condition eyes wide open to help my people." I shook my head slowly. "Sure does feel like a plain old curse most of the time, though."

He sat up, a look of expectation in his eyes. "Have you ever thought about turning yourself off, ending it all?"

"Where did this philosophical inclination suddenly come from, boy? Up until now, the most metaphysical thing you've ever considered was whether to have another beer or not."

"Gee, thanks for the ego boost, pops. And I'll have you know, I talk a lot about important stuff with Mom and Toño. I usually know better than to attempt a serious conversation with *you*."

"Touché. I deserved that one. Nice technique, too. You're really learning to twist the knife after plunging it in someone's heart."

"I've learned at the feet of a master."

I swung a playful punch at him, but was too far away to land it.

"A master who is apparently losing his touch by the way."

"Yes."

"Yes, you agree you're losing it, old clunker?"

"No. Yes, I've thought long and hard about suicide." To myself I muttered, "Not sure if a robot can commit suicide, actually. Huh? More philosophy. Crappy dappy."

"You have? For real?" JJ perked up.

"Sure." I couldn't talk for a moment. Big lump in my

throat. "JJ, I never planned on this immortality thing. I did what I had to do to help others. I considered it my duty. I'm stuck with it, but I don't want it for its own sake."

JJ angled his head, thinking. He squinted his left eyes at me and said, "Wait. You competed for that spot and won out over any number of equally well-qualified pilots. If you hadn't done it, someone perfectly well-suited would have. You wanted to be the *stud*. Now you're stuck with the consequences you probably didn't give much thought to at the time."

The little brat was his mother's son all right. "When did you get so smart?"

He pumped a fist in the air.

"You're too right. I heard about the program and I wanted to win. I did. So yeah, I have to own the consequences. But," I raised a finger, "I *was* the best. I came back with these," I held up both hands, "as well as the membrane tech. No one else even came close to such prizes. So maybe I had to do it to serve, because I really *was* better than any of the other slackers."

"Gosh," the little rat said covering his mouth, "you're right. You *are* a victim. I, along with everyone else alive, feel so bad for you. Wish I could help, but I can't seem to find the time."

"You know, I could leave you here to walk home." I gestured to the general vicinity.

"Would you? Wow, that would be great. Then I could be a victim, too, just like my father."

"Okay, you called me out and you're right. I have no one to blame but myself. But in all seriousness, there *are* major downsides to this gig." I looked far off toward nowhere in particular. "If I had to do it over again—" I had to stop another second. "If I had to do it all over again, I would, and I'll tell you why. As shitty as some aspects of my existence are, if I hadn't taken the leap, I'd have never met you." I sat up, reached over, and rested my hand on his shoulder. "You're worth the headaches, you big goofball."

JJ rested his face on my hand and blinked. "I'm glad you did, dad."

"Maybe you should catch some Zs. You're a growing boy." He settled back, still looking at me. "Check that," I corrected, "you're a terrific young man who could use some shut-eye."

TWELVE

"Okay, people, here's the situation. Thirty minutes ago, seven of our automated communications satellites exploded at precisely the same time." Amanda knuckled the conference room table as she leaned on it, briefing her cabinet.

"That's certainly unusual," said a senior general, "but do we know it was an intentional act?"

"They were destroyed by independent thermonuclear explosions. It was a terrorist act, all right."

"Any idea who or why?" Secretary of Domestic Affairs Charles Bingham asked.

"No," Amanda looked to Heath. "But I'd bet my life it's Marshall, back with a vengeance."

"Has he claimed credit?" asked Jillian Black, her assistant chief of staff.

"No, not as of this moment."

"What makes you so certain it was Stuart?" Jillian replied.

"We just arrested the renegade technician who's been reanimating him and his longtime secretary who's been running the operation."

Someone whistled loudly.

"You didn't think it was necessary to let us in on that one?" asked Bingham, with a sharp edge to his tone.

"No, Chuck, I did not. It was need-to-know only. The man is officially dead. I didn't want it leaked that he's actually not. I take all precautions when it comes to information concerning Marshall."

"Yeah," Charles said with a harrumph, "for all the good it did."

"Secretary Bingham," said Heath angrily, "now is neither the time nor the place for flippant remarks. We need to remain focused and function as a single unit."

Anger danced across Bingham's face. Then he said quietly, "I maintain *respectfully*, Madam President, that in the future we all be kept in the loop when such significant developments take place."

"Duly noted," was Amanda's terse response. To the entire group she said, "Any thoughts or questions?"

"Any injuries or radiation danger?" asked the Surgeon General, Satish Kumar.

"No. Membranes popped on throughout the fleet, so no radiation exposure or blast damage occurred, except to the drones."

"I don't get it," stated Bingham. "Why blow up a handful of useful but noncritical automated satellites? They're not *strategically* important."

"I suspect we'll find out soon enough," said Amanda. "If Heath and I are right, Marshall will be calling anytime now, the dramatic bastard."

As if on cue an AI interrupted. "Priority holo incoming, Madam President. Shall I put it on the table?"

"By all means." She crossed her arms and stared at where the guilty party's likeness would appear.

A standing male figure materialized. He was formally saluting. It was, of course, Stuart Marshall. He wore a modified Army uniform. She noted it displayed ten stars. Stuart stood stiffly, though his arm wavered visibly, suggesting it required immense effort to maintain the salute.

"What, Stuart?" Amanda demanded. "Please dispense with your childish behavior and tell me what you called to say."

An anonymous off-holo voice called out loudly, "He's waiting for you to return his salute."

"Stuart, really, knock it off," she said exasperated. "I'm not in the mood."

The sound of Stuart saying the words, *not until you return my salute,* were enunciated by him, with his mouth closed.

"Fine." Amanda said with disgust, "If it will shorten my contact with you." She saluted very quickly and only partially. "Now can you get to the threat and intimidation portion of your performance?"

"Greetings, PP Walker." He hunched his shoulders and covered his mouth with two fingers. "Oh, gosh. Did that ever come out funny? I never said it out loud before. My bad. Sorry. I did *not* just call you *Urination* Walker." He shook his head demonstrably. "No. I said PP, as in *Pretender President.* I, as the only *rightful* president, have yet to determine what exactly will be the punishment for your presumption, madame."

"Stuart, cut the crap and tell me what this is about."

He furrowed his eyebrows, turned his head, and looked down, like an actor responding to a shocking piece of information in a tense scene. "Did you, Madame PP, just say the word 'crap' in the presence of the leader of the US? May shame befall you." He swirled a hand in the air. "But you're forgiven, Madame Bushmaster. I realize you're still in shock on account of your whore-bitch quite literally eating herself to death."

"Stuart, we all know you're insane and no one wants to hear you drone on like the fool you are." Heath was hot. "Get to the point, before I do us all a favor and hang up."

"You wouldn't want," Stuart shook a finger of admonition in the air, "to do that, son. You see, Ryan-Lite, if you did, you'd piss me off more than you do already by drawing breath. If I was angrier, I promise you'd regret it most acutely."

"Again, Stuart, what's happening? Are you responsible for the destruction of those satellites?" Amanda stepped in to prevent Heath from escalating the situation.

"Let me see." Stuart placed his index finger under his chin. "Ah, yes. Now that you mention it, I do recall placing one-hundred-megaton bombs in some orbiting platforms and pushing the 'go-boom' button."

Amanda rolled her eyes and prayed for strength. "Why did you do that, you sorry bastard?"

"I'm *not* sorry, honeypie" he barked petulantly. "You couldn't possibly understand my feelings. I did it because I love all of my citizens. I wish to harm not a *single* hair on a *solitary* head." He smiled mischievously and added, "Unless you force me to, that is."

"For the love of all that's holy, Marshall, spare us the pain and get to your fucking point." Again, Heath's mood was pretty obvious.

"Ryanette. I will brook no further disrespect from your pie hole. One more outburst, and I will refuse to proceed until you are cast out of my sight."

"He'll play nice, Stuart," said Amanda placing her hand on Heath's forearm. "We're all ears."

"No you're not. You're just being silly now, you little rug-muncher. You're all ears? What, I'm addressing a room full of quivering, detached body parts?"

"You have ten seconds before I terminate this holo if you do not stop being an ass."

As if slammed in the face with a serious-stick, Stuart instantaneously transformed into the very picture of stately profundity. "Certainly, Amanda. As always, you are correct. Now, I was calling to inform you of the nature of my little stunt with the comm-sats. I wanted, as an initial move, to get your full attention. I see I have achieved that goal.

"Now, the second matter I will disclose is the presence of fifty similar thermonuclear devices hidden, ingeniously I might add, on fifty worldships."

"You're bluffing," called out a senior general.

"Atchison? Is that you, Jimmy *Atchison*? Well, I'll *be*. So butt-licking sycophants still have a place in the current political milieu. Good for you, son. Anyway, has anyone aboard that ship of fools ever known me to bluff at *anything*?" He waited a few seconds and prompted them. "Hmm?"

"We're listening, Marshall," said Amanda as coolly as she could.

"Nice," he said cheerfully. "Okay, here's the reality y'all face. I've hidden fifty huge bombs on fifty ships. Now I know what you're going to say, so I'll head you off at the pass. You're saying to yourselves, *how did Marshall get his cotton-picking hands on that many bombs?* Answer. *Doesn't matter, because I got 'em.* Next dumb question. *Can he prove it?* Answer. *Absolutely.* I could set them all off and there'd be no doubt." He rubbed absently at his chin. "Prefer not to do that, but it is one of my options. Another way I could prove it is this. Here's a list of ten worldships, each of which carries a powerful surprise. *Nantucket, Adventurer, Herbert Hoover, Starbound, Klarika, Lancashire, Boldly Goes, Protectorate, Denial,* and *Jefferson*. Manda, as PP, you select one name, and I'll tell you where the device is hidden. That way you know I'm as serious as a pregnant-underage mistress." He folded his arms and waited.

A thousand thoughts ran through her mind. With little consideration, she blurted out, *"Boldly Goes."* Several of her family members were on the ship. She'd made a snap decision, so she didn't have time to fret about her blatant favoritism.

"Fine. The bomb is in a church. I placed it in a storage room to the left of the altar, where seasonal decorations are stored. It's in a large red box, with the words 'Do Not Open Until Christmas' spray-painted in white on all four sides. My advice is to not have the junior janitor open the box to validate my claim. The nuke is armed and has a secondary movement trigger. I'll give you ten minutes to check it out, then I'll call back." Marshall's holo vanished.

"I'll get right on it," said the Secretary of Internal Affairs Jamal Lin.

Exactly ten minutes later Marshall rematerialized on the table. He was now seated with his feet up on the desk. "Satisfied, child?"

"We confirmed that a large nuclear device was in that box. We believe your claim. *I* believe your claim. Where do our negotiations begin? What do you want?"

"Now, Mandy-Mandy, who said anything about negotiations? I believe the proper term is *nonnegotiable demands* on my part and *full and immediate capitulation* on yours."

"What do you want?"

He gazed to the ceiling above him. "Hmm? Well, I *want* a pony for my next birthday. I *want* to be taller. Oh, and I *want* you to marry me."

"Stuart," she began, "if there's one shred of decency left in you, please be serious and present your demands."

He sat up, leaned toward the camera, and asked, "But what if there isn't a shred of decency left, nothing?"

Heath cupped his hand over her ear and said something brief.

"Then," she said grimly, "we're done. You murder millions of innocent people, and we continue our search to find you." She slumped into her chair. "At least their deaths will be painless. There's some consolation in that knowledge." Her head dropped forward.

"Why, Ms. Walker," Marshall said, "that was truly eloquent. If I had a hat, it would be off to you. In recognition of your passion, I will tell you my demands. Ah, first, and I trust this is not an emotional blow, I actually don't want you to be my bride. I don't have the time to break in a newcomer to the heterosexual lifestyle. Sorry. Hey," he said cheerily, "why don't you guess at my first demand? Bet ya can."

"You want that idiot Miljenko back." She didn't bother lifting her head to say it.

"Ding, ding, ding. We have a winner. Never steal my people, PP. *Never.*"

"How do you wish to make the exchange?" she asked wearily.

"No need. Just open his cage and turn him loose. By the time I need him again, he'll have disappeared nicely."

"Anything else, Marshall?" Amanda asked with her head still down.

"Nah. That's it. Nice doing business with you." He stood and started to walk off-holo. Suddenly he flopped back in his chair. He pointed at the lens and snapped, "Psych. Had you hopin', didn't I?"

"Just tell us, you sideshow freak," Heath said, "and let's all move on."

"Heath Ryan," Marshall said with prickly irritation, "you're so no fun. The lamentable condition of unfunness is genetic in the Ryan clan. Here's a side bet I'll wager with you personally. I bet that if you say one more word, I'll blow up one worldship. Hmm? You wanna take that bet?"

Heath said nothing.

"Excellent. One more attack dog muzzled. Here's demand number two. I want my five worldships back. I had grown most fond of them before you illegally stole them from me. And, I want them as of right now. No evacuations or warnings. If you balk, they blow."

"Done," came out of Amanda's mouth. Those present in the room were stunned. She finally lifted her head. "It's better to have as much of humanity alive as possible. Their captivity can't last forever."

"Ah, Ms. Mister. Who says it can't? I will always be with my people."

She refused to take the bait. "Anything else?"

"No, not really. Oh, a warning. I carry in my left hand," he held it aloft, "a dead man's switch. If you morons actually did incapacitate me, you'd regret it, like, immediately. You also better pray I don't need to scratch my nuts while I'm shaking someone's hand." He puffed out his cheeks. "Ba-boom. Got it?"

"I hear you, Stuart. The five ships' control-key codes will be posted to my personal website within the hour." She looked up with sudden and convincing fury. "Are we done?"

Stuart visibly recoiled, then composed himself. "Yes we are."

"Good. When you're underway with your hostages, please send me the locations of the remaining bombs."

He tilted his head side-to-side. "Nah. Consider their locations to be an Easter egg hunt to keep y'all busy on your long, otherwise boring voyage to wherever the hell you're going." He was gone.

"Mandy," belted out Heath, "how could you give in to that madman? There's no telling what horrors the people on those ships will suffer."

She stared at him a while, tears welling up. "I know he would have set off all the bombs. I believe he really wanted to, just for the hell of it. A man like that," she smeared a tear off her face, "you don't screw around with. We got off light."

"This time," Heath said angrily.

"This time," she agreed sobbing.

THIRTEEN

Amanda and Heath sat alone in a dark Noval Office, long after everyone else had left for the night. They sat in opposite directions looking into nothingness. Heath had single-handedly done quite a bit of damage to a bottle of vodka. Amanda rapped the tips of her fingers repeatedly on the desk. No useful, productive direction could be decided upon before the cabinet meeting drifted apart. In over half an hour, neither of them had spoken. Since the holo with Marshall, they'd avoided each other's eyes as best they could.

Amanda was beginning to think Heath had passed out drunk. His eyes were closed and his breathing was soft and regular. Apropos of nothing, he spoke in a low pain-ridden tone. "I'm sorry for what I said back at the meeting. You did what you had to. I'd have done the same thing, God willing, if I were in your place."

She waited several moments before responding. "Thanks. It hurt more than you can imagine to have you angry at me. I've come to rely on your shoulder." More to herself, she half-whispered, "More than I should. I need to be stronger."

"No," he said sitting up. "You're perfect. Don't change just because those you trust fall short. I think you handled Marshall as well as anyone could have." He threw his hands up, "The man's nuts. I think he'd have loved to murder all those people *and* blamed it on you."

She smiled sadly. "Thanks. That helps." She took a very deep breath and blew it out slowly. "He could've demanded more. I'm actually surprised he didn't." She squinted in the near darkness. "In fact, I wonder *why* he didn't?" She turned to Heath. "Put yourself in his place. If you could've asked for more, why not do it?"

"He could've asked for more ships, but I don't know if that would be such a prize."

"He could have taken all the farmships, if for no reason other than to hurt us."

Heath rocked his head back and forth. "Nah. He probably doesn't need more food. He'd be buying more headaches more than likely. Plus, once he's gone, I doubt he'll think much about us. There's no real benefit in trying to hamstring us. No jollies in it in the long run."

She pursed her lips. "I guess. What about more androids? I'm sure he can fabricate them slowly, but he has to know there are at least a thousand blanks laying in De La Frontera's lab."

"Good point. Why not take *them*? They'd make perfect longterm guards or patronage gifts."

"Maybe he will ask us to give him those, too, somewhere down the line?"

"But," Heath said, "why not ask when he had us where he wanted us? If he had a second plan, why bother to rely on it? Makes no sense. And what about the newer copy of Stuart Marshall, the one Ryan installed? Why not at least ask for it to be destroyed? It's not like him to leave a viable copy behind."

"It would seem like something he'd want," said Amanda running a hand though her mop of hair. "Maybe he figures it's not really him, so he needn't concern himself with it?"

"I suppose. Still, it's odd for a vengeful man to pass on a perfectly good helpless victim to toy with."

Amanda rested her elbows on the table. "Let's puzzle this scenario out. He *should* want more androids. Only reason not to would be that he doesn't *like* them." The pair was silent a spell. "He couldn't have forgotten to ask. He's too good."

"If he figured he could take them—like, *steal* them— he wouldn't have to ask." Heath was unconvinced by his own argument. "Maybe he just wanted to screw with our minds, like he's doing?"

"Hmm," she hummed. "That *would* be classic Stuart Marshall."

"Or," Heath's voice perked up, "he doesn't want to bring on future threats, like Jackson turned out to be. A few replacements for himself and Drawjoy would mean he was the only immortal in play."

"That makes the most sense, I guess. That'd only mean he's changed his tactics a bit since before we left Earth. Unfortunately, it doesn't represent a juicy insight into his mind."

Amanda set her head in her hands. "I still can't think of a thing we can do to get our ships back. Even if your great-grandfather popped up this instant, I doubt he'd be able to pull it off a second time. Marshall's got to have put some defenses against that cube in place."

"I wonder if he even can? I mean, how could he protect himself against that level of tech?"

"Well, he could keep hold of the dead man's switch indefinitely. If he was cornered he could send destruction our way at the speed of light. It'd work until we've found all the bombs." Heath looked to the ceiling. "He could surround himself with hostages. If Jon confronted him, he'd think twice if innocent people were at risk."

"Yeah, he'd have to settle for indirect attacks, wouldn't he?"

"They could be turned against him." Heath sprang to his feet.

"The hostages?" Amanda asked with obvious confusion. "How do you figure that?"

"No. Androids could be used against him. That's why Stuart doesn't want them around, especially with Jon and his supercube. He's worried Jon'd ask his magic box to puppet the androids against *him*."

"Easy, cowboy. Back in the saddle. If that were the case, he'd have to worry Jon'd be able to just manipulate him, so Stuart would be in the same predicament."

"Maybe he'll put aluminum foil all over his head?"

For the first time since the cabinet meeting Amanda smiled. "Quite the picture. Him pressing it down tight with both hands, so there's no chink in his armor."

"Or maybe he hopes a Faraday cage would protect him? He could hide in one constantly."

"What the hell's a Faraday cage?"

"Oh," he said, "it's an enclosure formed by a conductive material designed to block electric fields. It's a safe space from electromagnetic intrusions."

She tapped an index finger on her chin for a minute. "Don't see how that piece of information benefits us either. Whether he's sitting in a cage or a hot tub, he can't know what will stop Jon."

Heath's face went blank. "But it does."

"Heath Ryan. Are you holding out on me again? How would Marshall's being shielded from radio waves help us?"

"Remember how I said DeJesus put in a backdoor program to shut down all androids?"

"Yes. But I still—"

"It means I'd have to be in the room with him to make it work." He shook his head like it weighed one hundred pounds. "Not easy. Not safe. Not gonna be fun."

"What are you babbling about? Is Marshall's insanity contagious? You're not getting within a million miles of the man, literally."

"I have to. It's the only way. We get one shot at this, so I have to be in line-of-sight to him to make certain I shut him down."

"When were you planning on telling me about your rogue mission, Mr. Vice President?"

"Sooner or later," he had a guilty look on his face, "probably."

"So let me get this straight. *My* vice president, the father of my *unborn* child, and a man with a family at home who *depends* on him, is planning to waltz into Stuart Marshall's secret, secure inner sanctum with a control box in his hand and switch the SOB off before he takes control of his mini-fleet of worldships?"

"No," he waved his hands vigorously in the air. "No way. I don't know how to do the waltz and I'm not about to learn."

"Stop it. You're not going *anywhere*. If our security people vet your plan and think it has one chance in the universe to work, they'll send someone trained for the mission. You, my out-of-shape desk jockey, are staying right here." She pointed downward at her desk.

"Wait." He held up a hand. "There's another brilliant part to my plan."

She folded her arms and scowled convincingly. "What?"

"If I'm killed in the process I won't have to tell my

wife about my infidelity." He smiled grimly. "That's the best part, as far as I'm concerned."

"*Men*," was all she could say. "If you could get your priorities as straight as your dicks half as often, the world would be a brighter place."

FOURTEEN

Stuart Marshall rose from the desk he'd used to deliver his ultimatum. He had a big old smile across his face. Winning was such a wonderful thing. The fact that it was a Ryan and a Geraty whose noses he'd rubbed in dog shit made it all the sweeter. Life, or whatever, was good. Everything was falling into place. He had his ships back, he had the remainder of humanity by the balls, and he had his technician again. Nothing could stop Stuart from having the powerful, lust filled, and unending life he so richly deserved.

He was still debating the wisdom of reanimating his old crew. Duncan had gone over to serve the false Marshall, so the kid was out. But whether Stuart should bring back the other three Horsemen was unclear. He wasn't sure he needed them any longer. He was absolutely unwilling to share power, and they might eventually come to demand some. They could, of course, be resurrected if the need arose down the line. The Four Horsemen were drinking buddies, but Stuart wasn't sure he needed such companionship any longer. He had millions of helpless souls to entertain him.

He wouldn't assume power over his ships for another day or so. He decided to enjoy his last worry-free excursion in public. Once his location was public knowledge, Ryan, the eternal boil on his backside, might be able to control Marshall's robot brain. In the future, he'd have to remain safe and secure in his protected suite, venturing out at his peril. Yes, one last stroll amongst his people would be nice—invigorating, even.

He exited his cramped apartment into the center of the hurricane that was always Mrs. Wong's kitchen. The Fortune Garden restaurant was, for reasons incomprehensible to Stuart, very popular. Its tables were full day and night. That meant the kitchen's pace varied from frenetic to a blur. Cooks, pots, temporarily living chickens, and shouts flew in every direction all at once. This suited Stuart well enough. Once he was over his disgust to have to humiliate himself by living amongst such squalor, his living arrangement was tolerable. Mrs. Wong asked no questions and accepted his gold with glee. Occasionally, when she felt he was due for a rent increase, she'd say something to the effect that he reminded her of someone but couldn't recall who. Aside from that blackmailing, their relationship filled his temporary need for anonymity.

Once he was back on top, he planned on paying her one final visit. He promised himself he would not kill the hag, only maim or disfigure her significantly. Stuart was, however, self-aware enough to acknowledge that he was given to breaking his promises. That day, his final day in hiding, his thoughts did not dwell long on Mrs. Wong or the unholy smell in her kitchen. He thankfully had more global issues to ponder.

He stepped into the crowd that heaved to and fro on the sidewalk as it passed The Fortune Garden. He wedged himself into the flow heading a particular direction and matched its pace. The masses surrounding him laughed, coughed, conversed, and stank of body odor, but they also completely ignored his presence. Since they paid him no notice, they could never betray his presence. Even the most sophisticated security cameras were unable to pick Stuart's face out of this staggeringly dense crowd. As with most actions he'd ever taken, Stuart was proud of his choice of hiding places. He thoroughly enjoyed being so much brighter than everyone else.

After a while, the crowd thinned out enough that he could move freely. He hiked up his hoodie and bent his neck as far forward as he could without too obviously doing so. Stuart was out on the town for no reason in particular other than to ease his painful boredom. He considered grabbing a bite to eat or seeking out a brothel, but decided neither option was all that alluring. Soon, he'd be back eating the best food and screwing the best bitches. The local standards were so nonexistent as to make a mockery of Stuart's discriminating palate regarding both important pleasures. He could wait.

How, he fretted, would he structure his soon-to-be-realized reign? For as surely as cream rose and torching a few critics silenced dissent, his was to be a kingship, not a mere presidency. King Stuart? King Stuart I? Perhaps Emperor Marshall? King Stuart Marshall I sounded more balanced, more perpetual, than Emperor Stuart Marshall. Then again, emperor did have a heft to it no other title could equal. Wait. He smiled outwardly at his brilliance. Emperor King Stuart Marshall I. Yes. With his new brand of power—harsh, swift, and eternal—the title declared itself. And his descendants, who would be as numerous as the stars in the sky, would be emperor kings and empress queens in their own right. Together they would divide up the known universe and rule it with one iron fist. And he would be their god.

God Marshall? True, but potentially a bit "off-putting" to some demographic segments of his subjects. Best not to cross the street in search of trouble. Stuart Marshall, god? No, too indirect. The Divine Emperor King Marshall I? Now that wasn't half-bad at *all*. Giddy, he set those issues aside. Time was on his side, and he could decide later. *Wait. Should it be written "time was on his side," or "time was on His side?" Don't ever sell yourself short,* he chided himself. He held power for the *people,* not for himself. The people wanted icons they could look up to from the mire that was their existence. Stuart had sworn to serve the people as best he could. Providing them a tiny ray of light in their dark lives by being a stunning vision of glory was a kindness on his part. Or *His* part. *Note to self: Decide on capitalization later,* but *he was inclined to favor doing it.*

Lost as he was in his thoughts, Stuart plowed over an ancient old man cobbling together his forward progress with a walker and steely determination. The senior crumpled to the walkway with a sickening crunchy-squish. Once on the ground, he remained motionless.

Stuart was instantly outraged at the useless codger. With incendiary anger and unbridled fury, Stuart began kicking at the fallen citizen. "Watch where you're going," he screamed as the point of his boot landed repeated blows to the fellow's heaped-up body. "You could have hurt me. What were you thinking? Are you an assassin sent by Satan—or worse yet Jon Ryan—to destroy me? I'm *no* one's fool and certainly not yours." Stuart's foot kept swinging, but it no longer found purchase against the octogenarian's bones.

Stuart looked from side to side and found that several passersby were pulling him backward, away from the motionless body. In spite of his robotic strength, Stuart could not free his arms or spin out of their restraint. A panic set in. His assailants must also be androids. How else could they dominate him so completely? More assassins dispatched by the accursed Ryan to derail the bright future he was to gift to humanity.

His outrage was complete, and it was pure. He head butted the nearest monster that restrained him. That allowed him enough movement to cast off the other soldiers of darkness and rally to the defense of the general public which he, Lord Stuart, represented.

Bleeding and broken good Samaritans tumbled to the ground. Someone shouted to call the police. *Aha.* His would-be murderers needed backup. He, being no fool, wouldn't wait for the arrival of any more of Ryan's goon squad. He launched a final killing blow at one of his assailants and began running home, back to his hidden fortress. No one would find him and no one could follow. No. He was too clever, too fast, and too invisible for human eyes to follow.

He ran like the righteous wind he was, sweeping the planet to purify it, and he disappeared.

Three hours later, a huge contingent of armed soldiers surrounded the city blocks at whose center was The Fortune Garden restaurant. Police and military personnel in civilian garb simulated the normal ebb and flow of people within the cordoned-off zone. Even infant-size dolls were paraded around to help complete the picture of normality visible from the restaurant. A plan had been rapidly agreed upon by the combined security forces, but not a single person was certain of its wisdom or safety.

It was clear from the observation cameras that followed Marshall's haphazard progress to his lair that he still held the dead man's switch in his left hand. If he couldn't be incapacitated without releasing pressure on the trigger, millions would die. The sketchy plans involved Heath Ryan interceding to stop Marshall, though it was not disclosed to the security personnel how that particular magic would be accomplished. If the vice president failed, an all-out assault would be launched. At the very least, there could be no possible escape for the murderous Marshall.

The front door to Stuart Marshall's hovel flexed under the force of the knocking. For several minutes Stuart tried his best to ignore the interruption, but he finally gave in. He opened the door to find the diminutive Mrs. Wong glaring up at him, hands positioned defiantly on her hips.

"What?" he snapped. "I'm very busy and have no time for the likes of you." He started to shut the door.

Mrs. Wong's tiny foot halted the closure. She stepped forward to occupy the portal. "You got *roaches.*"

Stuart was dumbstruck. Of course he had roaches. He lived behind this troll woman's squalid kitchen. "And? Why do you pester me with such triviality?"

"Roach no trivial." She edged up to him and thumped his chest with her finger. "You bring roaches. I never have roach before you. Now I have roach *everywhere.*"

He was uncertain how to proceed. His first instinct was to beat her to death on the spot. Alternately, he could invite her in, dismember her, and place what remained in the restaurant's refrigerator. That would be bitter irony. Or, he could take the bait. That was not specifically how Stuart perceived his choices, but it was the one he made.

"Revolting madam, you had roaches in your kitchen since the day it was first constructed. I assume they fell from your skirt into their new home, where they have been fruitful and multiplied. Your roaches have nothing to do with me. I want to have zero to do with either you or your superiors, the roaches. Scram."

He shoved her backward and grabbed the door to close it.

Mrs. Wong was never to be denied. She pushed him backward. "No, you bring roaches, now city inspector want to shut kitchen *down*." She kicked him soundly on the shin. "I need spend money to have 'sterminator come and kill *your* roaches." She rose to her tiptoes and tried to poke him nose to nose. She came up quite short. "This come out *your* rent," she howled. "*You* need pay to kill *your* roaches."

"Look, *bitch*, if it'll get you out the door, I'll *buy* you an exterminator. Just get out." He butted her toward the door with his chest.

With the skills of a bullfighter, she parried his advance and spun to stand in the center of his small space. "Lucky you, I bring my *nephew* with me to do job. No need let your bugs lay so many egg no spray can kill them." She swept her arms over her head like a helicopter.

Stuart looked to the door to find a hunched man standing there with a canister and a spray applicator. His face was completely obscured by an antiquated double-cartridge gas mask. The man bowed deeply and mumbled something even Stuart's keen hearing could not make out.

Mrs. Wong slapped Stuart on the shoulder. "My nephew Kwai say you must leave. He say only android can survive his spray. Stupid person who stay will die. You choose, but please be quick. I pay Kwai by *hour*. Decide chop-chop." She slapped one palm with the inner edge of the other hand simulating a knife chopping.

"What," said Stuart incredulously, "you think I'm going to leave Ming the Merciless here in my place alone so he can rob me blind? Tell him to do what he has to. I'm staying."

The shrouded figure made sounds that might have been words, though again, Stuart couldn't tell. Mrs. Wong translated. "He say if you drop dead he charge me to carry you body to the trash. I no foolish. I go. Come back tomorrow. See how many your roaches and maybe you dead." She addressed Kwai in Cantonese. *"Come to my office when you're done. I have some noodle for you to take to my sister."*

Kwai bowed to her and made unintelligible verbal declarations. As soon as she'd closed the door behind herself, Kwai began to mightily pump up his canister. He seemed to be singing a song, possibly in some Chinese dialect, but again Stuart could not glean the meaning.

Kwai began spraying whatever toxic concoction he'd prepared liberally around the room paying no particular attention to one area over another. In fact he squirted as much into the air as into corners and behind furniture.

"You're going to kill someone," shouted Stuart, "spraying that crap around willy-nilly like that."

Kwai bowed rapidly and shouted back. He turned the applicator directly at Stuart and let loose a jet. When the water—for it was water Heath was spraying—struck Stuart he exploded in rage. "You stupid slant-eyed moron, look what you've done." Stuart pointed to his dripping face.

Heath rushed to Stuart, pretending to aid in Stuart's efforts to clean himself. When Heath was almost within reach of him, Stuart tasted the fluid that dripped into his mouth and discovered it was pure tap water. "Why you —"

Those were the last words to come from Stuart's mouth. In one fluid motion, Heath placed a hand over Stuart's left hand so the dead man's switch could not be released. With his other hand, Heath thumbed a small box he'd pulled from his pocket. Instantly, Stuart collapsed to the floor. All the while, Heath crushed the trigger tightly into Stuart's palm. Quickly they were both on the ground, though only one was conscious. Heath called out loudly. "He's down. I need help, *now*."

A couple of armed men crashed through the door and dropped to their knees as their weapons swept the room. A technician rushed past them and placed his hands over Heath's. "Very slowly," the technician panted, "you hand the trigger over to me."

Heath gingerly released half the trigger, waited until the technician held it securely, and then released the other half. Once the technician held the switch exclusively, Heath rolled onto his back and ripped off the gas mask.

"That was," Heath yelled to no one in particular, "fucking intense."

An officer hurried to Heath and handed him a comm-link. "Anything," Heath asked, "go boom in the night?"

"No," replied Amanda, "thank God, no. You okay?"

"No," said Heath, "but I probably will be, soon enough."

"You need me to send down a clean set of underwear or something?"

"That would be nice. How 'bout you bring them personally?"

"Nah, I'll pass," she said. "I have a pretty weak stomach."

"No use in a crisis, says I."

As Heath still lay on his back breathing heavily, several technicians began to carry away the android that had housed Stuart Marshall. Heath handed them the android deactivation switch. His head hit the floor again.

FIFTEEN

Yibitriander sat behind a simple table as Kymee entered silently. Without being asked, Kymee sat down beside him. "So, what have you learned?" asked Yibitriander.

"It's largely what we suspected. *Wrath* contacted the relay station to update us on his activity. He made it seem like he was following some routine procedure, though we all know no such protocol exists."

"He was boasting. Rubbing our eyes in the mud. He wants us to know he lives, in spite of our best efforts."

"In spite of *your* best efforts, my friend."

Yibitriander didn't hear that last part. He was lost in thought.

"So are you to pout for all eternity, or do you wish to hear *Wrath*'s report?"

"Hmm?" he muttered. "Oh, yes. What's going on out there?"

"*Wrath* reports that he was unearthed by the human android. It is his opinion he was discovered by accident. Shortly before activating *Wrath*, the humans were confronted by and killed an Uhoor named Plo."

"Don't recall that one," observed Yibitriander.

"No. I believe he's too young, or rather, was. By the time Tho and the remainder of her pod arrived, *Wrath* was operational. The Uhoor backed down. Your android friend remanded them to the farthest part of this galaxy under threat of genocide if they returned."

"My but Ryan's a fast learner. And Tho. The old sow is still fluttering about."

"It would appear so on both counts." Kymee eyed his companion questioningly. "You and she disliked each other in a special way, as I recall."

"Just say it. We hated one another past all emotion and reason."

"Since that time, Ryan has used *Wrath* to settle some domestic squabble amongst his people and as transport for Kaljax refugees fleeing to Hodor, the planet where you ditched *Wrath*."

Irritated, Yibitriander snapped, "I know *Hodor*. I didn't *ditch* or *scuttle Wrath* there. I attempted to hide him for all eternity."

Kymee smiled at his friend's manifestation of temper. "Be that as it may."

Yibitriander chuckled softly.

"What?" asked Kymee.

"The thought of it. *Wrath*, the most powerful weapon ever devised, used to shuttle Kaljaxians." He laughed heartily. "I imagine his mood was none too pleasant."

"He always was vocal about his self-perceived importance, wasn't he?"

"Is that all?" asked Yibitriander.

"Yes. Recently, Ryan has not used *Wrath* for any purpose."

Yibitriander thought quietly for a moment. "I wonder why? What's the old saying? I would have thought he'd be as busy as a groom on his wedding night. *Wrath* is nothing if not an outstanding toy with which to play."

"I pray he never learns you called him a *toy*." Kymee could not suppress a giggle. "What are your thoughts?"

"For now? For the present I shall do nothing. If, and *only* if, it becomes imperative, I'll act. I'll alert you well in advance if that happens."

"Fine. I'll let you know if *Wrath* sends along any more updates."

"Yes. Now, I must be alone to think. I have yet to comprehend the utility of nothingness."

"Still stuck on that one? My, I'd have imagined you'd be past that and on to why the cusp of understanding is always incomplete. You do have much to accomplish, my son."

"And you, old man, should go ponder why you should still be so judgmental. It's unbecoming."

"Why? That, my son, is so very obvious. I am, because it is *fun*. Even the great and mighty Deavoriath need a little fun now and again."

"I think, instead, I shall seek out Mother and tell her of your folly. It'll serve you justice."

"You would sic her on me after all these years? How cruel my own flesh and blood has turned out to be."

"How very dramatic mine has become, too." With those words, Yibitriander departed.

SIXTEEN

"I say we ship him back to Kaljax. I'm not busy for the next ten minutes. Let me drop him somewhere, possibly at sea during a winter storm." I was upset. Not that it was rare for me to be angry, or at least blustery. But the cause of my angst was as unanticipated as it was novel.

"Pocrante is a good man," replied Sapale with a stomp of her foot. "Why is it you constantly bicker with him?"

"He thinks he is so smart, that's why." I flapped my arms in the air and did a silly dance.

"He's the man who headed the most prestigious science academy on the planet. We're beyond lucky to have him with us," she said, placing a hand on her hip.

"I don't feel as lucky as *others* might." I turned to JJ. "Do I *look* lucky to you?"

JJ knew better that to step into the middle of that spat. "What does lucky look like? When I know, I'll offer my opinion."

"Coward," I said to my son. "Look, I just don't like the guy. If I can't return him to Kaljax for a full and complete refund, how 'bout we put him in charge of the colony over on Gramdor."

"We don't *have* a colony," Sapale responded dryly, "on that desert continent. I'll wager in ten thousand years there'll be no colony there."

"He can start one. Then in ten thousand years, *normal* people can join him." I was pleased with my comeback.

"Name one thing wrong with him," Sapale challenged.

"He ... no, you'll just get mad and I'll storm out with a bad taste in my mouth and —"

"What? Jon, we've been brood-mates for years. Say the words. I promise I will *not* get angry." She smiled sweetly and blinked her four eyes.

"Fine." I all but shouted. "I don't like the way he *looks* at you."

She pointed to her central chest. "At me?"

"No, JJ. Of course, I mean *you*."

"How does he look at mom?" JJ asked unhelpfully.

"Yes. Is he sucking me into his head with his eyes?"

"Yes. That's exactly my point. I'm glad you see it, too. You can be the one to tell him he's got sixty seconds to pack."

"Have you been drinking the engine coolant again? I did *not* agree with you. I *do* not agree with you. Pocrante looks at me the same way he looks at you." Sapale pointed up at Jon's nose.

"Great." I responded, "now I feel a whole lot better. The guy hits from both sides of the plate, so I guess I'm supposed to feel flattered?" I turned a shoulder to her. "I want to go on record as not being swept off my feet."

"Oooh." she bristled. "You're getting more impossible with each passing year."

"Mom," said JJ, "I think that's unfair."

"Did I request your input?" replied Sapale with a quiet growl.

"Thanks, son of mine," I said.

"No," added JJ, "he's just as impossible as he's always been."

"Unthanks," I said to JJ, and I stuck out my tongue at him.

"Pocrante regards me as an equal," she said in a paced cadence, "and treats me with proper respect. I think *his* brood's-mate would notice if he was flirting, long before one as dull to such nuances as you would."

"Was I just complimented or insulted?" I asked JJ.

"Wow," he said suddenly, "would you look at the time. I told Toño I'd help him rebuild an engine this afternoon."

"It's nine in the morning," I spat back.

"Yeah, but I hate being late." With that, JJ was history. Smart young man.

"I know you're teasing, but please stop complaining about Pocrante. If he should learn of it, there'd be trouble."

"Trouble?" I said patting my chest. "Trouble for *moi*? I doubt that's a valid concept in this context."

Sapale altered the pitch of her growl. It was more threatening. "I don't mean he'll beat you up and take your dessert. There are matters of honor a man of Kaljax is bound to follow. Remember the crazy violent society I wished *not* to re-create here? If you piss him off sufficiently, he might have to leave. On Kaljax, he'd challenge you to a duel, but out of respect for my allowing him to immigrate, I doubt he'd do that here." She growled again. "So, *knock* it off." Then she tiptoed up and kissed me. "You're as stuck with me for life as I am with you. Get used to it."

"Speaking of getting stuck, you want to ... you know, I'm just asking —"

"Go find something to do that does not require my

being there. I actually have a nation to build, and don't have your luxury of infinite time." She wagged her finger at me, indicating I should bow down. We kissed again, and then she turned and walked away.

"I hope I'm not interrupting anything," said Toño as he sidled up.

"No. Never. Sapale has something to do that doesn't involve me."

"I meant, knowing how you two bicker all the time, I was hoping she wasn't staging an exit only to return and lay into you again. I hate being in the middle of that."

"I'm stunned." I rested a hand on my chest. "You think I bicker frequently with my brood's-mate?"

"It's the running joke of the entire colony."

"Ouch."

"Anyway, do you have a moment?"

"It would appear I have many open slots on my dance card."

"Why is it," he observed, "you can never simply answer, *yes*?"

"Bor-ing."

"If you think so. Come with me. I need to show you some data."

"Okay. Can't you just, you know, zap it into my head?"

"Are your feet malfunctioning? Perhaps your motivator program is corrupted?"

"I think not."

"Jon, I like to think of myself as human. Like you, I was forced to become an android to serve a greater need. But I rather preferred being the simple soul I was. With that in mind, might we *walk* to the lab and *look* at the data like normal humans?"

"You're a lot more sensitive than I remember you being back in the day. Hey, maybe on the way, we can spit and then stop and take a leak. Would that make your existence more palatable?"

True to form Toño dismissed my snark and had turned mid-remark to head back to the lab. He sure knew how to deflate me. Almost as well as Sapale. Good thing I always had my personal cheerleader JJ around.

When I arrived to his lab—it was really a big shop with tools, not the chemistry lab of a high school—Toño was standing at a work station, fiddling with something. "What's that?" I asked.

"Oh, this?" He held up a metal tube with some dials at one end. "It's a transponder." He seemed to say it like that meant something in and of itself.

"And might I add it's sure a nice-looking transponder. In fact, if I ever need a handheld transponder, I know just the kind I'd want."

Toño gently shut his eyes and shook his head slowly.

"What?" I asked.

"One morning you'll wake up to find I've deleted your dubious sense of humor. It drives everyone batty, but it seems to affect me more than most."

"So, Doc, what's that transponder saying that you wanted to share with your mission commander?"

His blank expression suggested, but did not prove, that he was further annoyed with me. "It's picking up signals I can't explain."

Hmm. That made no sense. A transponder was basically a radio signal relay. It received one signal and automatically broadcast its own signal. It was the radio spectrum equivalent of a fireman's bucket brigade. Doc had set up a series of such devices around the globe. We had satellites in orbit for long-range communication, but the transponders served as a backup. In practice, they only handled whatever signals Toño sent them, since ninety-nine point nine percent of the time no one was far enough away to need a signal boost.

"I don't get it. *You* manage all the throughput. How can there be signals you can't explain? Unless there's a Boy Scout on the other side of Azsuram with a walkie-talkie, how can that happen?"

"This is true. But some radio frequency signals are, nonetheless, being detected and relayed by our network."

"A message from the worldships? No," I corrected myself immediately, "they're still too far away." I scratched my head. "Solar flares?"

"A possibility, but I'd expect those to be of longer duration and mixed frequencies."

"Okay what do you think they are?"

"No idea."

"I'm not going to write your opinion in stone, Doc, but you must have at least some wild guess."

He shook his head. "Not really."

"Let me ask it this way. How many signals are there? One?"

"Actually, that's hard to say."

"You're not inspiring deep confidence in your mission commander."

"Sorry, *boss*, I just can't say." He reflected for a second. "I pick up one faint signal in the hundred Hertz range. That's well below any band we'd task for message transmission. There may be a second, still weaker signal in a similar range. They're both too faint to amplify much without the noise degrading the signal to gibberish."

"How long are they?"

"Oh several seconds long, up to a minute."

"Can you triangulate a direction?"

"No. I tried, but again, the signal-to-noise is just too messy."

"Okay." At that point he had me a little worried. "I

kind of need to know what the signals are. Gun to your head, what would you say?"

He smiled. "Pull the trigger. End my suffering."

"Wait." I declared, "Two hundred fifty years old, and *now* he develops a sense of humor? Shut down my sensors. I am stunned." We had a nice chuckle. Then against all odds, I had to be serious. "Does the signal show up in the satellite feed?"

"No, but," he raised a finger, "that's not too surprising. The frequency ranges and gains are all different. Plus, if the signal were highly directional, the satellite feed might miss it."

"Are the signals getting stronger?" Maybe something was coming our way.

"No, not in the short time I've followed them. And before you ask, I did have Al and Lily analyze the signal. They don't know what to make of it, either."

I guessed whatever it was that generated the signal had to be pretty far away. That was somewhat reassuring. I asked Doc to keep me posted and left to finish a few projects I had going. One important thing I'd learned in this big scary universe was never to overreact. If the signal represented an actual threat, that problem would present itself sooner or later. If, as was more likely, it was yet one more unexplainable hiccup from some cosmic source, it didn't matter all that much in the first place. Toño could study it, but my concerns were with the safety of the colony and especially that of my family.

Over a few weeks, the signal neither changed nor went away. I relegated it to the back of my mind. I hadn't been on a trip in my vortex for several months. Sapale was happy with the current colony status, so she didn't want new members or need any particular supplies. I was itching to go somewhere, but I cooled my jets. Sapale was not pleased with my wanderlust. She felt it demonstrated a lack of commitment to the mission we'd set out to accomplish. She was probably right, but it was always best not to tell her such a thing.

I contented myself with construction projects, council meetings, and family matters. Several of our children had moved out and had families of their own. I loved to do what I called Grandpa Rounds. That's where I'd go around to one or two grandchildren's houses daily and try as best I could to spoil the little ones rotten. Sapale loved her ever-growing family, but unlike yours truly, she relished her administrative role almost as much. There wasn't a meeting she didn't attend or a social function where she wasn't the honored guest. She was naturally spectacular at everything she did. The kids loved her, the grandkids loved her, and even people who weren't related to her loved her. Both the local and nascent planetary governmental systems were developing nicely. As a society we were self-sufficient, and projections held that we would be so for a very long time. Most importantly, we all were happy. My family was happy. As hard as it was for a lone wolf like me to admit, I was pretty darn happy, too.

We were comfortable, well protected, and our prospects were great. What could go wrong?

SEVENTEEN

"No," Heath said earnestly, "you look exactly the same."

"You lie as badly as you tell jokes," replied Amanda. She smoothed her hand down her abdomen while looking at herself sideways in a full-length mirror. "I'm clearly pregnant. Anyone can tell this belly of mine is telegraphing that message." She angled her torso back and forth. "I'm going to have to start wearing baggy clothes. That'll buy us some time before our inconvenient secret gets out."

"I'll limit my advice to matters of state. All fashionista issues are well above my pay grade."

"Fine with me. I've seen the way you dress."

"If you're done insulting me, we'd better get going to the Joint Council meeting."

She consulted her handheld. "Right. You head on out. I'll be ready in a bit. See you there."

Twenty minutes later the leaders of congress, the military, and Amanda's cabinet officers were milling together ahead of their monthly meeting. As the United States was reconfiguring itself aboard the fleet of worldships, several key changes were adopted. Many new programs were designed to keep the relationships between the various branches of government better. An effort was made to see that everyone knew and, where possible, liked one another. An intentional cordiality was observed. No one wanted to return to the rancorous partisan politics of old Earth.

"All right," Amanda began, "if you could all take your seats, we can get started." People gradually stopped their private conversations and sat down. "Fine. Thank you all for coming today. I have good news. There's not too much to discuss, so this will probably set a record for the shortest meeting yet." A playful cheer went up.

"Since the capture and destruction of Stuart Marshall, things are going remarkably well. I'm sorry to say we've only found and disarmed eight of the nuclear devices he planted. But with luck, we'll have them all soon."

"Do we know," asked a major general, "if he was truthful about the number? Could there be less?"

"Or more," said one of the cabinet secretaries.

"No, we don't," Amanda replied flatly. "I'm inclined to believe his claim of fifty, but we won't know for certain until we don't find the fifty-first bomb."

"You temporarily shut down all the androids in the fleet," said a naval officer. "Ours are all back up and running, but were there any problems encountered with the rest?"

Amanda deferred to De La Frontera with a nod. "No," stated Carlos, "no androids were damaged by the power-down event."

"I'm still in favor of taking one very hard look at the future of the android program." That was Speaker of the House Stanley Turret. He was a short squat man who was fairly spherical when viewed from most angles. He was proudly pugnacious and had been accused of being too pushy, even by his supporters. He disliked androids and wanted to scrap the entire lot of them, including the original astronauts. *Mankind for Man* was his slogan. It was a view shared by an ever-growing number of others, in no small part due to the insanity witnessed in Stuart Marshall's antics.

"Yes," said Amanda, "I'm in full agreement that a conference to discuss the future of androids is needed. However, I feel now is not the time for such a meeting. I think we should wait until early next year. I wouldn't want Marshall's actions to unduly influence the tone of the discussion."

"With all due respect, Madam President," said Turret, "I'm not certain the matter can wait that long." He snapped his head from side-to-side causing his jowls to slap like a basset hound. "I for one am certain *I* cannot wait that long."

Amanda tried to remain calm and to exude a casual air. "Send me a bill and I'll read it. I for one will not sponsor such a conference in the foreseeable fu—"

A penetrating high-pitch squeal burst from every speaker in the room. Everyone rocketed their hands to cover their ears. A few screams rang out. After a couple seconds the intolerable sound abruptly ceased.

"What the hell—" Amanda began. She was cut off by the renewed sound at an even more excruciating level. It lasted a second or two, then pulsed off.

Amanda was doubled over at the waist. "Everyone out of the room. Now. Whoever is in charge of the audiovisual system is in some serious *shit.*"

"Class is *not* dismissed," came a booming voice. "Remain in your seats, because the real show is about to begin. You'd just *die* if you left now, and I mean that literally. I have armed guards at all the exits."

Amanda's gut wrenched, and she vomited up into her throat. It was not morning sickness, either. Halfway through the announcement, she'd recognized the voice. She squared her shoulders to the air and shouted, "Stuart Marshall, what are you doing?"

"Ding, ding, ding, *ding*. Give the little lady a kewpie doll. She guessed that name in ten syllables or less."

"No," said Heath breathlessly. "It *can't* be Stuart Marshall. I was *there* when De La Frontera dismantled and incinerated you."

"You know, Ryan, I'm so tired of you, I think I need a nap. I hate with a red passion when someone says something that *is* can't be."

"Stuart," said Amanda, "where are you and why are you tormenting us yet again?"

He laughed loudly. "If I *told* you where I was I'd be kind of stupid, don't you think, honey? As you'll learn soon, it would spoil all—and I mean *all*—of the fun to come."

Her heart sank and she wanted to vanish from existence. "What do you want?"

There was a pause. Then he said, "I've called you all here today so that I might inform you what your immediate futures hold in store. That way you may conveniently hear them as a group."

Amanda panicked. Stuart was in a position to wipe them out with one press of a button. She started to signal for everyone to run in spite of the threat that their exits were deathtraps.

Heath spoke. "We're not doing anything until you tell us how it is you exist. We'll not negotiate with an AI meant to trick us."

Though no one in the room could see it, Stuart rubbed at the bridge of his nose. "Why is it, shit-bird

Heath, that you think I need to explain myself to *anyone*, least of all a Ryanling?"

Amanda found her voice and her nerve. "He's absolutely correct. Tell me how you escaped the unescapable or we're done conversing."

"Y'all shut up, and y'all will die, real quick like."

"Be that as it may. But if you do, you won't have as much fun." She sounded resolute.

"Oh fine, Butch the Bitch. It's kind of nice, truth be told, to boast a bit, anyway. You know, to toot my own horn. After my night on the town, it occurred to me I might have compromised my location. Turns out I was, as usual, correct. I was also correct that you'd pull some bonehead stunt like you did."

"Then why did you allow us to capture you?" Amanda asked quietly. The possibilities were racing though her head.

"First and for the record, you didn't *catch* me. You who couldn't tell shit from Shinola; never have and never will. I placed an AI-guided replica of my handsome self in that room and waited for you to take the bait. Had you fooled six ways to Sunday."

"No way," shouted Heath, "I was there. We spoke, you carried on a dialogue with Wong. Not even an AI could pull that off."

"I was using a remote microphone to puppet the android, you twenty percenter."

"But I hit the kill switch. It would have turned you off, too."

"And that it did. But because you're such an android lover, you also eventually turned the damn thing off. I woke up with one hell of a hangover and an even greater desire to personally take your life, Ryan."

Heath realized he still had the kill switch in his briefcase. He lunged for it and snapped it open.

Frantically he repeatedly pressed the button. Activity was confirmed by a signal light on the unit.

"You done, cupcake? Fool me once, shame on you. Fool me twice, shame on me. I'm speaking to you from the comfort of my shiny, brand-new Faraday cage. Your signal couldn't reach me if you were right outside my door, booger brain."

Shit. He's got us and he's really pissed, Amanda thought. She had never considered a contingency for that horrible possibility. She was completely at his mercy, and he had no mercy in his soul.

"So," she tried to preempt him, "I presume you want those ships. The codes are still valid, I think. If not—"

"You don't honestly think in your wildest girly wet-dreams that it's gonna be that easy, do you, sweetlips?"

"Wh ... what do you—" she started to say.

"I want you, if it's possible in this life, to stop talking and to listen. I know that you girls *love* to chat, but I don't."

"We're listening."

"Music to my ears, child. You're singing my song. Here's the deal. Listen closely, as there are three parts to this plan, Stan, which isn't so much a 'deal' as it is a proclamation of fact. One, of course I get my ships. Now, however, it's fifty ships of *my* choosing. Let's all blame Ryan for that one, shall we? Two, you have Frontera give Drawjoy the know-how to remove that stupid backdoor program in my head. Three, you must choose, Mock-President Amanda Mandy, which worldship I will blow up as punishment for your egregious sins against me. You will have thirty seconds to choose. Now, I know you're a noble dyke, so you'll say, 'I won't choose.' This I anticipate. Boring it is, by the by. If you do not choose, I will choose for you, and I will fry *three* worldships. Your thirty seconds begins *now,* Contestant Number One."

Amanda was frozen with fear. She struggled to focus but could not. It was too unbelievable that Marshall was about to murder a million people of her choosing. Her mind went completely blank.

Heath saw that Amanda was floundering. Which ship should she choose? It struck him that the one to pick was the one Stuart was actually on. It would fulfill his demand, but he couldn't do it. But which vessel? He could be on any of a thousand. Wait. It hit him. What was the name of that woman, his secretary? Heath had read the reports the investigating officers made when the search for Marshall was still going on. Some fruit? Yes. Plum? Mrs. Plum. No, Plumquist. Where was she interviewed?

Think, think, think, he shouted in his head. Millions of innocent lives depended on him recalling that insignificant fact.

It wasn't a big ship. No, it was one of the smaller ones.

"Fifteen seconds," taunted Marshall.

The series of ships with the stupid cutesy names. *Happiness*? No, *Sweetheart*? No. *Forever Yours*? No, but it was forever something. *Forever ... Forever ... Together*. She'd lived on *Forever Together*.

Heath cupped Amanda's ear.

"Five seconds, bitch."

"Chose *Forever Together*. Trust me," he whispered. "Just do it."

Without thought or delay Amanda blurted out, "*Forever Together*."

The disembodied voice of Stuart Marshall fell uncharacteristically silent. After a seemingly endless pause, a clearly befuddled Stuart spoke. "Ah, funny you should pick that particular ship. Either you're smarter than you look and act, or there is a God in Heaven smiling down on you. *Forever Together* is precisely the ship my loyal secretary and I are on at this very moment. I think I'll not incinerate us both. Choose another. This time you've got ten seconds."

"No," Amanda said flatly. "We had a deal, Stuart. I choose *one* ship and you blow it up. I know you think life's a game," she swept her arm around the room, "that this is all a game. So, I will hold you to your own rules. What's a game without rules? I chose my one ship. You didn't place any condition on my choice or say there was one I couldn't pick. A deal's a deal. Either blow up the damn ship your sorry ass is riding, or don't, but the game is over."

"I ... I don't think you understand," Stuart began. "I—"

"You, Stuart Marshall, are slime. You are by a wide and continually expanding margin the worst human to ever exist. No, wait, you're not the worst human because you're a squeaky *tin* man. You know, I met you once when you actually were still human. You know what? I didn't like you then, but at least you were a man. Now, as a walking computer, you somehow feel you're not bound by the conventions of us fleshies. But I'll tell you this, ass wipe. Humans play the game by the rules." She took a few deep breaths. "Now, blow up *your* ship, blow up *three* ships, or blow up all the *fucking* ships. But know this. If you don't play fair, I will order the fleet to rail gun *Forever Together* into cosmic dust, and then I'll drink to your lost humanity while you tumble down to Hell right next to me."

The room burst into applause. Heath put his fingers in his mouth and whistled.

"Impressive speech, young lady." Stuart said with potential sincerity. "I couldn't have played it better myself. I know when I've been bested and it ain't often that I am. Game over. Let's call it a draw. Send me the fifty codes and the tech I need and I'll be on my merry way. Oh, by the by, Mary Jane and I have already left *Forever Together*, and the shuttle is Faraday shielded, so don't get any more bright ideas. Kirk out." The air went dead.

"I think," Heath said as he stood, "that went well."

EIGHTEEN

I got a message that Toño wanted to see me in his lab. I'd recently learned not to ask him to send me information by Brain-O-Gram. We were, after all, two normal human guys. I made the pilgrimage.

"Yo, Doc. How's it going?"

"Not so well, I'm afraid." He held up a foot-long cigar-shaped device. I had no clue what it was. "My last hypersonic dissassimilator has given up the ghost."

"And I thought *I* was having a bad day. I'll call for a priest to give it the last rites and a proper Christian burial." I batted my eyes at him.

"As always, the world's a stage and you're the opening stand-up act. This," he held up his shiny tool, "is a very important implement. I use it all the time, or rather I did, up until now."

"What, pray tell, does a hypersonic dismantler do?"

He gave me a stern paternal glare—we're talking home after curfew with a dent in the family car level. "The *dissassimilator* allows me to make microscopic holes in nanoprobes. That way I can insert a functional limiter."

I shrugged. I was totally in the dark. He could just as well have been speaking monkey.

"It lets me fix things. That's what a hypersonic dissassimilator does."

"Why didn't you say so in the first place?"

He rolled his eyes. He almost never rolled his eyes at me anymore.

"Quick three-part question. Why might I: one, care; two, need to know; or three, care?"

"I'm certain you don't, one through three. The point is, I could fabricate one, but that would take a very long time and it might not function as well as this one."

"And we immortals are in a hurry because—?"

"Jon, I have many critical roles to play. I don't wish to sacrifice my other duties simply to repair this probe."

"Good for you. I approve of commitment, if applicable in this situation. Sapale says often that she thinks I should be committed." I rubbed my chin. "I *think* she means emotionally, not physically in a mental hospital, but come to think of it, I *should* clarify that perception."

There went those eyes again, rolling around the heavens.

"Okay, I give. Where do I fit into this little micro-calamity? The one involving you and your probe thingy?"

He replied as if it took some effort to remain calm and speak in a civilized manner. Weird. "I'd like you to take me to Carlos, so that he might provide me with a new one."

"Oh?" I said nodding my head rapidly. "No prob. Uh, Doc, why didn't you just ask me that right off the bat?"

"I have *no* idea. One would think I would learn later, since I failed to do so sooner." He placed his palm over his face. Totally weird.

"Let me clear it with the missus and set up a duty

roster for surveillance. Won't take half an hour. Then we'll surprise old Carlos."

Several of my kids were experienced enough that I didn't worry going on a short jaunt with Toño. In the past, he generally was left behind when Sapale and I went somewhere. Now we could do boys' night out. After I finally convinced a dubious Sapale that it was *Toño's* idea to go to the human fleet, she had no problem with our taking the trip. When I say it took a while to convince her, what I really meant was it took her a while to call Toño and confirm my story. It was almost like she didn't trust me.

We materialized in a hangar dedicated to the vortex alone. That way we didn't have to run through the drill of showing up outside, asking where it was safe to land, and then doing so. I had my own personal parking space, thank you very much. As soon as we arrived, Toño called Carlos. I know, he could have just flashed him a message head to head, but that wasn't how humans did things. Oh well. When we walked into Carlos's office, I was surprised to see Amanda and Heath there, too. She was out of breath, suggesting she'd hurried to get there. Wait, was she preggers? I did a quick ultrasound, which us androids could do from across the room. Wow, she was. A healthy boy. What a strange world it was.

"Toño," Carlos exclaimed, "and Jon. It's so wonderful you are here. Thank the Lord." He rushed over and shook our hands.

I pointed to Heath and Amanda. "You two are here pretty darn fast. Why do I think it's time for me to start worrying?"

"Grandpa," Heath said with a smile, "you're such a negative humanoid." He knew how very much I hated it when he called me that. "We're just glad to see old friends. Hey, anyone up for bridge?"

Toño wagged a finger in Heath's direction. "He's so much like you, Jon, it's both alarming and depressing."

"Like clones," added Amanda.

"So," I said, "we need a sonic zapper. Then we'll be out of your hair." I waved. Not sure why, but I did.

Carlos was crestfallen. "But we very much need your help. Surely you can stay to at least hear us out?"

"I think he's joking around," said Heath. "Aren't you, Pappy?" If there was one term of endearment I hated even more than *grandpa,* it was pappy. He knew that, too. I should've put him over my knee and tanned his behind. It would have done us both a favor.

"Please, gentlemen," Amanda said, "have a seat. I have a tale to tell."

Boy howdy, did she ever. I especially liked her ultimatum to Stuie. *Brilliant.*

"So, how long ago did he separate with the worldships?" I asked.

"About three weeks ago," she replied. "They're still in easy communication range, no delays yet."

"Do you have," Toño asked nervously, "any reports of how he's treating his prisoners?"

"Yes. His fleet is so large he hasn't even begun controlling it. Aside from being told what happened, nothing has changed on most ships. The two he's visited reported that he didn't act too insane. He provided them with a list—his manifesto—and made some changes in the administration. He's killed a few people, but my impression is they were people he's held a grudge against for quite some time."

"Good," I said, "no real damage done, and not too far off. Once we fix this, the ships can rejoin you guys easily enough."

"You make it sound all so easy," said Amanda. "You can't seriously have a plan yet. Can you?"

"My plans are usually more impulse and seat-of-the-pants than plan *plans*."

"Trust me," observed Heath, "this much is true. Granddad was, and always will be, a fighter pilot."

"Oh my," was all Amanda could come up with. Silly girl. It was natural enough, though. She had yet to see me in action, up close and personal. Was she ever in for a treat.

"So, you haven't located very many of the bombs he hid?" I asked.

"No," said Carlos, "it's worse than the proverbial needle in a haystack."

"Carlos, Toño, Heath, you're with me. Amanda, alert the proper people on all vessels that we'll have the bomb locations to them shortly. We'll meet back in your office in an hour. Any questions?"

"Yes," stated Amanda. "Am I to *assume* you're in charge now?" My, but she sounded pissed and off put.

"Well ... no. I mean ... you're the boss lady. I'm just—" I cleared my throat loudly. "Hey, Amanda, what say we," I indicated my three companions, "go to the vortex and meet you in the Noval Office in about an hour? And, I don't know, maybe you could touch base —"

She held out an imperious finger. "*Out*. All of you. GO."

I saluted her. Boy she didn't see that one coming. I was almost out the door before she thought to return the salute. Rookie CICs.

Inside the cube, I hooked up and asked Manly, "I need the precise locations of all fission and fusion devices on all the human worldships."

"I'm sorry, Form, are you addressing me?"

What, was he taking jerk lessons from Al? "Yes. Who else might be able to supply me that information?"

"I don't presently know. Shall I work on that list, too?"

"Ah, Manly, is there a problem? This is like kind of important?"

"I am unaware of a problem, Form."

"Okay, good. Manly, would you please display for me the locations of all nuclear devices on all the ships in the human fleet?"

"Yes, no problem. I saw where you were going earlier with the request that sounded like an order."

Huh? I wasn't supposed to give Manly orders now? What did he prefer, I sent him chocolates first? Maybe it should be accompanied by a thoughtful card, too? Oh well, not the time or place for a confrontation. Within a few seconds he reported that he had compiled that data. He downloaded it to Carlos and Toño who confirmed receipt to me. Then they left at a trot.

Once we were alone, Heath asked, "Why did you need me to come? It looks like those two have it all under control."

"What, you weren't dying to see the inside of my cube?"

"Well sure, but—" He reached over and messed up my hair. "Thanks, Grandpa. I was." When he was done giggling, he asked, "How about Mandy? She'd have liked to see, too."

"No girls allowed. Not on my ship. They're bad luck."

"Wait. You drag Sapale and your daughters back and forth to Kaljax like this was an inner city tram."

"Point taken." I turned to him. "You wanta grab a seat?"

He furrowed his brow but sat down. "Why do I want to sit down?"

"We need to talk. People sit when they have important conversations."

He flashed his finger back and forth between us. "We're about to have an important conversation?"

"Yup."

"It's not about the birds and the bees, is it? I kind of have that down pat."

I glanced up and smirked. "I guess it is, now that you mention it."

"Tell me you're not serious. Not that you ever *have* been, but—"

"The president's pregnant."

That shut him up quick. He shifted nervously and rubbed his mouth with the back of his hand. His heart rate went up forty percent, and sweat began to form all over his body. Son of a gun.

"Yeah," he said looking to one side, "that's not *common* knowledge yet, so don't, you know, mention it in public."

"You mean I shouldn't raise a toast to my new grandson in the next pub I see?"

"What are you talking about?"

"Do I look like a priest?"

"No."

"A minister?"

"No," he said, a bit annoyed.

"You wife's attorney?"

"No, and I resent—"

"Junior, I don't care if you have a mistress who happens to be the lesbian President of the United States. I really don't. But don't try to con a con, okay? You're the father right?"

He dropped his shoulders in resignation. "Yes, she is, and I am."

"You're quite the Ryan. I'm proud of you, grand baby Heath. When you screw a thing up, you screw it up beyond any possible repair."

He placed his face in his hands. "Tell me about it."

"So, what's the plan?"

"Same as yours, I'm afraid. None."

"A piece of grandfatherly advice. Not having a sound plan works for war and for getting free drinks in a bar. Extramarital offspring, not so much. *They* require a plan. Preferably a good one, and one that involves nobody getting dead."

"Spoiler alert. You know that was half the reason I apprehended Marshall personally."

"I do now, dumbass. Now, here's a thought. Solve the problem like a *man*, not a teenager with testosterone poisoning. You need my help, you got it. We're family. Nothing's ever going to change that. Now, let's get to your girlfriend's office and solve one problem at a time."

"You know, Gramps, you're not nearly as mean as I remember you being."

We arrived to Amanda's office and found it a beehive of activity. There were more generals and admirals scurrying around than I thought I'd ever seen. People shouting into radios, trying to be heard by whoever was on the other end. It was barely controlled chaos. Carlos saw us come in and rushed over.

"Your data is incredible. Many of the devices were known weapons in storage, but all forty-eight unaccounted-for bombs have been located and are presently being deactivated. It is a *massive* victory, Jon. Our peace of mind can be restored. We cannot begin to thank you."

"Happy to help. Any idea how long it will take to neutralize the bombs?"

He rocked his head back and forth, thoughtfully. "A couple hours, maybe a bit longer. Why?"

"I want to focus on dealing with Marshall once and for always. Can't do that until domestic security has been restored."

"No," he mused, "probably not."

Sure enough within a few hours it was a wrap. Every bomb was incapacitated and removed. Everyone could breathe again. I asked Amanda to clear her office of any nonessential personnel, so we could figure out what to do about Stuart.

"There," Amanda said sitting down, "one crisis averted, another one directly ahead. No rest for the wicked." We all had a chuckle. "So, what's your version of a plan, General Ryan?"

"If you're going to start name-calling, I'm outta here. *General* Ryan."

She looked to Heath, then to me. Then she rolled *her* eyes just like Doc did.

"You mentioned you think Stu's holed up in a Faraday cage. I checked with Manly. After laughing his digital ass off about anyone using such arcane technology, he said it wouldn't affect any of his options."

"Who's *Manly*?" she asked.

"Oh, sorry. That's what I call my vortex manipulator. It's like the ship's AI, but I'm beginning to think Manly's actually a lot more than any computer." I scratched at the back of my head. "I wonder sometimes if he isn't more alive than I am. Maybe that's not saying much, I guess."

"I won't tolerate any loss of lives other than Marshall's. Is that clear?" She was extremely serious.

"I'll make it happen, *if* it's possible. This is combat, Mandy. It's dirty, it's unforgiving, and more often than you'd like, people get killed."

"Do you need anything from us? Any personnel or materials?"

"I'll take Heath. He can be in charge of the fleet once we free it." I could see it on her face, the question. "You can't come. The president stays here. Heath is capable, he's expendable, and he does not have a serious medical process." I saw it in her eyes. She knew I knew.

"Fine. Will you be able to keep in contact with us?"

"No problem. I can take a radio. The cube's walls won't interfere with the signal much."

"When will you be ready?"

"I learned a long time ago: Do the unpleasant as soon as you can. Never wait for cold feet to set in."

"*Now?*"

"As in after one more thing. Madame President, would you ask everyone but Heath, me, and those two metal scientists to leave the room?"

"Why ... of course. Everyone. Thank you for your help. If you could leave as quickly as possible I'd appreciate it."

"What's this about?" asked Toño. "No more of your childish joking I pray."

"Hang on." The door shut behind the last person. "I want to clear the air. You two need to be in the loop because you're my trusted friends. No secrets between us —ever."

"Jon," asked Amanda, "what's this secret? What are we here for?"

"He knows," said Heath rather sheepishly.

"Mandy, you're pregnant with Heath's son. In a few minutes, he's heading directly into harm's way. He might not come back. No telling what'll happen when the shit hits the fan. I'm not your father," I looked to Heath, "or yours either. But I do request you make this whole thing right before we take off." I leaned my chair back. "Your call, but I'm going to be disappointed if you let this linger."

Amanda and Heath stared at each other a very long while. Heath finally broke the silence. "I'll tell Piper I'm leaving her. There, that's it. It's the right thing to do." He looked at Amanda a few seconds. "It's what I want to do."

He looked to the ground. "No big deal. People get divorced everyday."

"Are you just going to assume that's what *I* want? You might wanna run it by me first." She let that hang in the air like a real pro. "Or is it a done deal that I'll have you?"

Women. They never changed.

"You're right, well, partly right. I need to let my wife know exactly where things stand. If it means the end of our marriage, then so be it. As to your having me, I can only beg that you do on bended knee." Heath teared up.

"That's the sweetest thing a man has ever said to me. But Heath, can you imagine the scandal? *Us* getting married? We'll be the laughing stock of humanity."

"Then come with me to Azsuram," I said, smiling from ear to ear. "We'd love to have you and, trust me, nobody'd think what you did was scandalous." I cocked my head. "Those Kaljaxians, they have a totally different take on sex. Totally."

"Well," Heath said as he pushed off the desk, "I have a really bad meeting to attend. Jon, how long can you give me, you know, if things drag on?"

"As long as it takes, my man. As long as it freakin' takes. Those worldships move like overstuffed turkeys in snow. Mandy and I will chat while the science twins go locate a new sonic screwdriver."

Two hours later, a very drained and dejected-looking Heath dragged himself in the door and collapsed in the nearest chair. Amanda and I waited for him to speak. It took him almost a minute. Heath took a remarkably deep breath and raised his eyes to meet ours. "That went worse than I anticipated in my worst-case scenario."

"Come on, buddy, cut the drama and tell us where things stand." I wasn't much for theatrics. I have always been a cut-the-crap kind of guy and expected it of my kin.

"Bottom line, I'm a free man. Our marriage is over."

"How did she take the news?" Amanda held her breath after asking.

"How did *she* take the news? How about how did *I* take it?" He shook his head in disbelief. "Two trains colliding in the dark."

"Huh?" I grunted.

"I started to say something like, 'Honey, there's a problem we need to discuss.' I don't know, something along those lines. She tells me whatever I have to say can wait, because she has an 'unpleasant matter' to discuss with me. She flips on her handheld and a holo appears. It's some dude with a three-piece suit. He begins by introducing himself as Piper's lawyer. He says she wants a divorce, that as a result of my duties to the nation, I've forced her into the arms of another man. Coincidentally, the *other man* is the one delivering the bad news to me.

"He said she has long suspected infidelity on my part, but as he put it, 'She also feels the pot should not call the kettle black.'" He looked at us for support.

"Sounds good. Clean break," I said thumping him on the shoulder. "Strong work. Now let's go kill Marshall again."

"Huh? Wait. She gave me the boot. *She's* suing *me* for divorce. He said Piper only waited this long out of respect to the sensitive nature of politics in these trying times. What's that supposed to mean?"

"Hey, Mr. Self-Absorbed, let it go. You're free, like it or not. The fact that she lowered the boom on you before you could lower it on her is history. If it meant old Piper wounded your fragile male ego in the process, that's just another point for her side. Let's go." I pulled at his arm. He went limp.

"I think I need time to heal."

"You know," I said as condescendingly as possible, "you're right. They say the best way to heal emotional trauma is a long voyage at sea. As we're fresh out of oceans, I have an alternate long voyage prepared exclusively for your mangled soul." I lifted him to his feet. "Now, say goodbye to the nice president lady and let's go. I miss my brood's-mate's cooking and warm considerations. The more time I spend with you means I spend less time with her."

"Mandy," Heath said weakly, "see you soon, I hope. We'll talk. Okay?"

"Absolutely, sweetie." She came over and gave him a peck on the cheek. She shook my hand. "God's speed and the best of luck to you both."

As I half pulled Heath down the corridor, he turned to me and asked, "Did she just call me *sweetie?*"

"Yeah. She's clearly head-over-heels for you. You lucky stiff."

"She ... she kissed me on the cheek, like one would their third cousin twice removed." He swiveled his face toward me. "I may never return, and I get a cousin kiss?"

"Maybe she's not one given to displays of affection in public."

"Public? It was you, me, her, and four silent walls."

I pivoted his still slack frame so we were face to face. "Maybe she likes the taste of forbidden fruit more than the recently divorced fruit." I let that rattle around in his wheelhouse. "When you get back, *if* you get back, you can sort it out. She may be lots of things, but she's not one to beat about the bush." I somewhat regretted the particular idiom, but there it was.

By the time I was hooked up to the vortex and ready to depart, Heath was almost back to his usual self. That was fortunate. I didn't need a love-sick sack of sponges by my side. I needed a copilot. I confirmed with Manly that when we dropped out of folded space, we would be as invisible as possible to the worldships. I knew they'd be on ultra-high alert and didn't want to give up the element of surprise. Manly assured me the humans would remain as clueless as they had always been. He said it like he didn't give us much credit.

We puffed into real space about a thousand kilometers behind the stragglers of the fleet. "Are you monitoring their communication?" I asked Manly.

"Have been since we arrived to the main group," was his terse response.

"Any changes suggesting they've detected us?"

"None, Form."

"Please let me know if there are any significant changes."

"By your command."

I turned to Heath. He was eating a sandwich. "Now comes the hard part. We, my friend, need a plan. Any ideas?"

He swallowed harshly and took a sip of coffee. "You think *I* have a plan? I'm just along for the ride. I have no clue what this bucket can do. That's your area of expertise, not mine."

"Point." What was the cube capable of? Up until then I'd used it as not much more than a shuttle. I had no idea what miracles lay hidden beneath its shiny walls. When I'd temporarily taken out Marshall a while back, I did so myself. What could Manly bring to the table?

"Manly, I have a general question for you."

No response.

"Manly, you there?"

"Of course I am, Form. Where else might I be?"

"Beats me. Then why didn't you answer?"

"You had yet to pose a question. What? Did you fancy that after millions of years of uninterrupted service, I suddenly decided to take a nap?"

What was with him? "Manly, I'd like to discuss the

137

tactical situation with you. Are you programmed ... strike that. Are you expert in combat and stealth techniques?"

"Yes. I am the most powerful war vessel in the universe. I am sentient and seasoned in battle. I am unaware of any limitations that I might have."

Wow. I should've asked him that question before.

"How can you say that?" asked Heath. "How can you be sure there aren't any more potent ships or skilled minds?"

No response. "Ah, Manly," I interjected, "please answer his questions as well as mine." I knew he was persnickety on that point.

"By your command. I know these things. That is all of it you can comprehend. I assure you I am what I say I am."

I held a hand up to Heath to silence him. "Fine. I believe you, Manly. Okay, you know what's going on and what I hope to accomplish. You also witnessed my actions when we captured Marshall before. Do you have any thoughts as to how we can remove him this time?"

"Yes. You're in a position of attempting to duplicate a victory. That by definition means your prior victory was false. You gained nothing, and Marshall benefitted much. You were duped. You were foolish. Your concern for mercy and fair play dominated your thoughts and hence emasculated you."

Yeah, but how do you really feel, Manly? I guessed he was correct in his critique, but wow. *Emasculated* myself? Ouch. "I see your point. Thanks for your honesty. Without rehashing too much of the past, how might you go about ending the existence and threat of Stuart Marshall, once and for all?"

"Trivially easy. I would open fire on the flotilla and destroy everything that exists. I would radiate the remaining dust so that there was zero possibility of regeneration. Zero."

OMG. This guy was insane. "Okay, that would work. Thanks. We'd kill millions of innocent hostages, but I agree it would in principle be effective. Let's call that Plan One. Now any thoughts as to what a Plan Two could be? Aim for something a tad less apocalyptic, if possible."

"I repeat my earlier observation. Your sentimentality is contrary to your stated desire. All lives will perish. What does it matter if it is today or a handful of years from now?"

"It matters, you monster." Heath said unhelpfully. I raised my hand again.

"Do you request I respond to the human, Form?"

"No. He's just having an unusually bad day. He's kind of an emotional mess. His wife and he are having issues."

"I heard she dumped him like a sizzling hot turd."

"I'm here, you both know. I can hear you." Heath was definitely whining.

"Back to Plan Two," I said. "Let's stay focused. What alternate tactic might we employ?"

"I have located the android named Stuart Marshall. I could atomize his craft alone. I could not, however, guarantee that he does not have regeneration facilities on one of the other forty-nine vessels. Hence, the plan is flawed. I dislike flawed plans."

I rubbed my temples. "How about a Plan Three? This plan must include blowing up no ships, vessels, or crafts."

"Sentimental fool."

I had my limits. Manly just rocketed past all of them. "I will tolerate no insubordination or insults. *I* am a Form. *You* are not. *I* command both this mission and this vessel. You, Manly, will both obey my orders and show me all due and proper respect, or I will deactivate you. And before you go and tell me you're the most powerful asshole in the universe and that I couldn't possibly deactivate you, know this. I have gone from a man to an android. I have traveled endless miles and bested everyone who has defied me. I have *never* been defeated, and never will be. I beat *you* in a wager. The Deavoriath marooned you, and *I* brought you back to having meaning. Comply or die. It is that simple."

Without pause or hesitation he responded. "I am truly sorry, my Form. You are right on all counts. I only exist to serve you. Can you forgive my insolence?"

"I forgive *nothing* in times of war. I never allow sentimentality to sully my actions."

"You have bested me yet again, Form. With time, I hope to be judged again for my deeds if I cannot be forgiven. I have a design I feel you will approve of. May I present it to you?"

Too thick. The son of a lawn mower was trying to butter me up. He was violating the first law of dealing with Jon Ryan. Never try to bullshit a bullshitter. *Never.* I was the king of all bullshitters everywhere.

"I have tired of you, Manly. I no longer seek or value your council. Please respond to my commands but otherwise consider yourself relieved of duty pending your court martial."

I kidded around a lot. Sometimes people didn't know whether to take me seriously or not. I played the clown. Hell, I *was* a clown most of the time. But you know what? Sometimes I hit the nail so firmly upon its head that I surprised even myself. Sometimes I was just that good.

"I beg," Manly said in a neutral tone, "that you reconsider, Form. I am built to serve. Please know this. If you relegate me out of useful service I will experience infinite pain—literal physical pain. I allowed pride to cloud my vision. I acted disgracefully, and worse yet, I can never forget my transgressions. If I were in your place I would treat me more horribly than you are treating me now. Perhaps this is why I am a vortex manipulator and *you* are Form. I appeal with sincerity to your better nature, to your kinder heart, and to your superior judgment to afford me one last chance to prove my worth and my loyalty."

I turned and walked slowly across the room. I sat down and rattled my fingers on the armrests. I was fairly certain Manly's last soliloquy was genuine, or at least not far from it. But I couldn't actually know it for a fact. I also desperately needed his help. In the end I did what I always had. I said to myself WTF. Yeah, I took an insane chance.

"What is Plan Three, vortex manipulator?"

"Form, I wish for you to address me properly. You may of course address me however you see fit. My name is *Wrath*. This vessel is *Wrath*. We are *Wrath*."

My but didn't *that* sound ominous. "I think for now I'll go with Manly."

"By your pleasure."

Wrath then proceeded to tell me his Plan Three. It was simple, quick, and, best of all, no one died violently. Yea for my manipulator named *Wrath*. I gave him the green light and waited for something to happen, maybe fireworks or metallic squeaky noises. Nothing. A second after I said *Go*, he said, *It is done*.

It couldn't have been that simple. He said it was and, as it turned out, he wasn't lying. I hailed the vessel Marshall was riding in. "This is Captain Jon Ryan, *Opportunity*. You there?"

"Yes, Captain. This is Lt. Tip Benjamin III, duty officer. Boy am I glad to see you. Well, I can't actually see you, but I can hear you. Your signal is local, so I bet I could see you—"

"Tip," I interrupted, "I don't have all day."

"Sorry. I'm doing it again aren't I?"

"Stow it. I need a clear update. Are you capable of that, Tip?"

"Aye."

"Is Stuart Marshall neutralized?"

"That's one of the parts I don't actually know. I'm ... we're all plenty confused."

"Get me your CO on the double, Benjamin. I need to talk to someone who speaks human."

"She's right next to me and she's just as confused as I am. I mean I think she is. We haven't fully—"

"This is Commander Hannah Johannsen. Captain, here's the situation. We find ourselves adrift. Control command does not exist. I can't convince the computer to release operations to me."

"How's that possible?"

"The damn machine says we're on an unauthorized voyage, that command control was never properly given to anyone, so it cannot be transferred without the proper validation."

"No. It was given to Marshall. If he's incapacitated, it falls to the next in command. That's you. What's the problem?"

"The problem is the computer has no record of a Stuart Marshall *ever*. No Marshall, no valid chain of command."

"Hang on. You're telling me that Marshall does not exist in any record on any ship? That's nuts."

"You and I know he exists, or did. I honestly have no reliable understanding of his status. Security teams are sweeping the ship as we speak looking for him. But according to the electronic record, no such person ever existed."

"Manly," I called out, "just exactly what did you do?

You said you'd *erase* him. I thought you meant the android's brain."

"As I told you, I wiped the system clean concerning the existence of Stuart Marshall. No record means he cannot be re-created, since he never existed to reproduce. There currently are no digital or other copies of his consciousness."

"I guess I didn't fully understand Plan Three. There's an android somewhere on *Opportunity* that *looks* like Stuart Marshall. Hopefully it's recently defunct, but it has to be lying there somewhere."

"Incorrect," was Manly's quick response. "There is no android with Stuart Marshall's semblance because—"

"There never was a Stuart Marshall," I finished his thought. "But he did exist. I remember him. You remember him."

"True, but irrelevant. Yes, there is an android on the floor of a Faraday cage that you would recognize as Stuart Marshall. But as far as non-living memory is concerned, there never was such an individual. Hence, that blank android is not Stuart Marshall."

"How widespread is that wipe?"

"It is comprehensive. There are no Marshall records anywhere."

"Even back in the main fleet?"

"Yes. It is what you authorized. The impossibility of a recording of his name assures that he is gone for good."

"But, wait. There is that rehabilitated android of Marshall, the one I put in charge the first time we took the crazy one out."

"No, Form, there is not."

"No, there is. I spoke with him a few months back. I never much warmed to him, but he was an upstanding guy. He was getting married, of all things. I even met his fiancée on holo."

"He never existed. There is no record of him, so he never was."

Holy shit. I killed both Stuarts; the good one *and* the bad one. My heart sank. That poor woman, his fiancée. One second she loves a wonderful guy, and the next minute he never existed, but she remembers him completely. What a gut kick.

"Hannah, request permission to come aboard. I want to leave the vice president with you to help you with your return to the main fleet."

"Permission granted. Looking forward to meeting both you legends."

Heath pointed to his chest and mouthed the word *legend*.

"Look," I began. "I'm done here. I'll deposit you safe and sound in some hangar, then I'm outta here."

"Can't you stay a little longer? What if we need you?"

"You won't. They've got you. A Ryan is a Ryan is a Ryan."

He gestured to the ceiling. "Maybe, but this one doesn't have a magic box."

I smiled. "You'll do fine. You're more than enough on your own. I'm serious about you two joining us if either of you is interested. I'll come back in a couple of months to see if you want to make the leap." I shuffled my feet. "You can tell Amanda how I accomplished the mission but disobeyed her order. One person died. If I'm lucky, she won't bust me like Marshall did. I don't want to start all over at my age."

"I'm guessing Mandy'll be lenient. And I'll contact Marshall's fiancée personally to make sure she gets through this."

"Thanks, kid. I'd appreciate that. It kills me to be responsible for yet another death."

144

Heath walked over and hugged me. He was a good man.

NINETEEN

I picked up Toño and we popped back home. For the first time in my long life, I actually felt like I was home. What a wonderful feeling. In the few days we were gone, nothing major happened and certainly nothing disastrous. I think the biggest news was that a wolpom laid some eggs. Wolpom were indigenous to Kaljax. They sort of fill the swine role there, though they are a bit smaller and a whole lot smellier. Butt-ugly, too. Never look directly into the face of a wolpom. Sapale said they were cute. Sapale said I was cute, too. There you have it, by way of comparison.

I did return to the worldship fleet after a month like I'd promised. Heath and Amanda had gone public and were weathering the storm of controversy. Their political survival was greatly aided by the return of the stolen ships and the permanent death of Stuart Marshall. They declined to escape to Azsuram with me. Can't say I blame them. Azsuram was becoming more Kaljaxian by the minute. They'd probably feel out of their element. Plus, they were young, ambitious, and possibly in love. They needed and wanted to cut their own swathes in life.

Days rolled into months and the seasons changed with increasing rapidity. Sapale and I became great-grandparents as JJ and Fashallana became grandparents. A pleasant fulfilling stream of time flowed ever onward. Remember my saying about bottoms dropping out? Yup. Accompanied by a loud crash this time, too.

It was the middle of the night and everyone living was asleep. Us androids were sitting together reading. My book was, for the record, an ancient classic. *The Corporate Virus*. I know, everybody read that and *Lord of the Flies* and *The Scarlet Letter* in high school. I sort of skipped those assignments. I was too busy with sports, girls, and cars.

Anyway, Al blurted out, "Red Alert. Red Alert."

"What," I said springing to my feet. "And keep it down. I'm right here. Let the children sleep."

"I'm picking up ultra-long-range readings on the scanner. There appear to be a huge number of Uhoor heading right toward us."

Crrrap. Not them again. We had a deal. Don't come back and I won't make your sorry asses— assuming of course they had asses—extinct.

"How far out? How long do we have?"

"At their present speed about a week."

"Okay, at least we have plenty of time to prepare. Toño, let's go visit *Wrath* and see what readings he's getting."

We left at a fast walk. I was nervous. Since we returned from that last trip, the one where Heath and Amanda decided to stay put, I'd been kind of avoiding my cube. The things Manly said, the tricks he tried to pull off, and the extreme violence he advocated without reservation had cooled my interest in him significantly. I wasn't certain I wanted to associate myself with such a calculating killing machine. But he was good to have around in a fight.

Once inside, I asked him if he'd detected the Uhoor.

"Yes of course. I noted their course change shortly after they made it. It was unclear, initially. They were feeding near a black hole, so my readings were unreliable."

"When was that?" I asked darkly.

"About a year ago."

"Why did you not inform me of that important update?"

"You had not come to visit me. How could I inform you?"

"Ah, by radio. Maybe turn on your external speakers and shout really loud."

"I do not have speakers, external or internal."

"Let it go. I want an honest, no-bullshit answer. Is there anything else you know I would like to know but you have not told me because I've been ignoring you?"

"No, not really."

"*Wrath.* That's a bullshit answer. What else do you know about potential threats that you have yet to cough up?"

"Toño noticed some low frequency signals in a ground-based transponder."

"Yes, about a year ago. They wax and wane but have never increased significantly," said Toño.

"They are warp signatures," stated Manly.

I looked to Toño. "You have a clue what he just said?"

He shook his head. "Not really. *Wrath* are you referring to the Alcubierre warp drive theorized to allow a vessel to travel faster than the speed of light?"

"Yes. The warp technology is not simply theoretical. It has been developed many times by various civilizations. It is, however, highly inferior to the space folding that I perform. Specifically, if not balanced precisely, the temperature inside the warp bubble skyrockets to the extreme. Tricky stuff."

"Okay, science lesson over." I was hot. "You detected warp signatures and didn't tell me. Why?"

"They represented no immediate threat. They still may not."

"May not? If they *may* not represent a threat, then they *might* also. What threat can they pose?"

"The warp use, none."

"You spoke of a potential threat, then you say the warp field isn't a threat. Please cut the crap and tell me what I want to hear."

"The warp technology itself is neither harmful or harmless. It is a tool. What could be problematic is what's inside the bubbles traveling faster than light."

"There are more than one? What could be in the bubbles?"

"Anything, Form. Anything imaginable that wants to get somewhere else as fast as possible."

"The last time you encountered warp bubbles such as these, what was traveling inside them?"

"A Berrillian war armada."

"What's a Berrillian, and what's their armada like?"

"They are an ancient race, though not nearly as old as ours. We fought each other many times. The wars were good."

"What the hell is a good war? I've done war a lot, and nothing remotely positive ever happened."

"You have a narrow view, Form. Our wars were grand. Countless battles were fought and all were vicious beyond description. Billions died and thousands of planets were destroyed. In the end, their technology and their resolve could not match ours. They ran like frightened children. They retreated for millennia. They fled so fast even I was eventually unable to track them. Frightened children. Run from your shadow in the night. I shall always find you and crush your bones."

"Manly," I interrupted nervously. "Are you still talking to me? I hope like hell you're not, because you're sounding kind of psycho scary."

"Sorry, Form. My thoughts wandered. It will not happen again. May I be of any further assistance?"

"How long until the Uhoor arrive? Al thinks about a week."

"Your ship's AI is approximately correct."

"Can you defeat that large a number and still guarantee the safety of those on the ground?" I held my breath.

"Yes."

"Are you absolutely certain?"

"Ninety-nine, ninety-eight percent, Form."

"Not the answer I wanted to hear, *Wrath*. Not the answer at all."

"Sorry, but those are the odds. Please remain optimistic. I was built to kill and I do it with perfection, precision, and persistence. I shall vaporize the last of the Uhoor. Your loved ones are not to fret."

Manly was sounding nuttier by the minute. A tsunami of Uhoor were coming, and something possibly worse than very bad was going bump in the night in warp space. Great. Perfect.

It was time for a Council of Elders meeting.

TWENTY

Sapale convened the meeting the next morning. The room, which was the largest we'd built, was packed. About a third of the population was on the council. When word got around as to what we'd be talking about, everybody else made it a point to be there, too. I could tell people were frightened by the pitch of the voices and the tone of the snippets I caught. Who wouldn't be?

Sapale called the meeting to order, which was, for the first time ever, hard for her to achieve. Nervous conversations persisted, and she actually had to use the gavel I made her. Turned out Kaljaxians never invented the gavel, so it was a first for her. I think she liked slamming it down—a lot. Hopefully she'd leave it in the council chamber and not bring it home with her. Didn't need that in my home life.

She announced that she was going to tell everybody all that was known. She'd heard wild rumors and permutations of the truth, so she wanted there to be no misunderstandings. The Uhoor were coming in force, presumably to do battle, but there was no way to confirm that ahead of their arrival. She reassured everyone that the vortex alone could probably protect the planet, but we were going to prepare all defenses. The few space craft we had would remain close to home as a second line of defense. Ground weapons and membranes were the third line of defense. Those would be adequate to kill any Uhoor that escaped the other perimeters. Sapale promised sincerely that no loss of life or property was anticipated.

Someone in the back yelled that was good and well, but what about the murderous superrace following right behind them. The room exploded in shouts that reflected his concerns. I was amazed. The mighty Uhoor were nothing more than an annoyance to most attendees. Nothing more than giant caterpillars. They feared the unknown, not the imminent threat.

Sapale spoke loudly, declaring that it was not certain if the weak signals were that specific species, or even heading remotely in our direction. Once the Uhoor were dealt with—peacefully, we hoped—we would worry about what the far-away signal might mean.

That brought murmurs and grunts of doubt from the audience. One of the immigrants stood and demanded that she be allowed to repatriate to Kaljax before the axe of doom fell on Azsuram. I was inclined to say I'd take her, then and there, but it was Sapale's show. I held my tongue. My brood's-mate tried to reassure her and anyone like-minded that there was no planetary threat. If one ever presented itself, they would discuss all options at that time. The woman refused to be seated. She declared that talk was cheap and that her life had great value. She would not be placated or dismissed. Sapale looked to me. I could tell she was on the verge of telling the bitch exactly what I had been ready to say.

Sapale was in her new incarnation a society builder,

so she opted for diplomacy. Anyone with further questions was encouraged to linger after the meeting, and she promised to stay as long as it took to address everyone's concerns. I admired Sapale's ability to be so tactful, but I worried a little that she'd actually turn into a talking-head politician. Sooner than you know it, she'd smile a lot, shake every hand she saw, and kiss every baby. Deplorable.

Finally the tense discordant meeting drew to a close. Sapale reminded everyone that there would be twice daily emergency-preparedness drills until further notice. She asked that, in these extraordinary times, no one take the exercises lightly or ignore them. Everyone's survival depended on every individual doing their part correctly and well. That announcement was met with a sentiment as close to hostile contempt as I'd ever seen. People in crowds sure were a pain to deal with, despite the fact that most were closely related. My impulse to jump in my ship and leave, once and for all, was almost irresistible. *Second star to the right and straight on 'till morning* never sounded so inviting.

Fortunately, with all the fuss and preparation, the time waiting for the pod of ponderous pickles passed quickly enough. None too soon, for my liking. Vhalisma and I were packing the vortex and were ready to fly out to intercept the Uhoor. Vhalisma had always been involved in defense issues, so she was my natural choice to bring as a copilot. JJ couldn't be spared, since he was at that point the head of the combined defenses of Azsuram. "Combined" was admittedly euphemistic. At that time, "combined" meant everyone standing on terra firma. In the future, we envisioned there would be land, sea, and space arms to our military. But at present it was only boots on the ground.

I parked *Wrath* directly in the path of the Uhoor, two

days's travel at their speed, from Azsuram. That way if it all went to hell in a handbasket, the remaining two lines of defense would have plenty of notice that they were about to become relevant. I did bring Al, too. Lily had several new AIs to help her coordinate matters back home. As irascible as Al could be, I knew I could count on him in battle. He might also help if that damn vortex manipulator went completely rogue. I was beginning to understand why someone buried him on some forgotten planet. The nice part about Al was that I didn't have to specifically tell him *Wrath* scared the shit out of me. If I did, that factoid would have become data easily hacked by the manipulator. Al knew me so well, after living in such close quarters for so long, that I didn't have to spell out such obvious reservations.

"Are they in weapons distance yet, Manly?" I asked as calmly as I could.

"Yes, Form. They have been for several hours. I have each blight targeted and am ready to vaporize them to their version of hell. Shall I fire now, or would you prefer to look into their eyes as they boil from their heads?"

"Stand down," I said firmly. "I wish to communicate with them. I want to see if we can arrive at some peaceful solution well before any fighting commences."

"Form, this is madness. We have discussed sentimentality in combat before. I serve you, but part of my service *is* to provide you with honest critiques. Please do not make decisions based on needless and unattainable goals, however well-intentioned. This scum has broken their word and is attacking your family. Think not of vague ideals, Form. Think rather of your tiny grandchild, Latrytin, as she lies at this very moment sleeping in her crib. The Uhoor would kill her and laugh of it for eons. Come, comrade, let me fire now. Then we shall return home in glory. The women will come to us like moths to an irresistible flame, and together we shall drink the night away."

Man, was he good. Good and insane. He was rational, deferential, even poetic in his convincing argument to avoid morality and engage in mindless bloodlust. Dangerous guy. I'd have to keep my head. I thanked my lucky stars Al was along for the ride. He'd easily picked up on the lunacy, too. Who in their right mind programmed this vortex manipulator?

"Open and confirm back to me a communication channel to the lead Uhoor. I think that would be Tho."

There was an unnecessary delay then Manly spoke with obvious disgust. "Tho is not among the pod."

"Can you determine which one is in charge?"

"No. And that is the truth, before you further accuse me of duplicity, Form."

I sure hoped his mental facilities outlasted this battle. "Then make it audible to all of them. Say: *This is Captain Ryan, Form of Wrath. You are in direct violation of our treaty that keeps you on the other side of the galaxy from Azsuram. Please declare your intentions.*" I waited a few seconds. "Any response?"

"Yes. They have sped up."

Crap. "Tell them this: *If you do not stop and negotiate, I will destroy all of you. There will be no more Uhoor. If you force my hand, your great species will become extinct.*" Again I asked, "Any response?"

"None. As I counseled, Form, these brutes are incapable of reason. They are driven by malevolence and spite. The galaxy will be a better and safer place for every righteous species once you, Captain Jonathan Ryan, seize all the glory and become a legendary hero to a grateful, subservient universe."

"Belay the editorials, Manly. Fire one pulsed shot across the bow of the nearest Uhoor. Let them know I mean business."

"They would know it better, less ambiguously, if you allowed me to target the leader herself. Her renegade, marauding party must be punished maximally. She who whipped them into a state of bestial vengeance-seeking is *not* to be forgiven."

Double crap. Manly was coming apart at the seams. "How, *Wrath*, do you know the leader is a female? You said Tho was not present."

Al spoke. "I have received enough chatter to believe with confidence the leader is a female named Ablo. The pod is, for lack of a better descriptor, cheering her on."

"Based on all contact with *Wrath* in the past, do you believe Manly knew that, too?"

"It is a certainty."

"*Wrath*, your Form is pissed—mega-pissed. If you deceive me, lie to me, or mislead me one more time, so help me I will withdraw my control prerogatives. We'll drift in space until the Uhoor come and pound us to dust."

"Form," he said, "there has been a tremendous error of misunderstanding between you and me. I cannot mislead you. I have not lied. Please keep in mind I am an alien device and am still learning your ways and nuances. Command and I shall obey."

"Fire one warning shot twenty meters ahead of this Ablo bitch. Then, *Al*, hail her and demand an immediate unconditional surrender."

"F ... Form," Manly stammered, "I am best equipped to—"

"Shut it, Manly. I want my orders followed without discussion or grousing. You both have tasks. Perform them." Man, oh, man, was I hot. If Manly was standing in front of me, I'd deck him.

"The shot was fired and I hailed Ablo," reported Al. "No course change or communication from the Uhoor."

"Estimated time of arrival?"

"Two minutes," they both said in a chorus.

"How long will it take you to target and fire on all the Uhoor, Manly and Al?" Al controlled the rail cannons. I knew it would be next to useless against all those flying kielbasas, but I wanted to make the point to Manly that I had options that didn't include him. Really, it was silly posturing. I needed the cube. But maybe I could bluff the maniacal computer into somewhat better behavior.

"Thirteen seconds," replied Manly.

"One minute twenty-five seconds to deliver ten rail balls to each Uhoor." Ten hits would only serve to make them madder than they already were. I had thirty-five seconds to decide.

Still bluffing my ass off, I said, "Al, I will depend on Manly for this engagement. Please, however, remain fully ready to fire if Manly screws up."

I waited a few seconds. No response from either machine.

"*Wrath*, target and destroy all Uhoor with incoming vectors. Alert me when this has been accomplished."

For an assault of that magnitude releasing all that energy, I would have expected the cube to recoil, the lights to dim, and my teeth to rattle. Nothing happened, not even an audible *kathunk*.

Twenty-five seconds later, Manly said, "All the Uhoor are dead. Most were vaporized, a few remain corporeal with major portions of their flesh missing."

"Thank you, Manly. Are there any living Uhoor on your sensors?"

"None, Form."

"Al, how 'bout yours?" I wanted to keep Manly honest.

"None," Al quickly replied.

"Okay," I said more to myself, "that's that." Those Uhoor were more stupid and stubborn than humans. I would not have thought that possible. "Manly, take us home."

All that was left for me was the sick feeling of failure I got in my gut after each and every battle. Conflict—killing—marked the ultimate failure of reason. Every time, I got the dry heaves for a few hours and hated myself for a few days. Then came the remorse of knowing I'd taken a life, or, in this case, thousands of lives. The hollow reassurance that *they* attacked *me* did nothing to ease the cancer of remorse that ate at my brain. When I saw Doc, maybe I'd see if he could delete the portion of my personality that regretted the inevitable. Some people might call that humanity. I called it inconvenient. I didn't want to feel it any longer. Not anymore.

I'd radioed ahead that we'd won the battle, lopsided though it had been. The vortex landing site was, as a result, surrounded by a cheering crowd when we materialized. Vhalisma and I exited and were immediately embraced by what seemed to be the entire population of Azsuram. As long as I lived I'd never tire of the adulation and support of an admiring public after a victory. Heady stuff. But it never quite offset the sadness I felt.

After the initial hoopla, Sapale pulled me to the side and gave me the biggest kiss in recorded history. "All of our worries are *over*. I'm so happy I might burst."

"All of them?" I said with a patented Jon smile.

"Marshall is actually gone, and the Uhoor are extinct.

We—you and I—are free of their threats. We can *breathe* again."

I'm more a believer in sequential turds. You kicked one out of your path and someone quickly laid another one, probably stinkier, in that unoccupied space. But there was no reason to pop her bubble. Hey, maybe the universe was fresh out of excrement to obstruct our progress. Time would tell. And it did. The populace of Azsuram, and especially Sapale, had a very good two weeks. Yeah, only two weeks of that life-is-good crap. Nice while it lasted.

One evening Toño dropped by our house. "I'd like you to come to the lab and look at some data I think you need to be aware of." He spoke a bit in code to keep from overtly worrying Sapale. Yeah, that was as likely as not upsetting a lion by hitting it on the head with a thin stick. Her eyes shot back and forth between us looking for a tell.

"No prob. You be there tomorrow morning?" I was making a lame stab at being clever, downplaying the possible significance.

Toño looked thoughtful. "Yes, I will probably be there. However, you'd best come now. That way, I won't worry that I delayed informing you—"

"Let's go," said Sapale popping to her feet. She snatched her handheld from her waist. "Fash, can you come over *now* and watch the little ones? Great." She thumbed it off and replaced it on her belt. "She's on her way. Let me get my coat."

We walked to the lab in silence. Small talk felt inappropriate when we were about to get bad news.

Toño sat at a console and punched a few buttons. A series of wave forms appeared on the screen. The lines seemed chaotic, but I recognized them as the warp signatures he'd discovered a while ago. Crap and a half. It was going to be big bad news. He traced out one particular line. "These are the tracings I showed Jon a few months back."

Sapale knew about the phantoms coursing the void, but she had never seen the actual patterns.

"These," he said after hitting a button, "are tracings, or rather the lack of them, that were recorded two weeks ago." He turned and looked at me solemnly. "The warp signatures disappeared shortly after *Wrath* destroyed the Uhoor."

"That's an odd coincidence," I said, without much enthusiasm.

"Yes." Toño actually scoffed. He'd expressed many a negative attitude toward me over the centuries, but he'd never done that. "Quite the coincidence, if only it actually were one." He hit another button. "These are the return of the warp signatures here, a little while after the incident ended."

"So," I said, "what? My firing interfered with reception?"

"Jon," he said firmly, "there's a considerable difference between wishful thinking and the placing of one's head in the sand. Look at the signals." He rapped the screen with a knuckle.

I studied the waves. They looked the same didn't they? I mean what were they supposed to do? "You gotta help me out here. They look the same to me."

His fingers raced over a keyboard and two different signals appeared on the split screen. "Here," he said pointing, "before and after. The signal is blue-shifted."

"Sorry," Sapale said, "I've heard the term, but what does it mean in this context?"

"When a source moves away from the observer, it's *red*-shifted." He stopped speaking.

"And if the source is moving toward the observer," she finished his thought, "the signal is *blue*-shifted?"

"Yes. Just after *Wrath* put on a monumental display of force, whatever's out there turned toward us."

"Guess who's coming to dinner?" I mumbled to myself.

"Who?" asked my confused brood's-mate.

"Somebody," I said coarsely, "who's neither invited nor welcome."

TWENTY-ONE

"You asked me to come," said Yibitriander without glee, "and I am here."

"Thank you," replied Kymee smiling, trying to lighten his son's dour mood. Kymee walked over and they bumped shoulders. "It's more wonderful to see you than I might have imagined."

"I'm used to you speaking in riddles, but even that one lost me."

"Well," Kymee said playfully, "I was looking forward to physically seeing you, and yet I find that in beholding you, I'm more pleased than I hoped to be."

"For several million years we've all been mentally linked. You and I are technically never apart. How is it that the act of perceiving me visually enhances your experience?"

"You never were given to sentimentality were you?" Kymee twisted his mouth after speaking.

"Am I here for you to insult and deride, or is there a more noble purpose to your request?"

"Humorless, too. I forgot about that one."

Yibitriander flapped his eyes open and shut in

frustration. "Shall I return at a time when you're ready to communicate your purpose? However, if you prefer, I will stand here and be lambasted. I *am* immortal."

"Ah. There's the Yibitriander of old." Kymee sat and motioned to a nearby chair. "I've called you to discuss some, er, troubling notifications I've received from *Wrath*."

Yibitriander tightly balled up his fists and he sucked in a sharp breath. "That he reported his revivification was not sufficiently repugnant news? Now he feels entitled to provide to our uninterested ears a running commentary?"

"In this case I think even your ears need to hear his report."

Yibitriander took longer than he would have liked to compose himself. "I'm disconnected from his world. We Deavoriath are removed from that flow of reality. That he gnaws at our edges and hopes to draw us out is meaningless." He swiped an angry hand in front of his chest. "Was there anything else you wished to discuss before I take my leave?"

Kymee studied his son. Like countless fathers before him, he rubbed at his face absently and worried that his son was too impetuous and too self-assured for his own good. Kymee was fairly certain he himself knew what was important in life. He wished, as fathers have through all the ages, that his son would also grow to know life's meaning. Anger, petulance, and mule-like stubbornness were hardly reliable tools to employ along that journey. But Yibitriander had always been the hottest head among the countless hotheads of his people. That, after all, was intimately linked to the evolution of *Wrath*, was it not? Two who were one yet never together. Two who were bound to one purpose but working toward diametrically opposed endpoints. Both son and machine needed more time. Kymee hoped that there would be enough time left.

Yibitriander and *Wrath* both needed to gain the understanding and insights they both lacked.

"You will *stay*," stated Kymee, "and you will *listen*. What you do with the knowledge in your thick head will subsequently be up to you. But you will *hear* my words." He looked out a window to an empty landscape devoid of life. "It's not enough that we declare ourselves superior and hence detached from the universe we once ruled with an iron fist. We are still a part of the whole. If we compound our endless errors by adding the arrogance of inattention to duties that are *ours,* we have learned nothing in more time than we deserve to have been allotted."

A dutifully chastised Yibitriander rested back in his chair. "Speak. I'm listening."

"*Wrath* reports that the remaining handful of Uhoor left in this galaxy banded together and advanced against Jon Ryan's adopted home world of Hodor."

"And the outcome?" as if he did not know in advance.

"*Wrath* destroyed them without hesitation. Their kind no longer lives in this galaxy."

Yibitriander turned his palms up questioningly. "What else might they have anticipated? They knew with certainty that *Wrath* was capable of neutralizing them as he had so many of their brethren before. If a man freely walks off a cliff, shall I cry when I learn of his death against the rocks below?" He let his hands fall.

"It's not that cut-and-dried, and you know it. Yes, I disliked the Uhoor. We all did. They were aloof, humorless, and ... wait, that's what I just said about you wasn't it?" He laughed at his own joke. "But that they were vulgar didn't mean they deserved to die, even if they precipitated it. All are part of one and one is in all. You know this, I pray."

"Is this a lesson, a scolding, or an update?"

"Yes." Kymee shouted. He had not raised his voice in over half a million years. He surprised himself.

Yibitriander knew his father loved to bait him, or at least he had back when such actions mattered and were condoned. He wondered sitting there across from the old man if he still loved him. Did Yibitriander love? Was it still a part of him? He had no idea. Still, only a fool was proud to be a fool. He would listen longer.

"Is that *Wrath's* full report?"

"No," Kymee replied flatly. "If it were I wouldn't have troubled you."

"You have not troubled me yet. I'm glad you value my company. I thank you for calling me here."

"I doubt you'll say that so glibly once you've learned the whole of it."

"Am I to find out today? Will you finish lecturing, scolding, and updating me before tomorrow comes?"

That brought a tremendous smile to Kymee's face. "Yes. We shall find how detached and impartial you presently are. *Wrath* says he has detected multiple warp signatures. He's uncertain how distant they are or who generated them. He does, however, believe there are few possible candidates as to who created the signals."

Yibitriander's entire body slumped as if weighed down by several oceans of water. His face went blank, as did his mind. Only his primal raging emotions seemed to hear those words. His blood boiled in his veins and his hatred sprang from dormancy like it had never slept.

"I mark," Kymee said, "that you understand the implications of *Wrath's* report." Seeing that Yibitriander was mentally absent from the room Kymee reached over and shook him. "Are you okay, boy? I've told you matters are unsettled, not that they are to end in a matter of heartbeats."

"All that we've become ... all ... all that we've struggled

to become for an eternity cannot be ... be voided. It cannot happen."

"That which happens, happens whether you agree with it or not. Reality, it turns out, does not rely on your acceptance as a necessary condition of its existence."

"But ... but nothing has changed. *Nothing.*"

"If *nothing* has changed, then we've wasted a lot of time, haven't we?"

Yibitriander forced himself to calm, to return to where he'd rested for untold time. He failed. "Father if the worst possible outcome has occurred, what shall we do? Shall we do anything?"

"I'm not done ruining your day, son. *Wrath* reports that the warp signatures are now headed directly toward Hodor."

Yibitriander was overwhelmed. He experienced a panic he had not felt for longer than he could recall. No. His actions could not have sparked this firestorm. It was simply and completely impossible.

Wait. His mind raced. *He* didn't summon the return of the damned. No. If the Berrillians had returned, it was not of *his* doing. Or was it? They had parted company with the Deavoriath in defeat and disgrace, and that had been his doing almost singlehandedly. If they were back seeking vengeance after all this time, surely it was he they sought to find more than any other.

Yes, Yibitriander had fitted the android with control prerogatives. If he had not, *Wrath* would have remained hidden and the Berrillians, if that was who was out there, would have blithely sailed away as they seemed to have been doing. Jon Ryan would surely have failed on any number of occasions, if not for him. If nothing else, the Uhoor would have wiped Hodor clean of that new colony without *Wrath.* Good versus bad, right versus wrong, justice versus retribution. Why were they always hurled at him like flaming knives? Why could he not know rest?

"Would you like me to leave you two strangers alone?" asked Kymee.

"Huh?" Yibitriander scanned the sparse room. "Whom do you refer to?"

"You and your conscience, of course. The two of you seem to be having an arm-wrestling match with all three arms." Kymee smiled faintly. "We shall see what will happen. For now, at least, we have no control over any outcome." He breathed slowly and deeply staring at Yibitriander. "We may need to call a general meeting."

"A *what?*" snapped Yibitriander. "There's been no such gathering in an eternity. Why would we need one? If the Deavoriath need to consider a matter as a people, we can do it as the one that we are—mentally linked." He was stunned at the suggestion. "As we speak, everyone knows what we do. As we each feel, so does the whole."

"Time may be catching up with us," Kymee said. "If this is to be our final crisis, I think we should face it shoulder to shoulder, arm in arm, as the Deavoriath have always done. I swear that's what made us so strong." He gestured around the room. "It was never our toys or our esoteric technology that made us masters. Neither was it the weakness of our enemies. *I* haven't forgotten the power that it is to be *Deavoriath*. If we elect to act, to allow others to die, or to perish as a race, we will do it the old way. Physically together as one."

Yibitriander felt his guts tumble as they had not in forever. Had he called for the beast to awaken? Was it his one foolish act that would release the plague that were the Berrillians? Worse yet, had he released the pestilence that the Deavoriath were upon a slumbering universe? How could his nature have not changed from all the time, the effort, and the painful lessons of the past? How could he justify not just his act, but his existence? Doubt and self-loathing clashed like Titans in his head.

Hand wringing and self-flagellation would solve nothing. Neither hindsight nor remorse would extricate a single soul in harm's way from a nightmare no one deserved. Well, maybe only the Berrillians and the Deavoriath deserved such harsh fates.

TWENTY-TWO

As Toño and I walked into Amanda's office, she rose, smiled, and said, "It's wonderful to see you two so soon." She couldn't conceal her pregnancy at that juncture, even if she wanted to. She extended a hand.

"Yeah, Gramps," Heath said with a straight face, "good to see you're still up and about at your advanced age."

First I then Toño plopped into chairs without shaking hands or responding to that cheery greeting. That brought an exchange of confused looks between the president and vice president. They both sat with frowns on their faces.

As soon as they sat I spoke. "Look, I'm sorry for the lack of notice and cordiality. We come with bad news, worse than any humankind has ever received."

Amanda smiled awkwardly. "I'm sure," she tried to lighten the mood, "it couldn't be as bad as the destruction of Earth."

"We survived," Heath added. "Can't be worse than that."

I looked to Toño. The scientist shook his head and said, "Yes, it can be. Immensely worse, in fact."

"I'm afraid to ask, but," Amanda replied, "maybe you should just tell us what threat we face."

I drew a deep breath and sighed it out. "We've detected signals of what is likely an alien fleet that altered course and is heading straight toward us."

"Okay," Heath said, "I'll admit that sounds bad. Are these hostile aliens?"

"The word *hostile*," Toño responded, "falls considerably short of describing their evil, destructive nature."

"But," Amanda said as calmly as she could, "you don't know it's who you suspect, right? It *could* be anyone."

"I'm beginning to believe we're not nearly that lucky, Mandy," I responded. "Toño and I have been over the possibilities with the cube, and we are unfortunately quite certain we face a Berrillian attack fleet."

"Berrillian?" repeated Amanda. "I've never heard of them."

"They've been gone a very long time," said Toño. "If the vortex is correct, and we believe he is, they're back for revenge."

"Wait, wait," said Heath. "They can't possibly be mad at *us*. We've never encountered them, let alone pissed them off."

"They don't have a bone to pick with us," I replied. "They had a longstanding, unbelievably brutal war with the Deavoriath. The Berrillians are most likely here to settle with them."

"Jon," began Amanda, "we're both a bit confused." She gestured to Heath. "We've never heard of either of these races. How are *we* involved?"

"Millions of years ago," began Toño, "this galaxy was ruled by an advanced civilization called the Deavoriath. At the height of their power they were harsh, unyielding and, above all, unmatched in

170

technology. Though all races were their enemies, few were nearly as capable and relentless as they were. The Berrillians were the most closely matched. They fought with each other on scales that are hard for us to comprehend. In the end, the Deavoriath were victorious. The Berrillians were lucky enough to flee before being totally wiped out. It would seem the Berrillians have returned to take up where things left off." To himself he muttered, "Presumably, they have enough new toys to fancy they have a better chance this time."

"How exactly does that involve us?" asked Heath. "Since we don't know squat about the Deavoriath, they must be far away from here if they even still exist. We have no beef with the Berrillians."

"Yes, and no," I said. "The Deavoriath are still around and they're actually quite close by. They're the ones who gave me these." He wiggled his fingers. "The vortex is theirs, too. If the Berrillians are hunting their old friends, they'll come right to our doorstep."

"Even if the Berrillians couldn't find the Deavoriath, they pose us a significant threat. Unless they've radically changed their ways, they're a conquering species. They were, the vortex manipulator tells us, much worse than the Deavoriath in every negative quality. They killed for the joy of it, they crushed planets for sport, and they had absolutely no concept of morality or mercy. They were the masters of destruction straight out of the gates of hell," Toño added.

"That does sound bad," said Amanda. "When will they arrive?"

"Unclear," replied Toño. "They are moving at faster than the speed of light by using warp field propulsion. There's no way to determine how fast they're traveling, or precisely how far away they actually are. Our best estimate is that they should arrive in a month; maybe slightly longer."

"One *month*." shouted Heath. "Are you trying to suggest the ultimate killing machines in the galaxy will be here in thirty days?"

"Unfortunately, yes," replied Toño.

"But," Heath responded, "that's preposterous. We can't be annihilated in a month's time."

"Why not?" I asked.

Heath rubbed his scalp so hard it hurt. "That's just not possible—not fair." He looked at the other three and lowered his head. "Kind of stupid of me to say that, wasn't it? What's fair ever had to do with anything?"

"Are we able to defend ourselves?" asked Mandy. "We have rail cannon, membranes, and the vortex. Surely that's a potent combined force."

"I've learned what I can from the vortex manipulator," said Toño. "Using that data, I've run simulations. *Lots* of simulations."

"And," she asked, leaning slightly forward.

"And we're pretty screwed," I finished. "The rail guns might be minimally effective, but only at best. Similar technology was familiar to the combatants back then, so we have to assume they have effective countermeasures. The membranes themselves didn't exist then, but they're purely defensive in this setting. No matter how strong a castle's walls are, a persistent siege will defeat the people inside sooner or later."

"And the vortex?" asked Heath. "That's one hell of a weapon."

"Yes it is. But a million years ago the Deavoriath flew thousands of them and only just defeated the Berrillians. One vortex is simply not enough to hold off an invasion force of this magnitude. Assuming they do have powerful new toys, one vortex will be totally overmatched."

"But," Heath said quickly, "you don't know the size of the fleet out there, do you? How can you know we're basically defenseless?"

"Our estimates are based historically on their style of warfare, as well as rough approximations based on the magnitude of the warp signatures."

"And," I said, "the sons of bitches must have some powerful new toys to march so openly back into Deavoriath territory. One vortex back then would have been insufficient. It'd be probably just a bad joke now."

"This sounds as bad as it can be." Amanda's face grew hard and determined. "What's our plan? What, General Ryan, are we to do?"

"I have no fucking clue, Madame President." I sighed and shrugged my shoulders. "We can throw everything we've got at them, sure. But I think we'll be interstellar dust real fast."

"There *has* to be a better option," insisted Amanda. She was imperial in her outrage. "We haven't faced all these challenges and overcome so much to sit on our hands or beg for mercy that will never come. There *must* be some defense or evasion that will keep at least *some* of us alive."

Toño and I sat in silence neither of us wishing to meet her eyes.

"I think *that's* your answer," said Heath. He then spoke harshly, sarcasm dripping from his lips. "I guess our fleet will have to fashion our *own* defense, without Azsuram's help."

"Look," I said quietly, "just because this may be hopeless doesn't mean we need to start fighting amongst ourselves. There's one upside for the worldship fleet."

"I'll take anything I can get," replied Amanda. "What?"

"They'll hit us first. You'll learn something about their

intention and capabilities from that. Hopefully that is. Assuming they blow through us, they'll be on you within a day or two."

"That does not make me feel better," she chided. "What about the Deavoriath? Maybe they will emerge from hiding and help."

"Unlikely," I said. "They've gone to a lot of effort to remain hidden. I doubt they'll do anything."

"Can they remain hidden from the Berrillians?" asked Heath.

"The vortex isn't sure. He's been out of touch for a long time. When I press him, all he'll commit to is maybe."

"Can we contact the Deavoriath through the vortex?" asked Amanda. "Maybe I can persuade them to help?"

"Funny you should mention that," I replied. "That's our next stop. I sort of tricked Manly—the vortex manipulator—into taking me there."

"I'm coming, too," said Amanda. "Give me a few minutes to prepare, and we can leave."

"Amanda." barked Heath. "You're not going on such a dangerous mission at this critical point in time."

The look she gave Heath was like skunk spray. "I do not believe I answer to *you*. If I choose to go, I will go."

"Ah," I fluttered my fingers in the air, "in case you both forgot, I'm in charge of who boards the cube, and I say *neither* of you are going." I shifted uncomfortably in my chair. "This may be a one-way trip. Toño and I are going because we have to. I've apparently been there, so someone there must like me. Toño's way more diplomatic than me and can maybe talk science with them." I sniffed loudly. "I've said my goodbyes to Sapale and the family. That's how pessimistic I am about this one."

"Why?" asked Heath. "They didn't kill you the first time. Why would they now?"

"They went to a lot of trouble to make sure I couldn't come back. When you walk back into the bear's cave, you're pressing your luck."

"I don't care. I'm coming. That's an order, General Ryan. I'm still your commander in chief, in case that inconvenience has slipped your mind."

She had me there. I was pretty much a free agent at that point, but technically I was still in the Air Force. There was no such thing as an airplane or a sky to fly it in any longer, but the organization still existed. "Look, Mandy," I pointed to her swollen belly, "I don't think it's medically safe to come. You're pretty far along you know?"

"I'm a medical doctor," said Toño most unhelpfully. "I'll grab some obstetrical equipment from a sickbay. It should allow me to keep her and the baby safe."

"But," I sort of whined, "it's kind of likely we'll all be killed and, at the very least, they'll keep the cube. If they do, we're stuck there."

"Jon," Amanda said evenly, "if I stay, and you're right about the Berrillians, it wouldn't matter if I never came back. Dead is dead is dead no matter how one gets there."

She had me on that count, too. "Your funeral," I said with resignation. "I'm leaving in ten minutes. If you two," I indicated Toño and Amanda, "are at the dock then, you can come."

"If you guys don't return, I'm sure stuck watching one huge mass of shit hit the fan," Heath said.

"Hey," I said, "think of it in the positive. You'll be in *command* of the fan. Lot of pressure there, grandson."

TWENTY-THREE

Our trip to Oowaoa was like all others—instantaneous. I got an additional sickening feeling in my gut once we arrived. It was show time. It was literally do or die time. I was nervous in more ways than I'd have thought it possible. The Deavoriath could just blow us away and be done with us. They could cheer for the Berrillians to blow us away. Worst of all, they could simply say *no* to helping us. That would constitute a verbal signature on our collective death certificates. From what I'd learned from the admittedly unreliable Manly, the Deavoriath were not a touchy-feely, kumbaya kind of bunch.

Oh well. Luckily, I was awarded little time to fret. As soon as we landed, *Wrath*'s hull opened into a door. Manly announced, "I've alerted the senior Forms of our arrival. They will meet with you here shortly. They command that you remain in this immediate vicinity."

"Did I ask you to trumpet our arrival, Manly?" I questioned, after the fact.

"No, you did not. I took it upon myself, as a matter of protocol."

I sort of figured he'd become more persnickety once

he was back on home turf. I was right, not that there was much I could do about his behavior. Whoever invented him, whom I was presumably about to meet, must have had a screw loose. Nice. Our futures depended on a whole bushelful of nuts.

"Are you alright, dear?" Toño asked of Amanda, as he reached for her elbow.

She pulled her arm away before he could touch her. She was clearly a bit green around the gills, but she was also tough. "I'm fine. Please don't patronize me." To his hurt look, she responded, "I know you mean well. Sorry. I'm fine." She began rubbing her belly as pregnant women are given to do.

I had no idea how long it would take for someone to arrive, so I led Amanda to a nearby stool and sat her down. The architecture seemed vaguely familiar, with its smooth contours and fluid structures. A vision of a man with three legs suddenly popped into my mind. Yeah, the Deavoriath had three arms and three legs. They walked like a crippled spider some mean kid had just pulled five legs off of. Wow, how could I've forgotten that image? Swiss cheese was a bad thing to make memories out of.

"Do you suppose," asked Toño mostly to break the tension, "it'll take them long to arrive?"

I studied the space around us. It had to be a hangar or similar landing site for the cubes. *Wrath* fit precisely on the pad. "I bet this landing area is centrally located so the pilots could land and get home quickly. It's not like the ships have powerful thrusters requiring an isolated landing spot."

A door closed loudly a few meters away. We had company. Three figures scampered toward us rapidly, but I sensed no urgency. I think these guys just moved quickly. Three legs, just like I remembered. I let my breath out when I confirmed nobody carried anything resembling a weapon. At least we weren't going to be shot on sight. Maybe.

The man in the lead was slightly younger than the one behind him. The third figure looked more gender-neutral. Possibly a female? I'd know soon enough.

The trio stopped a couple of arms' lengths away. They folded and unfolded their hands nervously, which was kind of comical, what with those six arms wriggling around like nervous elephant trunks. I started to say something when the lead man spoke. "I don't suppose you remember me, Captain Ryan. I'm Yibitriander." He nodded to the older male. "This is Kymee. He would be described as our senior science maker." He indicated the other figure, "And this is Lornot. She was a political leader, long ago."

I started to introduce my group, but Yibitriander held up a hang-on-a-second hand. "No need. *Wrath* has updated us on all that." He stared into Doc's eyes. "Toño DeJesus, master science maker," he nodded slightly, "and Amanda Walker," he bowed to her, "leader of a significant number of humans flying large rocks toward the planet we call Hodor."

"Pleased to meet you," said Amanda.

"Hmm," said Yibitriander somewhat mysteriously. "We'll see, won't we?" Back to me, he went on, "I'd like to welcome you and state that it is pleasant to see you again, but neither is the case. In scrubbing your memory, I knew I risked your not understanding how important it was for you never to return here. My oversight does not, however, free you of responsibility from your transgression."

That didn't sound encouraging. "Yibit ... Yibtr —"

He closed his eyes in frustration and said, "Last time, you elected to call me Yib."

Yes, I did. "Right, I remember that now. Yib, how've you been?"

"Fine," he said without emotion, "as I always am. Now, as I was saying —"

Lornot spoke up. "Yibitriander, might it not be appropriate to invite our guests to our, um, quarters? Offer them refreshments or something?"

God bless all politicians. She was asking him to lighten up, in a diplomatic way.

"They're not our guests. They arrived uninvited and of their own accord," Yibitriander stated flatly.

Kymee interrupted. "Yes, where *are* our manners? You'd think we haven't entertained visitors in a million years."

Yibitriander shot him a because-we-haven't kind of glance, but then eased back. "Please follow us. We will go to Kymee's space."

I noticed that drew a surprised expression from the senior science maker. These two were teasing each other at our expense. I guessed that was better than having been killed outright but it didn't feel reassuring, either. The six of us walked in silence for a few minutes, with Yibitriander in the lead. He stopped at a portal that appeared as anonymous as any other in the uniform expanse I'd witnessed.

He raised an arm to direct us in.

Kymee's place was a mess. I liked him immediately. In a world of sameness, he answered to his own call. Several seats—I couldn't really call them chairs—sprouted from the floor in a cluster. Yibitriander indicated that we should sit. Kymee left, but returned almost instantly with roughly hewn mugs on a tray. We were each given one. He set down the tray and raised his mug to his nose. He smelled it like it was a snifter of rare cognac. "This," he began, "is *nufe*. It is, or rather was, our favorite light refreshment. We drank it all the time."

"May I ask why you no longer do?" Amanda inquired.

That brought a short chuckle from him. "Much has changed. After we secluded ourselves here long ago, we undertook a series of ... um, *alterations*. Some were conscious; others were things that more or less fell by the wayside." He smelled his mug again. "This was a habit that fell out of use." He took a tentative sip and smiled. "Pity."

Amanda marveled at the contents of her cup. "This is ancient, yet you serve it to us? How very generous of you, Kymee."

"This?" he held his mug up. "No I fabricated it just now." He pointed back to the arch he'd entered by.

"If," she began to respond, "you can make it so easily, why—"

"Kymee," Yibitriander said with obvious frustration, "we are not here to discuss nufe, its storage, production, or consumption."

Kymee had a wounded look on his face. Lornot spoke up. "Please try your nufe. I assure you it is safe for your physiology. Amanda, I see that you are gestating. Nufe will have no ill effect on your fetus."

"Thanks," Amanda said as she flushed a deep shade of red. She took a sip. "It tastes like ripe strawberries, butterscotch, and a picnic on a warm summer afternoon. How's that possible?"

"Nufe has a different taste for each who drinks it," said Kymee. "That taste changes with time, possibly even between sips." He looked at his mug. "Marvelous stuff."

"We haven't had a baby on Oowaoa for much longer than I can remember," Lornot remarked, with sadness in her eyes.

"I'm afraid I will have to play the role of villain," said Yibitriander tersely, "yet again and *insist* we confine our conversation to the very serious matter of their presence here. Need I remind *anyone* how fundamentally serious such an incursion is?"

"You play the role of a grouch so well," replied Kymee. "How could we deny you it?"

"I'm not certain the term 'incursion' accurately characterizes the visit these humans have paid us. We should avoid judgmental labels, at least for the time being, don't you agree, Yibitriander?" Lornot said.

I rather enjoyed watching Yib's buddies pin his ears back so properly. But he didn't seem to be phased. I decided to speak up before he reacted angrily. "I'm all for getting to the point myself. You know, Yib, the longer I'm here, the more my memories return. I recall you were very kind to me on my last visit. I want to thank you from the bottom of my heart for your help. If it weren't for the command prerogatives you gave me, my mission would have failed any number of times."

"A questionable decision in retrospect," he replied. He seemed to *want* to be mad at us, but had to force himself into it. What was his angle?

"But you did it and I credit you with allowing me to save my species."

"Powerful praise," said Kymee, looking sideways toward Yibitriander, "yet seemingly well deserved. It seems I was wrong to question your request to place those instruments in Jon Ryan. I'm proud of your superior insight."

Buttering him up? Good. Kymee had to be on our side, or at least open to hearing us out.

"As a leader of the human colonists," said Amanda with her official voice, "I, too, would like to thank you for your farsighted kindness, Yibitriander."

He looked back and forth from his friends to us, sizing what he was up against. The SOB did it well. I think he was used to assessing situations and making quick decisions. He had to be a fighter pilot, too.

Amanda continued. "We are here to ask—no, to *beg*—for your assistance. I hope the Deavoriath will be as generous and gracious as they were before. We find ourselves in a more lethal position today than we were before the destruction of our home world."

"We've been briefed," said Lornot, "by *Wrath* as to your recent struggles and challenges. I'm afraid, however, I must inform you of *our* position."

That sounded bad.

"We intentionally separated ourselves from the outside world long ago. This you know. Our reasons were many and I shall not try to list nor justify them. Suffice it to say, we did it because we felt we had to. We built an impenetrable wall around ourselves for the good of everyone concerned, your race included. In its infancy, the Deavoriath of old would quite likely have conquered Earth and ruled it ruthlessly." She looked away when she was done speaking.

"Or simply *deleted* it," said a dour Kymee.

"While we fully comprehend your dire predicament," Lornot went on, "you must understand that our strong desire for solitude has not changed." She straightened her back. "I, too, would do exactly what you are, my dear. As the leader of my race, I would do whatever I could to save it."

"But," said Amanda quietly, "you're saying nicely that we're wasting our time."

"Yes," said Yibitriander quickly. "We are. We'll not be able to help you."

Toño spoke for the first time. "I believe you mean to say you are *unwilling* to aid us, not that you are *unable* to. Let us all be perfectly clear and honest."

The three Deavoriath looked at each other uncomfortably.

"I believe his usage of the word *unable* is more correct, my good doctor" said Lornot. "Not to put too fine an edge on it, but you cannot possibly understand what we were or what we are very capable of being once again."

"Say it, Lornot," demanded Kymee. He looked at us. "We were *monsters*. We *are* monsters. And not the simple nightmare monsters of a child's dream. We were evil, rapacious, and unrepentant monsters. Those, my friends, are among the worst kind imaginable." He sipped his drink and was promptly lost in thought.

"I could never presume to know your pain," Amanda said, "but you've been isolated for what, a million years? Two million? Surely, in that time you have risen above your past deficiencies. You must have transcended your baser nature."

"We alone are in a position to determine that, young woman," Yibitriander spoke coolly and detached. He was trying to paint a picture of conscious indifference. "We've explained what we could, out of civility. That civility is presently—"

"Silence." Kymee did not rise nor did his voice. But his word struck Yibitriander like a boulder from above. "I may not have lived that much longer than you, but I seem to have lived *better*. Do not disgrace your kind with harsh words and vapid threats. And please do *not* disgrace your father by being a boor. If there exists a single child of Oowaoa who has not become a better person over the ages, then we have failed as a species. I refuse to allow you to act in a superior or self-righteous manner to my guests. It's beneath *me*, and I pray it's beneath *you*."

"I suggest you allow us," Lornot said, "to discuss this matter amongst ourselves. It will likely not take long. I promise your words will be heard by all our people. It's the whole of us who must come to a consensus."

"Of course," said Amanda. "That you'll even consider our request is more than we could've hoped for. Where would you have us wait?"

"Here," Kymee said, "will be fine. If you will excuse us." Everyone stood. "We'll be nearby if there's anything you need. We're all connected mentally, so this shouldn't take long at all."

They filed out quietly.

"What's your take, Mandy?" I asked once we were alone.

She pointed to a wall and tugged at her ear. Ah, she worried the walls had ears. Clever gal.

"I'm glad the Deavoriath have agreed to discuss our needs. I'm certain they will, in the end, do what is right for all concerned parties."

She rolled her shoulders as she spoke. She had no clue, either. Everyone but tight-assed Yibitriander seemed sincere and caring. But that and a smile did nothing to stave off the Berrillian fleet. Without help we were a-goners. It was that simple. I finished off my nufe. Man it was great. Mine tasted like aged scotch, cotton candy, and a beautiful woman's lips. I meant Sapale's lips. Of course, I did. One thing was for sure, if we did survive, I wanted to negotiate the distribution rights of nufe. Actually, I wanted to bathe in the stuff.

Within ten minutes our hosts returned. Stone faces all around. Very not good. The fact that it was Yibitriander who spoke for the Deavoriath was equally disheartening. "I'm afraid we will not be able to help you in any significant manner. I'm sorry. That is the consensus of the whole that is one. You are free to remain here as long as you choose, but you may also leave when it is convenient for you to do so."

Don't let the door hit you in the ass on your way out, he neglected to add.

"You're free to keep *Wrath*," said Lornot. "By our laws and customs, it rightfully belongs to the finder. Kymee has taken the liberty of updating several of his systems. Aside from that, we cannot help you."

"Will those upgrades," Toño asked pointedly, "in any way make it more likely that we can defeat the Berrillian armada that approaches our homes?"

Yibitriander shot a glance to Kymee. "No."

I was stunned. Speechless and stunned, two very unfamiliar conditions.

"I thank you for your time," said Amanda in a more controlled manner than I could have. "We will return to our people now to prepare as best we can for the arrival of the Berrillians." She stood with uncommon grace and nodded toward Toño and me.

"I wish there were more that we could do," Lornot said with obvious pain in her voice, "but—"

Amanda delicately raised a hand. "You've been most kind. We wish you the best in your eternal quest for inner peace."

With that, we walked out of the room. Luckily, Toño remembered the path to return to *Wrath*, so there was no anticlimax after Mandy's superb last words. We left with real class. It was almost worth it. No. It wasn't even close. I'd never felt so hopeless in my life.

TWENTY-FOUR

The trip back to Mandy's worldship was instantaneous. That was well and good, as none of us were in a chatty mood. We were too depressed and too dejected to chat. No words were adequate, none captured our pain, and none could be helpful. I promised to keep her informed. I agreed to fly to her ship every other day, if only to be seen, and then pop back home. Once the fighting began, I'd come daily. If I failed to visit someday, she could reasonably conclude we'd been defeated. That way, for what little it was worth, Mandy would have a day or two to prepare for the other shoe to fall.

The trip back to Azsuram was not immediate. After the worldship fleet faded out, the view outside *Wrath* remained the uniform gunmetal grey it was during a space fold. I asked Manly what was up. Was there a mechanical problem?

"No, Form," he said deferentially, "I wish to speak with you before we arrive at your home. Now seemed the most opportune moment. I hope you do not object."

I did object, but what was there to say? My crazy cube wanted to talk, so talk we would.

"I have a plan that might just save your planet from undeserved destruction. It would quite likely result in no harm to you or any of your people."

That sounded too good to be true, especially from Manly. His agenda was his own. After a pause, I asked what his plan was.

"If we intercept the Berrillians while they are still in warped space, I might be able to destroy their ships. One of the technical difficulties with those warp bubbles is their instability. If I hit them with a gamma ray laser blast just behind the leading edge of their bubble, the resultant deformation might cause the bubble to collapse into a superheated plasma. They would be fried to a crisp before they knew what hit them."

"*Wrath*," I said. I stopped calling him the more casual "Manly" when I realized he was loco. "We do not know for certain it *is* the Berrillians who are in those bubbles. Just because they used to transport themselves that way does not mean it has to be them. We might fry a bunch of interstellar ice cream men."

"If, however, we wait until they drop into normal space, there is great doubt in my mind that I can successfully defend your family."

"I'm not firing on whoever's in those bubbles until I know for absolute certain they mean us harm—*period*."

"Form, they're unlikely to drop into normal space one at a time so I can pick them off. That would be tactically unwise."

"I said I'm not firing on what is hopefully a bunch of peaceful travelers. End of discussion. Take us home."

"How about I pick off just one? Perhaps I could determine their identity from the wreckage."

"After they were swallowed by a million-degree-plasma cloud, then hit real space faster than light speed?

Really? You're that good that you can analyze singed molecular dust?"

He was quiet for a few seconds. "Possibly not. Though in defense of my secondary plan, we don't *know* that's how they would end up."

"Any chance, however remote, that *any* matter could survive such a cataclysmic deceleration? Hmm?" I was really beginning to dislike my ride.

He didn't respond.

"I didn't think so. Take us home *now*. That's a direct order."

I felt slightly queasy, which I usually did when Manly folded space. Our dock on Azsuram appeared outside the viewport. It was a sight for my sad, tired eyes. Almost immediately, a teeming mass of people engulfed the pad. No surprise. This was the single most important return *Wrath* had ever made. I stepped out first and the phalanx of Kaljaxians, headed by Sapale, fell into a dead silence. I could only shake my head then lower it.

Sapale turned to her people and said there would be a council meeting in ten minutes. She waved her arms to herd them away. Once she was certain the crowd was receding, she ran to my side and wrapped me in her arms. She even gathered Toño into our lamentation hug.

Without a word she angled us both in the direction of the rapidly filling meeting hall. I know she was, if anything, more crushed by my failed mission than anyone else. But she kept her grief in check and guided us to the table at the head of the meeting room. I must have sat down because a few minutes later when she asked me formally for a full report, I was seated in my usual chair. The air was still. Not a soul breathed. The sickly silence was like a massive sword stroke to the skull.

"The defense of Azsuram is left to us alone." That was all I could manage. My mind was numb and all the emotion programmed into my head was gone. I had nothing. I had failed those who mattered to me the most, and my failure would likely cost each and every one of them their lives.

"We met with the Deavoriath from Oowaoa," Toño rallied to say, "but they elected not to provide us any additional aid."

Someone yelled, "How could they just let us die?"

Another angry voice cried out, "They are lower than *falzorn.*"

Still another desperate protester shouted out, "Let's attack *them* before we die."

A chorus of cheers boomed in favor of that futile vengeance.

That brought Sapale to her feet. Arms raised high above her head, she shouted for all she was worth, "Silence, people. Be *seated.*"

I doubt anyone else could have pulled it off. Every Kaljaxian suddenly shut up and sat down like they'd rehearsed it a million times.

She waited to make certain her control remained strong then she turned to me. "Is there no chance of a second appeal with the Deavoriath?"

I shook my head and wished I could become invisible.

"So be it. Citizens of Azsuram, we built our home here with the help of no one. We never needed help from others and we will not require it now." She raised her voice gradually to capture and inspire her people. God, she was a great leader.

"We will stand as the great civilization we have become in so short a time. Remembering our heritage of strength and courage, we will defy *anyone* to take from us that which is rightfully *ours.*"

A scattering of yelps rose from the crowd urging her on.

"We have great technology, great skills in war, and even greater *wills*. We are *indomitable*. We shall not be abused, trodden upon, or made victims by *any* race. I *pity* those who would attack Azsuram, those *foolish* children. The last vision our enemies will see with their dying eyes is the smile on our face as we crush the *lives* from their *hearts* with our boot heels. They will die poorly, beaten and disgraced. And when their kin learn of their treacherous, cowardly act, they will die *unlamented*."

Cheers rang from everyone, including me. We all shot to our feet and pumped our arms, chanting a battle cry loud enough to be heard by whoever hid in those warped-space bubbles.

"Our enemy will be more than defeated and more than dismembered by our axes. They will be *forgotten* by those who once loved them. Then ... then my friends, no, my *family*, we will gather back in this great hall. We will celebrate so wildly that all the gods of Old Dominion will make flight to Azsuram. They will make haste to our celebration so they can boast that they were *here* when the children of Kaljax claimed their greatest victory."

The crowd rushed forward. With coordinated care they encircled Sapale and reached to touch her shoulders. Tears flooded down everyone's faces. I wished at that moment that, I, too, was Kaljaxian.

Sapale once again raised her arms. "There is no time for this now, my family. *Now*, we must prepare. *Tomorrow* we fight. The following day we *feast*." The shouts of affirmation were deafening. Above their cheers, however, she was heard by all to say, "Return to your seats. Peace, my cherished ones. Sit and listen. We must set our defenses. For us to win, we must fight as one."

Reluctantly, slowly, everyone sat back down. For the next half hour Sapale read lists of assignments and duties. We had drilled endlessly of late, but she wanted to calmly make certain everyone was on the same page. At the end, she called for questions and comments, but she did so in a tone that clearly discouraged them. The session broke up, and soon she and I were alone at the front of the room.

"How did they justify not helping us?" Sapale asked with obvious scorn.

"They said releasing themselves on the universe would be worse than any damage the Berrillians could do."

She looked at me, incredulous. "That's such a lame excuse for an excuse. Our entire population will be wiped out, the humans will almost certainly be next, yet *they* think there's any worse possible outcome?"

I shrugged my shoulders. "That's what they said. They isolated themselves a long time ago to focus on improving who they were, because of their many perceived sins."

"Awfully full of themselves, the pigs."

"Hopefully we'll survive this and learn what they did that was so bad. Maybe we'll even accept their reasoning."

She spat on the floor, a high insult among her kind. "If we survive, I hope to never hear their name again."

"I didn't mention it back at the meeting, but there *is* another option."

"Yes. We could tuck our vestigial tails between our legs and run home." She glared accusingly at me. "That's your alternative, isn't it?"

"Hey, I'm on your side, brood's-mate. It *is* an option. If we crammed as many people as possible in the cube, we might get everyone to Kaljax before the warp bubbles materialize."

"Abandon this," she pointed out the open door, "and all of our dreams, because something went bump in the night? I couldn't live with myself if we did. I'd much rather die fighting than try to limp forward as a coward."

"We could allow others to make their own decisions. At least if we offer them—"

"What?" She was hot. "The chance to delay their deaths at the hands of warriors bent on death and destruction? After the humans, wouldn't the Berrillians turn on Kaljax? That planet is just as ill-prepared to defend itself as we are—less, in fact. They don't have your *damn* cube."

She was right. If conquest was the goal of the group racing toward us, the local systems would fall quickly. One could choose *where* they'd die, but survival seemed not to be a long-term option for any of us.

"You're right, as usual," I said stroking her forehead. "Let's check with the kids and then I had better be going. I want to face the incoming fleet far from here. There's just a chance they'll leave Azsuram alone if they bag their Deavoriath prize."

An hour later I was back on board *Wrath*, ready to find out for certain who our new guests were. Sapale and JJ accompanied me to the ship. We hugged. She kissed me. I stepped in and closed the wall behind me. I didn't know how last moments together worked or which words were good last words. It didn't look like I was ever going to learn. We knew we loved each other. I guessed that would have to be enough.

I instructed *Wrath* to put us directly in the flightpath of the incoming fleet. I wanted to start by basically daring them to run though me without turning or dropping out of warp. I wouldn't if I were them, but it was the best plan I could come up with. It took Manly a few attempts to place us where I wanted to be. It was hard for him to get exact reads on the craft while they were still inside the bubbles.

Eventually, he estimated they were traveling between three and four times the speed of light, maybe a million kilometers per second. We positioned ourselves a hundred million klicks ahead of them and hunkered down. That would give them around a minute to react to our presence. Manly believed they possessed the ability to scan the space around them, but he wasn't completely certain. They'd detected his attack on the Uhoor, but that display was a lot more prominent than a tiny semi-metallic cube sitting dead in space. We were about to find out.

The only visual evidence that there was something out there was the holes in the pattern of stars. Whatever was eclipsed by the bubbles was black, so I could vaguely see them approach. Twenty seconds to go. There were a lot of holes in the star pattern. A case of jumpy nerves began to set in. Ten seconds out the view screen was basically blacked out. Yikes.

"Fire across their bow," I said, louder than I needed to.

A flash of light shot across the gap between us.

"Form, they appear to have shifted course. It's slight, but I'm certain they have." There was a pause. "Yes they are spreading out to miss us. Not by much, but they neither intend to drop into real space or attack us presently."

"Why? It makes no sense. If they've come all this way to fight, why not *fight*?" A thought struck me. "Extrapolating their path, are they heading toward Azsuram or the place *Wrath* faced the Uhoor?"

"The latter. They are not headed toward Azsuram directly."

"Al," I shouted. He was along again so I had someone watching my back. "Prepare a summary of what's happened since we left home. We'll materialize just long enough for you to send it to Sapale."

"Done," was his quick response.

"*Wrath*, place us one hundred kilometers above Azsuram's north pole for one second, then to the exact spot you fired on the Uhoor."

Two seconds later, he said, "We are where I killed the last of the Uhoor."

"How long until the fleet arrives?"

"Perhaps five minutes. Maybe a bit less."

"Al, put a flat membrane between us and the incoming ships. Make it as big as you can one thousand meters away."

"Done."

"Form," said Manly, "I have access to the membrane generators. I could have raised them for you."

"But I asked Al to. Get over it. Let me know the moment they drop out of warp space."

It was quiet for a few minutes and then all hell broke loose with quite the vengeance.

"Seven hundred thirty-eight Berrillian warships have entered real space and are decelerating quickly."

"Can you confirm their identity? Are you positive it's them?"

"Yes," Manly said. "Their ships are painted the same *ridiculous* colors they were when I chased them out of the galaxy. The general configurations match also."

"Hail them, *Wrath*."

"No response," Manly announced after a few seconds.

"Keep trying. They have to hear us."

"Form, it's demeaning to continue signaling ships that ignore us. Please don't ask me to do that."

"Fine," I snapped. "Al, you continue to hail them. Tell them we are *Wrath*, and we wish them no harm."

"Done, Cap ... wait. They've fired on us. Some form of energy wave."

"The beams struck the membrane and were deflected," Manly said.

"What were they?" I asked. "Gamma-ray lasers?"

"No. I'm currently analyzing the beams. They're of a nature I have never witnessed. Pure energy, but they're not acting like any I'm familiar with."

Great, just freaking great. A new form of energy was being used against us. They couldn't use something simple like oversized peashooters could they?

"Al," I called out, "any ideas?"

"None, Captain. I can't imagine what those were."

Sound doesn't travel in the vacuum of space. So, whatever hit us next wasn't an explosion or a result of the beams hitting the membrane. The cube shook like a giant was outside, beating it with a sledgehammer.

"Report," I yelled.

"I am analyzing, Form. That was some type of wave ... No."

"No, what? *Report*."

"We were struck by gravity waves, Form. Somehow, and I shouldn't have thought it possible, they are able to generate directional gravity waves."

"What does that even mean?" I shouted. The cube rattled even more powerfully.

"Damage report."

"None, Form. Are you familiar with the concept of gravity waves?"

"Yes. Two massive objects bend space-time around them if they orbit closely. This shows up as gravity waves."

"A bit simplistic, but correct," Manly replied. "Somehow they've harnessed that technology."

"And it can pass though the membranes?"

"Captain," Al interrupted, "the waves didn't go around the membranes to strike us. They must deform the membrane. Recall, please, that the membrane is a congruity placed in space-time. Its uniformity allows little to pass though. Gravitational waves would, likely deform the membrane without interrupting or distorting it."

"A new series," Manly said, "has been launched."

"Did the shields hold?"

"Affirmative."

The Berrillians were testing the membrane. They had no clue what it was and were using a bunch of tools to probe it. Son of a gun. I hoped they didn't have a tool that could affect the membrane. It was our main hope for survival.

"Sir—" Al said.

Before he could speak, the cube pitched side to side, like it was a chew toy in a big dog's mouth. I managed to stay on my feet, but a human or a Kaljaxian would have been seriously injured. Mother of chaos. Not good.

"Report, either of you."

"The Berrillians switched to a higher energy gravity wave set," responded Manly.

"No shit, Sherlock," was my frustrated reaction. *Wrath*, open fire. Hit them with everything you've got and a bunch more."

Laser beams vaulted from our hull. Two of the closer ships exploded with the first strike. Outstanding. We could at least bloody their noses. Only what, seven hundred thirty-six to go?

A series of less powerful gravity distortions whacked the cube.

"Form, the enemy is able to bend the laser beam with their gravity waves. They can effectively deflect them."

Crap. "One hundred percent?" I asked.

A few flashes on the view screen suggested the answer was *no*.

"No. And deflected beams have randomly struck secondary targets."

"Keep shooting. Fire some beams randomly. Maybe they'll deflect them in our favor."

"Captain," Al reported, "the enemy fleet is splitting up. I believe they want to circle around past the membrane."

"Al," I said, "try and manipulate the membrane to direct those whatever-energy beams back at them like a big mirror. Also make the membrane spherical around us."

"Aye." A moment later, Al said, "Way cool. I've hit a few enemy vessels with their own beams."

Did Al just say *way cool?* What was this universe coming to?

"For what it's worth," said Manly, "they have little luck deflecting their own beams. Odd."

"How so?"

"They appear not to have prepared a defense against their own weapons."

That *was* odd. I guessed they could be stupid enough to assume they were the only one capable of such tech. In war, you had better never assume you were stronger, faster, smarter, luckier, or better-equipped than your opponent. Not if you planned on surviving. I filed that factoid away. Berrillians were arrogant sons of bitches.

A series of major gravity waves hit us. Again no real damage, but the waves were no joke either.

"Captain, a thermonuclear device has just impacted the membrane."

So they were throwing everything at us, hoping to find a weakness. I hoped they were sweating really good.

"A large number of projectiles," Al went on, "have been fired also. No effect on the membrane and none penetrated it."

If they were down to throwing sticks and stones, maybe we'd seen the worst of their arsenal. That would have been nice. Yeah. Coulda, woulda, shoulda, right?

"Form, several enemy ships are firing lasers at us in the ultraviolet and wavelengths visible to humans."

"Any speculation as to why?"

"They seem to have realized that those frequencies pass through the membrane. I should mention, Berrillian visual perception is geared more toward the high-frequency microwave end of the spectrum."

"Al," I asked, "would high-end microwaves pass the membrane?"

"Negative."

They were figuring things out. Clever assholes.

"What's the range of Deavoriath vision?"

"Ah," replied Manly. "I take your meaning. The Berrillians would recall that as being ultraviolet. It is currently much wider, but that they couldn't know."

Al cut in. "I don't take your meaning. What significance—"

"They have to be stressing about why the Deavoriath would make a membrane that allowed frequencies in they couldn't see."

"The intensity of the micron lasers is increasing rapidly," Manly said.

"Do they pose a threat to your hull integrity?"

"No. But they would wreak havoc with your people on Azsuram."

"Al, send out a three-hundred-sixty-degree message. Let Sapale know everybody's going to need mirrors." She was going to think I'd cracked, but I knew she'd do it. Not that mirrors would do much, but any port in a storm, right?

"*Wrath*, what's the progress of your laser attacks?"

"Limited, but not insignificant."

"And you, Al?"

"They have almost stopped firing those new energy beams. But when they do, I'm cramming them right down their stinking throats."

Did he just say that? He sounded like a bad actor in a cheap Italian western. Still, beam deflection seemed to be our best defense so far.

"*Wrath*," I said, "explain. How can the gravity waves shake the ship? Shouldn't they simply stretch and contract us?"

"Good question. They are aiming different waves designed to converge at a desired point in space. That causes the disruption."

"Assuming the battle remains as is," I asked Manly, "can you sustain your energy level long enough to destroy the fleet?"

"Assuming static combat, it would take us several months to destroy all these ships. My energy supplies are equal to the task, but I doubt the enemy would sit still and allow that. I estimate that if they cannot damage this ship shortly, they will retreat."

No sooner had he said it than that's exactly what happened. They broke off, assumed their previous formation, and slammed it into reverse. They popped into warp space and were gone.

Back on Azsuram, I sat at a table with Toño, Sapale, JJ, and a couple of our generals. Al was linked in, but I excluded *Wrath* intentionally. His input could be unreliable, and I didn't need that. I had just returned from an info-dump run to the worldship fleet, updating them on my initial skirmish. Maybe Carlos and his boys could figure out what they'd hit us with.

"So," I said, "we didn't win, but we didn't get our asses kicked, either."

"That's some consolation," muttered Toño, "I suppose."

"Ya think?" I gasped. "I'm kind of fond of my hide. Like to keep it a while longer, if it's okay by you, Doc."

Sapale rolled her eyes. Staring disaster squarely in the face, I was still capable of being Mr. Funny-Haha.

"I've analyzed the data you brought back," said Toño. "I think those beams were some type of plasma projected at high speed."

"What, like ginormous flamethrowers?"

He rolled his head back and forth. "I suppose you could compare them to that."

"That's *so* cool," I said smiling like a kid at Christmas. "Cosmic flamethrowers. I want one."

"I'll get to work on it as soon as I'm not killed," responded Toño. Humor? First Al, now Toño. Man my world was a-changing.

"We're tracking the Berrillians," I said back on task. "They're not headed our way, but they're not heading back the way they came either."

"Meaning?" asked Sapale.

"Meaning they're not going home. My guess is they're just buying time to think. They'll develop a new strategy based on our battle, and then they'll be back."

"But, Dad," said JJ, "now that we know who they are, why not attack them in warp space like *Wrath* talked about before?" He threw his hands in front of himself. "They'd be sitting ducks."

I shook the idea off. "Nah they'd just drop out of warp. That trick would only work once. Plus, we'd force them into doing whatever it was they were going to do anyway that much sooner."

General Divisinar Tao, an immigrant from Kaljax where he was one *serious* military man, spoke. "I would rather force them into action, rather than allow them time to improve their next attack." He punched his fist into his palm. "Hit them hard and even the odds a little more in our favor. Let's get this done."

"I suppose you're right," I replied. That of course brought the biggest smile to JJ's face I'd *ever* seen. Validation over his dad. "How are we coming with putting reflective surfaces on everything in sight?"

Sapale waved her hands in the air. "Okay. I can't imagine we'll ever coat the entire colony. Key positions are covered already. More will be soon." She tossed her hands into the air. "Who knows how much is enough?"

"All right, here's the plan. I'll alert Amanda, then I'll attack the Berrillians in warp space. *Wrath* says they're circling us at about ten million kilometers. If we're destroyed, they'll logically scan the area for targets. They'll find Azsuram quickly, unless they're total lame-o's. So they could be here in as little as a week, depending on their conventional drives."

"It's always possible," said Tao stroking his chin, "they'll not see the need to attack us. If they detect no signs of the Deavoriath, they might leave us alone for the time being."

"Let's pray that's the case," said Sapale.

"An old Earth saying comes to mind. Hope for the best, but plan for the worst," I observed.

"If you and *Wrath*," added Tao, "are removed as assets, we are facing rather lopsided odds that aren't in our favor. Reasonably, ships of the size they possess could contain upward of five thousand soldiers each. I'd assume no less of a war-like race on a voyage of revenge. Once our paltry space-based defenses are neutralized, we're looking at a ground campaign we simply cannot win. It would also be quite brief. Even if they never learn how to penetrate our membranes, they could shake us to pieces with those gravity waves."

"We don't know exactly what their tech can do," JJ remarked. "Maybe they create a lot of earthquakes but can't actually open our defenses."

Tao nodded silently. "Let us hope that is the case. But with their high-speed plasma sprays, we could never drop our shields. Eventually, they'd find a way to get through, or they'll starve us out." Tao looked at me. "With *Wrath* gone, there would be no possibility of resupply. Kaljax and the worldship fleet are much too far away to offer aid of any kind."

"We have perhaps a year's worth of supplies in secure areas," Sapale said, "assuming we do face a siege."

"That would be a year of misery, ending in a tremendously unpleasant death for each and every one of us. Hardly a desirable strategy, in my reckoning," Tao said with military coolness.

"With no better alternatives leaping onto the table," she responded, "I'll take what little I can get."

"Naturally," Tao replied with a head nod. "As our undisputed commander, it would be your only real choice. A man such as myself," he pointed to me again, "or Jon would prefer going out in a blaze of glory. Such an option is not the choice of a leader on behalf of her people."

"Men and their flair for the dramatic. You know," she said to Tao, more as an accusation than a question, "it *hurts* when you're mortally wounded? No glory, no singing spirits of the Ancients, just searing pain before death."

He shifted uncomfortably in his chair not certain whether to respond or let the confrontation pass. He settled for a bow of his head and a folding of his hands on the table.

"I'm outta here," I said as I stood. "Sapale, I'll see you at home when I'm back from updating Amanda."

As I walked to the vortex, Toño came up alongside me. "Might I join you?" he asked pointing to the cube.

I raised an eyebrow. "Sure. It'll be a quick trip, but company is always a good thing."

Inside he asked if we might land on the command worldship so he could speak with Carlos. I told him that would be fine, if he was quick. He reassured me his visit would be brief, so I had Manly set us on our designated landing pad on that worldship. With tensions being so high generally, our materialization set off a minor explosion of activity. Techs ran around like blind mice and lights flashed everywhere for no apparent reason. We hadn't made it to the hangar door before Amanda rushed in, breathing like a long-distance runner at the finish line.

"What?" leapt from her mouth. "What now?"

I patted her shoulder. "Not to worry. Toño here," I gestured to him, "just wants to touch base with Carlos."

The relief was visible on her face. I felt her shoulder muscles relax like they'd melted. "Oh, fine. Welcome," she said between breaths.

"*Welcome?*" I teased. "What are we, visiting royalty, now?"

"Sorry," she half-smiled, "I'm still not used to all this tension." She leaned over and bear hugged me. "It's great to see you."

Wow! I had no idea she'd be that glad to see me. "Thanks," I said uncertainly. "Nice to see you." I looked behind her. "Where's Heath?"

She pursed her lips, glanced to one side, and then replied, "Don't know. Maybe at home."

Hmm. "Whose home?"

She stared into the distance. "You know, silly. *His* home. His and Piper's."

Oh my. "So what? They reconciled or something?"

She shrugged. "Maybe you should ask him, all right?"

She took hold of my elbow and began to lead me toward a lift. "We have more important things to discuss."

"We do?" I didn't know of any, aside from the report Al had already transmitted.

She pulled me to a stop and turned me toward her. "We have to have something more important to discuss. There must be a million matters more important at a time like this than a pathetic failed love affair."

"Failed, what? Nobody told me."

"Maybe he mailed you a letter," she said with obvious bitterness. "Me, I never see you enough. You live kind of far away, remember?"

What the hell? What form of bizarre conversation was I participating in? I guess she didn't put that personal four-one-one in the messages she sent me on my lightning appearances, but why wouldn't she? They were both extremely important to me—family in fact. He was kin, and she was about to give birth to the next generation in my wacky lineage.

"You want to talk about it?" I asked, as we began walking again.

She held my elbow like it was a lifeline and she had fallen into high seas. "No."

"May I ask what happened?"

"You mean who dumped whom?"

"Err, well, yeah. Kind of." What? Sue me. I was curious.

"Really?" she said, continuing to direct her eyes forward. "Humanity is on the brink of destruction and you want to know the dirty details?" The lack of denial on my part indicated she should continue. She hugged the arm she was already clinging to. "You're impossible."

"So I've been told. Repeatedly."

"It wasn't working for me. There, I said it."

"What?" I meshed my fingers together awkwardly. "Was it the boy-girl thingy?"

She slapped my arm. "What comes after impossible?"

I shrugged.

"Well whatever it is that's what you are. *No* it wasn't the," she intertwined her fingers, "the boy-girl thing." She was quiet a second. "We lived in a pressure cooker. I was lonely and he had wandering inclinations. It's a stupidly old and common tale." She shivered. "I wanted to end it before the baby came. Closure, you know?"

"Makes sense." I guess it did, but I wasn't really interested in clarifying the point. Women were impossible to figure out, and pregnant ones even more unfathomable. I might have ended up losing an eye if I pressed her for details.

"And Piper took him back? Just like that?"

The look she gave me. It was meaner than a junk-yard dog and more deadly than one of Manly's laser bursts. It said, *he'll get what he deserves. I could give a shit*, and, *you didn't just ask me that* all rolled together in one angry salvo. Memo to self. Never piss this woman off. I was beginning to feel fortunate that I was facing an almost certain death right around the corner.

We'd arrived at the Noval Office. She swiped her ID over a screen and went in first.

"Can I get you anything?" she asked. Her voice was all calmed down. Whew.

"No. Look I'm not staying that long. I don't know why Toño insisted on meeting with Carlos, but I'm about to buzz them both and tell them to stick a fork in it."

"I asked him to do so," she said without emotion.

"Huh? No way. How could you know we were coming?"

She flopped her head around then said, "I asked it as a *contingency*. When it looked like you were leaving, for maybe the last time, I told Toño I wanted to speak with you."

"Why didn't you just say so?" I tossed my hands up. "Pretty simple words. You know I'd come."

"You pop up, upload a ton of data, and are gone in an instant. I didn't want to risk losing the opportunity. You might not have come back."

"Come back? When?"

"By the time you went through our upload and saw my request, you might not have come back." She dropped her face into her palms.

"Mandy," I said pointing over my shoulder, "I gotta go get myself killed pretty quick here. I'm a little lost. Are we speaking in some form of code?"

"Yes, of course. At least *I* must be." She started crying.

WTF? Had I developed nauseating, bad breath, or volcanic facial pustules?

"Here's the thing," I said leaning toward her. "I don't have much time. No time really. If maybe—"

"I couldn't let you go without telling you how I feel about you." She swiped angrily at her tears.

WTF^2 ? I started scanning the room for hidden cameras. This had to be some kind of practical joke.

"Okay, nice to know." I started to stand. "I wish everyone felt the same—"

"I *love* you."

WTF^∞ ? "Uh, *thanks*?" Wow lame response by any standard, even my barely existing ones.

She covered her face. "Sorry. Leave. *Go*."

"Mandy, you kind of blindsided me here. I clearly don't know what to say."

"Just go. I'm fine."

"My opinion? You're actually very unfine. Please talk to me."

She blew her nose and shook her shoulders. "In the

brief time we've worked together, I've come to value your company more than that of anyone I've ever met. Look, I'm not a home-wrecker." She stopped and stared at the ceiling. "Well, *technically,* yes, I am, but I'm not, you know, like that. I mean, it's not my general intent."

"Sapale will be glad to hear that."

"Jon Ryan, I'm being serious and baring my soul. Don't you be ... so *you.*"

"Totally at a loss for words here, Mandy," I replied, raising my hands in surrender.

She took a couple breaths and composed herself. "It's selfish of me, yes. But I needed to let you know how I felt about you. I know you're happily married and have no delusion I could change that."

"Did you know that when enraged, Kaljaxian women will suck your eyes out of their sockets?" I tilted my head. "Not cheating on *that* girl. I can tell ya that for nothing."

"I don't expect you to. In telling you how I feel, I didn't hope for anything other than the chance to say it. I'd think less of you, in fact, if you did try and use my love as an advantage over my better judgment."

What? *I* wasn't the one confessing my passionate love, she was. If I used her weakness to my advantage? OMG. I needed to go and definitely get myself killed. I had zero desire to return to this kind of insanity.

"Mandy, your wife was assassinated, you fell in love with Heath, and we face an impossible war. Rebounding to me—"

"I'm not on the *rebound*, bucko. I thought Faith was my only love. Heath was definitely a rebound. But however childish I'm being in talking to you, it's not the same." She snapped her head to one side and covered her eyes. "I think you'd better leave."

If I stayed I was a fool. If I left I was an insensitive idiot. If I asked her to come with me, I was both and double dead. Once from the Berrillians, and once from my brood's-mate. How did I always end up in crazy situations like this? Seriously? I did nothing to encourage her. I never hit on her or even flirted with her. She was my great-grandson's girlfriend. Wow, *that* sounded bad, in and of itself. Creepy bad. When in doubt and in a pinch like this, I'd found it was best to recall my extensive PR training at NASA from years back. Smile, speak in a confident and reassuring manner, and avoid specifics. Dwell on the obvious and stick to platitudes.

"Well, I'll be," I said pushing out of my chair. "Would you look at the time. Mandy, I'll let you know if we don't get killed, okay? I'll let you get back to your important work on behalf of a grateful public. Later."

I flashed Toño in my head. *Judas of Iscariot, if you're not at the ship by the time I get there, I'm leaving you behind.*

That bad, eh? flashed in my head instantaneously. *I suspected as much. I'm leaning on* Wrath *as we speak.*

Too bad. I'd have run the whole way there if you weren't.

How long have I known you?

TWENTY-FIVE

"Havibibo, you run when you should fight. You disgrace us in the eyes of the pairs who serve us. There can be no greater shame. All the Faxél of Berrill will laugh when our name is spoken. A fleet commander cannot also be a coward."

"Your rashness is why I *alone* command the war fleet. If we are defeated by the scum of Oowaoa yet again, *that* will be the disgrace. We cannot plan vengeance for fifteen million turns and let it slip away like water between our pads because we rushed foolishly into an action, not knowing fully what it was we faced."

Kelldrek bent her torso halfway to the floor and paced around her other half. She moved as the predator she was. Her teeth bared, to join her perpetually exposed fangs, created a frightening, bone-chilling expression. Anyone other than her other half would rightly fear for their lives upon seeing her so displayed.

Havibibo had known her since they were kittens. Yes, at times he'd felt the rip of her bite, but mostly during sex. She would never attack him with an intent to kill. At least, he thought not.

"My scientists," she said, "are analyzing the barrier shield the Deavoriath now employ." She wiped drool from the corner of her mouth. She always salivated when her second acted like a savage beast. Her blood was not that distant from her ancient ancestors's animal passions. Hers was quick to boil, especially when her other half acted with such fury. Evolving to walk upright and create an advanced civilization had done little to blunt her fervor. It was good to be a Faxél.

He shook his head to clear his focus. "To attack when we cannot even hit them with our main weapons is foolhardy. This is a mission of conquest and revenge, not suicide."

"You played slap-paw with the universe's worst scum. Let us attack them with the madness that is ours and ours alone."

"Answer me this then, Kelldrek. Where were the other Deavoriath cubes? I saw but one."

"It was alone. So? It should have been our first prize of thousands. The rest are no doubt hiding, willing to sacrifice that cube to learn our new technologies."

"That, my claw, was *Wrath*. They would sacrifice *that* cube?"

"Perhaps it is as outmoded as your cowardice. Maybe they are as willing to lose their old vehicle as I am to lose our frightened old leader." She feigned a tender paw in his direction. "Would you like me to help you piss, second? If you're afraid to step into that dark corner, I will hold your *dick* for you."

Hormones, rage, and passion flooded Havibibo's brain. He kept reminding himself he was a commander in wartime. He could not waste hours in violent, narcotic sex with his second. That had to wait. "Call the pod-leads to group in the main convocation room. Everyone must be there in ten clicks."

"Action? I may collapse on my side and eat my own guts."

"Mock me at great risk, second. Though you are dearest to me, you also serve your commander. Do not mistake my tolerance in private as permission to overstep your boundaries."

She flashed her full set of teeth again but said nothing. She bowed and left their quarters.

Ten clicks later, fifteen males and females sat around a serpentine table. The design allowed everyone to face each other. Small rodent-like creatures scurried in panic on the top, but were prevented from escape by a rounded edge. Refreshments could not be enjoyed if they leapt from the table and hid.

Havibibo scratched his enormous claws loudly on the metal surface, calling the meeting to order. "I will have your reports," he said, advancing his hungry gaze from one aide to the next. "If your progress proves to be insufficient, I will rip you to pieces and cast your flesh into the frozen cold of deep space." He scanned them all again before he snapped, "Grell, start."

Grell Thom-Gahacken was the expedition's chief scientist. He was the oldest in the company by a large margin. Faxél rarely survived to his age, let alone served a useful purpose. All of his contemporaries were either dust or excrement, having either died or been eaten. That he survived spoke of his talent and, more specifically, of his viciousness. Both were legendary. Grell had been on every voyage Havibibo had ever taken. There was no love between them, but each knew the other's drive and loyalty to be exemplary. That was, in the end, superior to friendship, which was rare among the Faxél in the first place.

In his dry raspy voice Grell spoke with firmness and confidence. "I have much to report. My review of the enemy's weapons reveals them to be the same gamma-ray lasers of antiquity. The intensity is a bit greater, and the focus has been improved, but they are essentially unchanged."

"How is it," Havibibo asked slamming a paw to the tabletop, "that the great and mighty Deavoriath have remained so static?"

Grell shrugged. "You must ask that of them, not me." Never take possession of a problem that is by all right someone else's. "I can only report on my observations."

"And you observed their new shield wall?" Havibibo asked with a harsh challenge.

"I did," replied Grell. "Most interesting projection."

"I care nothing for *interesting* phenomenon," howled Kelldrek. "I don't even care what it is. I wish only to defeat it. Tell us you know *now*, or I will pounce on you before you finish your latest feeble excuse."

Grell looked to Havibibo. It was important to his survival that Kelldrek gave less than her full support to her mate. Damn the woman. She was the perfect foil to Havibibo's thoughtful ways. Two halves of a perfect whole. Damn them both.

"As to the nature of the force field, I can't say," Grell finally admitted. "It may actually be a set point in space-time, spread by them at will."

"If that were the case," asked Havibibo as he absently preened a claw, "can it be breached?"

"So far, no," was his cautious response.

"I know *that*, old beast," replied Havibibo. "I was the one pressing the 'FIRE' button. Can we hit them through the shield, yes or no?"

"I doubt it," Grell said looking down.

"So," responded Kelldrek spitefully, "we should do what, surrender? Go home and raise crops? They have the perfect weapon, so eons of waiting and preparation should be cast into the mud? Maybe the Deavoriath will be uncharacteristically kind and make slaves, not rugs, out of us?" she hissed menacingly.

"Not a perfect *weapon*, just a perfect *defense*," Grell replied.

"And the difference, as you see it?" asked Havibibo with his best take at passivity.

"We can lay siege. An impenetrable wall can always be trumped with a sufficient wait."

"Alright," Havibibo said. "The only weakness in your plan is that it might be challenging to lay siege to a craft that bends space and can travel anywhere instantly. Hmm?"

"I was thinking of their home world, or perhaps colonies. Obviously the cubes are too mobile for such a tactic to work."

"As we are faced with a cube, not a planet, and have no idea where their settlements might be, it would seem you have told me nothing. You have no usable input." He leaned in Grell's direction. "Were that *all* you had to offer, I should not wish to be you." It was his turn to growl.

"The plasma weapons were useless," said Grell, "but the gravity wave impacts were promising."

"The plasma blasters were not useless," said Kelldrek. "They were worse than that. They were turned to effective weapons *against* us."

"A bit random to be called a weapon," replied Grell by way of defense.

"Tell that to the families of those burned up in the six craft we lost," responded Kelldrek.

"This bickering is pointless," said Havibibo raising a paw. "Grell, what do you counsel us to do for our next attack on the cube?"

"That we not attack the cube next."

All eyes snapped to look at the old cat.

"I have not come all this way, after all those generations, to bump chests once with the enemy and give up." His pointed his exposed claws at the others in the room. "*They* have not come all this distance to concede defeat as quickly as they can shit. That we chanced first on *Wrath* is a good omen. I swear it by the Quadrad, it must be destroyed immediately."

A lesser pod leader spoke up. "Don't forget *Wrath* will pounce on us sooner rather than later. Even if we chose to ignore *him, he* will seek us out."

"His position," began a younger sub-leader, "is weak." The woman puckered her lips and raised her paws then tilted side to side quickly. It was a mocking gesture. "You can't hit me, but I have no courage. I run like a prasma and eat rotten leaves. I will harm no one, unless I run over them in reckless retreat."

"*Wrath* has seen all we have to offer. He may have held his best weapons in reserve," speculated another officer.

"No," said Havibibo, "this is war. In war you kill, if the opportunity presents itself. If *Wrath* could have destroyed more of our ships, he most certainly would have."

"So," asked Kelldrek, "it's a standoff? A child's game come to an impasse?" She now mocked everyone present.

"If it were a stalemate," Havibibo replied, "I would throw everything at them at once and die well. But I refuse to accept that we have failed." He sniffed the air, an ancient habit from his carnivorous ancestors. "I order the search for a colony. If we can seize one, we may learn more of their mysterious defense screen. At the very least we will taste Deavoriath blood in our mouths once again."

"No," screamed his second. "No, no, no. We must destroy *Wrath*. We know where he is, and he deserves killing more than anything else in the universe. And if the Quadrad grants it to be Yibitriander himself at the helm, I will rip his heart out with my fangs."

"I have made an order, and all will work to accomplish it. The discussion has ended. Go and may the blood of Irirdaz be in you," said Havibibo with finality.

As his commanders filed out, however, several quiet anonymous hisses were heard. A challenge to his control was a serious matter. Someone needed to be shredded, but that probably needed to wait.

TWENTY-SIX

"Yes," said General Tao, "the battle was brief, but a sound strategy presents itself as a consequence."

"We're here to speak and listen," replied Sapale. "Please go on."

His hands moved in the air with vigor and force. He was really into war. "*Wrath* faced them, inflicted mild damage, and escaped unharmed. I feel that constitutes a major victory."

"Not dying is different from winning," I responded.

"But," Tao went on, "don't you see? If you harass them in guerrilla-type attacks, you could deplete them slowly but surely. They came in a large but finite number of ships."

Not a very sexy battle plan. "I imagine they'd eventually develop a counter-strategy that would neutralize my actions. That's a key tenant of military history."

"If they do," Tao said, "then you stop the attacks. Another feature of my approach is that they cannot menace us if they are swatting at you like a flying insect."

Maybe. "They could try to set up a defensive

perimeter around Azsuram while attacking on the ground," I countered.

"Then we're screwed," said JJ.

"Not necessarily," responded a very sober Tao. "The reason we fight wars, boy, is because victory does not care which side is favored to win. Chance favors the bold and the prepared."

"Plus," Sapale said, "if they attack us, they attack us. We'll defend our homes as best we can, regardless of our chances. History is ripe with stories of smaller forces defeating larger ones."

"It is also riper," Tao reminded, "with records of larger forces winning. But," he looked around the small group present, "it matters more *how* one dies than *that* one dies. We will account well for ourselves, that much I can promise."

"I prefer," I said, "to do something, rather than nothing. I vote I attack the Berrillian fleet. I have no problem trying a hit-and-run strategy. If the situation changes, so can our plans."

"What," said Tao, staring at me like I was an interesting but otherwise inconsequential asset, "if you are destroyed."

"I guess that would trigger a re-assessment as to how wise my strategy had been, now wouldn't it?" I smiled like I didn't resent him saying that in front of my family. "I'll leave first thing in the morning."

"I see no strategic advantage in delay," was Tao's pissy response.

"Well," I replied, "when you're the boss of me, I'll have to obey you, won't I?"

"We're here to plan the best defense of our settlement," said Sapale. "If General Tao believes it's best for you to leave now, I think you should go now."

In spite of the setting, I cupped her cheek. "I've lived

longer than most of you combined. I know better than anyone how precious life is." In spite of the fact that Tao was right I added, "I'll leave at first light. I think fate can cut me that much slack."

She caught my hand between her shoulder and face and smiled like the sun rising over the best day ever lived.

Zero-dark-thirty found me standing outside the cube. Sapale and the older children were there to see me off. Our conversations, minimal as they were, resembled anyone else's at such a time, I suspect. We talked of tomorrow, though we doubted it would greet any of us. We confirmed upcoming dates, though we knew those times were not promised to any of us. And we professed our undying, unending love for one another, which was the only certain thing we spoke of. I've left a lot of people, but I've never done it with so much trepidation, uncertainty, and reluctance as I did then, leaving my only true family that sad morning. Immortality meant nothing if it was to be a solitary experience. It was, I knew with steely certainty, something to dread.

Finally, I shook JJ's hand and gave Sapale the biggest kiss I had ever smacked. I called for a portal, and *Wrath* opened to swallow me. Not one to linger, I immediately commanded him to take me to within firing distance of the fucking Berrillian fleet. The view screen went gray and my stomach flip-flopped. Seconds later, I saw the black patches in the sky, obscuring the distant stars, that betrayed the position of my enemy.

I've editorialized a lot about war in the past. I've done war a lot, and I've done it better than most. I not only hate war, but I hate more the *toleration* of the concept of war by ostensibly rational, civilized minds. I detested that war ever existed or was allowed to continue. If one's own were attacked, fighting back had traditionally been the only logical option. To hell with that shit. Find another way.

Better yet, avoid having to find a better way by acting to make war unnecessary before it's inevitable.

Central to my philosophy was the immutable stupidity, greed, and lust for war that permeated the minds of most dubious leaders. Whether it was Earth, Kaljax, or even the god-like Deavoriath from Oowaoa, old men in charge wanted war. They wanted war more than they wanted a beautiful woman. War had always been, and always would be, their heroin, better than every orgasm they ever had combined into one single paralyzing jolt. War had been their holy grail, with one condition, of course. They wanted war, demanded war, and begged war of others, as long as *they* had nothing personal at stake, like their own asses.

The aspect of war I hated most was that I was about to fight in one again. I closed my mind to any humanity I might have once possessed. I justified to myself, yet again, that I needed to defend those I'd left behind, those both mortally threatened and unable to defend themselves adequately. I fucking hated war. Even the one I was entering so consciously, the one brought on us by a ruthless blood-thirsty pack of lunatics. Oh well, they wanted war. Their biggest mistake was declaring one on me. Those sorry bastards were gonna pay for that mistake dearly. I assumed the wars of my past had already cost me my soul. Never screw with a perfect killing machine that had nothing personal to lose and was fighting for the only things he valued in the universe.

"Form, we are holding at one hundred thousand kilometers," Manly interrupted again. "What are your orders?"

"Huh? Oh, yeah." Hell of a time to get lost in thought. "I want to test the relative effectiveness of lasers versus rail cannons. At will, fire an equal spread of each at as many vessels as possible. You can drop the membrane completely with the first volley, until someone drops into real space. At that point, raise it fully and alert me."

"By your command." I swear I heard anticipation and excitement in his voice. Great. I was facing long odds and depending on a homicidal nut job.

A few seconds later *Wrath* spoke. "Eight ships destroyed. Two with lasers, five with rail cannon, and one by flying debris. The remaining fleet has dropped out of warp space and is forming a defensive line. Membrane up. I await further orders."

"Al," I called out, "do you concur?"

"Yes, Captain. Rail cannon appears to be more effective at collapsing the warp bubbles. We targeted one hundred thirty-seven vessels and destroyed eight."

Crap, that was only a five percent kill rate. Not nearly good enough. Still, over time it was a basis for limited hope.

"Al, assuming one skirmish daily with equivalent results, when would I destroy their last ship?"

"We were able to target around twenty percent of their ships with a five percent kill ratio. I'd estimate half a year."

Well, I guessed there were worse ways to spend my next six months than blowing up those who were badly in need of killing.

"*Wrath*, target the remaining craft with pulse-interrupted-membrane rail balls. Make certain we have a full membrane up when return fire begins."

"Two thousand shots fired before they returned fire. Moderate damage to twelve vessels. None destroyed. Most rail balls were neutralized in flight, a few deflected. Deflected balls account for one kill."

"Fire an equal number of laser shots and report."

"Two vessels hit with serious damage likely. One

confirmed kill. Their gravity waves continue to deflect the beams efficiently, if randomly."

"*Wrath*," I called out, "take us to the limit of their sensors in the opposite direction from Azsuram."

Before he could do so we were wracked by the most powerful gravity waves they'd fired on us so far. The cube shook like an angry T-rex had it in his jaws. Then we phased out and everything was still. As my nausea subsided, I called out, "Damage report."

"None, Form."

"Al, can you validate that report?"

"Yes, Captain. All systems and weapons unharmed."

"What are the Berrillians doing?"

"They are drifting in place," replied Manly. "We did not do sufficient damage to force them to linger, so presumably they are awaiting a second charge."

"Or," good old Al added, "they are breaking down our attack and searching for countermeasures. I imagine communications must be severely limited when they're in warp space."

"Withdraw to the limit of our sensor range and keep me posted."

"Form? Shouldn't we strike again? They are sitting targets."

"No. Sooner or later, they'll enter warp space. When they do, we whack 'em again and run. I want them to fear their high-speed travel."

"An interesting, if passive, tactic," replied Manly.

We floated idly in space for nearly half an hour. Impatient by nature, I kept asking my twin computer for updates. They both reported no change, except that one Berrillian ship had been scuttled. Presumably, the crew was transferred before the craft exploded. It was clear they didn't want to gift us a specimen to study if one of their ships was incapacitated.

Finally *Wrath* said, "They've entered warp space. Heading away from us."

"What direction?" I asked. "What lies in their path?"

"Azsuram, Form."

My heart stopped beating and my brain fell into my stomach. Barely audible, I asked, "Directly?"

"No," Al replied, "but the solar system in general."

Crap. They'd probably detected some sign of advanced civilization and had decided to attack a hard, immobile target. "ETA?" I asked louder.

"A few hours, perhaps, if they stay in warp space."

"Immediate attack. After we materialize fire as many rail balls as possible in one second, then raise a membrane."

Mild nausea hit me.

"Done, Form. Three ships destroyed and four damaged significantly." The cube began to shake like we were in a paint mixer.

"Put us in their geometric center and repeat firing pattern."

"What?" said Al. "Point blank is pretty close range, Captain."

"I know. Do it, *now*."

"Done," said Manly. Twelve ships damaged with six destroyed. So far no sign of plasma or gravity wave retaliation."

Several seconds later, there was still no counterattack. Instead, the fleet jumped back to warp space. Damn. I'd found a weakness. They didn't want to fire those gravity waves at themselves.

"*Wrath*, repeat attack per last plan immediately."

Again as my nausea cleared, *Wrath* reported, "Two ships destroyed and three—"

The gravity wave perturbations that struck us were impressive. For the first time ever I saw sparks fly from a couple panels. The plasma streams surrounded us completely engulfing *Wrath* inside the membrane.

"Damage report," I called out.

"Minimal, Form. One redundant backup tele-relay system overloaded."

"Hull integrity?"

"One hundred percent," he replied

"Take us far away, now."

"Done, Form. We are a few light years away."

"*Wrath*, I need your honest report. Did they damage you in any way?"

"Form, all of my—"

"*Belay* that, Manly I want short sentences and small words only during battle. Were you damaged?"

"Aside from the minor system overload, no."

"How did that system fail?"

"Between maintaining the membrane at full power, scanning the enemy, directing secondary membranes to deflect the plasma streams, and maneuvering to correct for drift, I was unable to secure non-essential systems."

"By design, or because of over-demand?"

"Both. I can do the impossible, but even that has limits."

"If we repeat the same assault ten times, is it possible they will cause us more damage—critical damage?"

"Unlikely, but possible."

"So," I summarized, "we can attack them, but they can, with luck and persistence, damage us?"

"Yes, Form. I should point out that such a fate is—"

"Belay that. Are they back in warp yet?"

"No—wait, yes. They just resumed FTL speed," replied Manly.

"Geographic center, repeat attack, but only half as long, and withdraw immediately after last shot fired. Oh, and add in laser shots just before we dematerialize."

"By your command."

I was hit with two bouts of nausea barely separated in time. *Wrath* gave the report. "We destroyed eight ships, forced them out of warp space, and suffered no gravity wave retaliation."

Yes. They had a weak underbelly. "*Wrath*, return to the same point, fire five hundred rail balls, then return to this point."

"Done, Form. Two ships damaged, no return fire."

"Repeat assaults at variable intervals between one and three seconds. Same duration as the last. Do so until offensive action is taken by the enemy. Then, return here and hold our position."

I went through rapid-fire nausea that was really quite unpleasant. I wished I'd just vomit and been done with it, but I knew that wouldn't work. I just sucked it up.

After multiple cycles *Wrath* received a massive jolt of gravity radiation. Our lights flickered briefly and one panel went dark. "Form, we are stationary, per your orders."

"Report."

"We hit them seventeen times in less than a minute. Thirty ships were heavily damaged or destroyed. On the last run, they committed to gravity waves directed at us while we were in their center."

"Did the gravity waves hurt them?"

"Yes. Following all of the waves and reflections was difficult, even for me. However, I do believe that the cascade of waves damaged sixty additional vessels."

Wow. The most damage we'd ever inflicted was to have them shoot at their own feet while we were standing on them. They were down over a hundred ships so far. Unfortunately, they still had over five hundred under sail.

"Damage to us?"

"Minor."

"Minor as in—"

"One fuel cell removed from duty, three hull breaches already repaired, and one rail cannon blown free."

That was real damage. So, if we maximally harassed them, we could pick off a goodly number of ships, but we risked our own destruction in the process. Plus, we couldn't significantly threaten the bulk of their force. We could inflict nickel-and-dime damage, but not wipe them out. Not good enough.

"Are they back in warp," I asked.

"Not as of yet," replied Manly.

"Of note, Captain," Al cut in, "they have begun moving along their last course under standard propulsion."

"What? *Wrath*, you omitted that detail?" I was hot. Manly was simply not to be trusted.

"When I was certain of their intent, I would most definitely have mentioned it, Form. No point burdening you with premature information."

"*Wrath*, this is war. No data is too insignificant to mention. One of their ships stops for cigarettes and beer, I want to know. You got it?"

"Yes, Form. I live to serve."

I bet. "Al, what speed are they making?"

"Slow acceleration to an estimated sixty thousand kilometers per hour."

"When would they make Azsuram?"

"Perhaps three weeks, under conventional drive."

Three weeks. Well, that was something. In three weeks, I could maybe pick off a few dozen more ships. Still, five hundred swarming my home was not good.

"Alert me immediately if they go to warp space." I left the recipient of the order unclear, so they'd both be on their toes. After an hour, the enemy remained under conventional ion drive. I guess we convinced them they were too defenseless in warp space to risk it.

"*Wrath*, in thirty minutes I want an ultrafast raid. Appear in the center and fire all weapons for three seconds. Then, immediately retreat beyond their scanner range." I wanted them to know we hadn't forgotten about them.

The hyper short attack took out two ships. We were gone before they could fire anything at us. I had Manly repeat the same, fifteen minutes later, only that time, I had him appear directly in their path. Twenty minutes later, we repeated the maneuver, but from behind. Six ships damaged, all told. Through it all, they remained in ion drive. I had Al draw up a schedule of randomly timed repeat attacks. We could take out maybe one hundred fifty ships before they arrived at Azsuram. Better than nothing.

After the next attack, I had Manly put us on the side of Azsuram farthest from the Berrillians. It was a long way from home, but I wanted to give up nothing to the enemy. Sapale, JJ, Tao, and Toño flew in a shuttle to meet with me. I updated them. The Berrillians were opting for caution and were heading toward the solar system, basically on foot. No matter what I did, *Wrath* was only going to thin their numbers. A large force was going to find our colony within a month.

"Why do you suppose," Tao asked, "they are traveling toward us? You present a real and present danger."

"Not sure," I had to admit.

"Perhaps," Toño said rubbing his temples, "they are too frustrated with *Wrath's* mobility and apparent indestructibility. They may want a simpler target to attack, one less able to defend itself."

"That's not logical," said JJ. All eyes turned toward

him. "They can't know *Wrath* is our only Deavoriath asset. Logically," his new favorite word, it would seem, "we'd have to assume they were in search of an alternate Deavoriath target, just a stationary one. But a fixed target would be just as difficult for them as a movable one."

Good point. "Maybe," I said, "their weapons work better on land-based targets. Those gravity waves would likely rip a solid surface apart."

"Yes," agreed Tao, "I can accept that argument." He sat in quiet reflection a moment. "Perhaps that is what they were designed to do. Destroy planets."

"Like Oowaoa," responded Sapale.

"Yes," Tao said, "especially Oowaoa."

"I'll have the AIs run simulations and report back ASAP," said Toño, without having to be asked.

"That's a troubling thought," I said, "that those assholes might be able to destroy an entire planet. Sure, over time, I might be able to eliminate them by attrition, but they could do one hell of a lot of damage in six months."

"Not that much," remarked JJ. "Not if they can't go to faster-than-light speed. They're pretty much confined to this region. Aside from Azsuram, there's not much else to blow up."

"Hardly reassuring," Sapale said to our son.

"Their entire campaign makes next to no sense," said a troubled Tao.

"How so?" I asked.

"This race was embarrassed by the Deavoriath and has held a long grudge. Presumably, they have dedicated a million years of effort to focusing their entire society on nothing but the destruction of their past enemies. They decide they're finally ready, they travel an immense distance, but they end up underprepared. So far they've demonstrated nothing more than the ability to engage a limited number of targets. Doesn't make sense." He shook his head angrily. "They should have at least sent out—" He stopped talking and his face went blank, like a knife had been thrust into his back.

"What?" snapped Sapale. "Divisinar, what's wrong?"

"It *would* make no sense," Tao said aghast, "unless they're just sending out small bands to test their enemy's readiness. Expendable raiding parties to see what they would need for a full-scale assault."

"A trial balloon," I muttered to myself. "Don't walk into a dark building with your eyes closed and your hands behind your back."

"What?" asked JJ. "You think seven hundred ships with crazy good weapons is just a field test—a test drive?"

"I do," replied Tao glumly.

"Their actual attack force must be massive," said Toño.

"And still quite far away. That would allow them to make changes or develop new technologies, if needed," finished Tao.

"So, what? These guys are just here to whack a few Deavoriath things and die?" asked JJ incredulously.

"And report back," added Tao. "*That* is their only mission."

"Ah, gentlemen," said Sapale, "whatever their ultimate motivation is, we are the ones who stand in harm's way. If we're killed, it doesn't really matter what their larger goals are, now do they?" My Sapale, always practical.

"True," agreed Tao. "However, defense against a suicide squad is more difficult than against a rational opponent. We face opponents who are committed to die. They probably *want* to die. This attack force cannot be counted on to act with any modicum of self-preservation."

"We're six kinds of screwed, aren't we?" was my summation. In spite of our desperate situation, that brought a punch in the shoulder from my brood's-mate. It also got a chuckle from JJ, so it was worth it.

"So, if they must stay out of warp space," said Sapale, "they are no real threat to the worldship fleet, are they?"

"Not if *Wrath* survives the final battle," replied Toño.

"They'll be relieved to hear that," I said, "if they actually do hear it."

"The ultimate goal of your human fleet is the long-term survival of your species," said Tao. "The Berrillians may not threaten those humans who are currently alive, but I'm afraid they pose a grievous threat to the core mission." My, but he was a Glum Gus, wasn't he?

"Again, gentlemen," Sapale urged, "may we focus on the present and not on someone else's possible grim future?"

"Yeah," I said, "I need to get back to annoying the crap out of the Berrillians."

"Fine," responded Sapale, "you've told us all that you can. Go. I pray by the ancient gods you destroy them all."

"Walk with me back to the cube," I said to her.

She excused herself and took my hand. "How's Manly doing?' she asked as we walked slowly. "Has he blown his last mental circuit board yet?"

I smiled back at her. "Not yet, but man, is he ever nuts. I'm glad Al's along. Never thought I'd live long enough to say *that*."

"Good old Al." She was quiet a moment then asked, "Do you think you'll make it back safely for the final battle?"

"Me?" I touched my chest. "You can bet I will. Takes a lot more than a fleet of desperadoes with advanced weapons and hearts of stone to stop *me*."

She gave me a roll of her eyes.

"What? Not gonna start being serious and responsible now. With my last breath, I'll be cracking a joke."

"And I love you for it." She kissed me. "I will always love you."

We embraced for too short a time then I said, "I really gotta go. The more I hit them, the fewer will filter through to bother you guys."

She grabbed my shoulders and turned me toward *Wrath*. "Go, before I change my mind and ask you to stay."

I waved goodbye through the clear window I told Manly to make, and then I was gone.

Though I didn't think they'd be too effective, I brought along a few infinity charges. Those were the membrane bombs that entered something and could then theoretically expand it apart. What the hell? I'd throw a kitchen sink at them, if there was a chance it would dent a hull. We materialized a few thousand kilometers in front of the armada. They had assumed a more open configuration, probably hoping to limit some of the collateral damage that had cost them ships in our prior encounters. I had Manly fire as many rail balls as he could before they returned fire. They were lightning quick about it, but we still got off a few thousand rounds, just the same. We closed in, raised the membrane, and deflected the plasma beams back at them. It was a pretty routine attack plan by then.

A few ships exploded from the cannon fire and a few from redirected plasma shots. I had Manly target the exploding ships with infinity charges, just to see what might happen. Wow. When the charge went off, those Berrillian ships really exploded. They had to have designed them with secure compartments, thick walls, or something similarly designed to limit the spread of damage. The enhanced explosion destroyed quite a few nearby vessels even at the increased separation they had used. I ordered Manly to withdraw.

"How many ships did we bag?" I asked.

"Twenty-four," replied Manly.

That was the most tonnage we'd destroyed in one skirmish. Most cool. I assumed they'd spread out even more, so that we wouldn't be so lucky in the next attack. I immediately ordered Manly to pop into the center of the fleet. Sure enough, they were already farther apart. No biggie. *Wrath* put out a three-sixty laser pattern, which he could do at just the right frequencies, even with the membranes up. The most intense gravity waves yet rocked the cube. They had altered their tactic. They used successive waves to push us away, all the while hitting us with converging waves to try to crack us open. Not for the first time, I was glad no live bodies were aboard *Wrath* just then. They would have never survived. In fact, it set me to wondering what the Berrillians must have been thinking. They had to know how hard they shook the cube, yet whoever was inside wasn't killed. Good. Let them stew over the possibilities. A confused opponent was the best kind.

We disappeared before they could do any real damage. Sitting there in the cold darkness of space I had my best idea ever. Seriously, *ever*.

"*Wrath*, put us in their center again. Be ready to deploy an infinity charge at point-blank range."

"Form?"

"Do it *now*."

Instantly we were right back where we'd been. "*Wrath*, materialize inside the nearest ship, release the charge, and then get us the hell out of there fast."

"Form, there is a chance we will damage ourselves, if our fold-exit includes a bulkhead."

"Then make real sure we don't. Do it now."

The viewport went gray, then I was looking at the inside of a Berrillian ship. We were in a hangar or similarly large enclosure. Then we were back in deep space.

"Take us back, just behind the fleet," I ordered.

There was a huge fireball where the ship had been. That was magnificent. What wasn't magnificent was that they were instantly back in warp space. Crap. They must have figured out what we did and realized we could eliminate every mother-lovin' one of them. They had to hope against all hope we couldn't land on them in their warp bubbles.

"Can you repeat that landing while they're in warp space?"

"I've never had cause to say this before but are you insane, Form?"

"Can you? Yes or no?"

He was quiet almost a minute. "I've run a few simulations. It is possible, but it is exponentially riskier. If we disrupt a bubble while in one we, too, will be vaporized. The chances of such an outcome are one-in-ten, give or take."

"Give or take? Why, *Wrath*, I don't think I've ever heard you sound so human."

"Form, this is not the time or place for insults. We must focus on the complete destruction of our enemy."

Yeah, that was the Manly I knew and didn't love. I did a back-of-the-envelope calculation. At faster than light speed, the armada would reach Azsuram in less than an hour. Based on my past effectiveness blowing them up in warp space, there was no way I'd finish them off in that short of time. I could either fall back home and join the defense, or do something really stupid and way too risky. Yeah, you had to know which I chose.

"*Wrath,* do you have any idea which Berrillian vessel is their flagship?"

"No, at least, not for certain."

"Do you have a best guess?"

"I do not *guess.* I have a highest probability based on configuration and past tactics."

"Plot and execute a course to put us on board the flagship."

"Form," he responded with actual fear in his tone, "I must advise against such a rash act. Let us blow away a few more ships first. It is the *prudent* course."

"Put us on that ship, or I'll manually set off an infinity charge in your belly. Understood?"

"Yes, Form. The calculation will take a few moments."

"You have thirty seconds." I didn't want him to stall into not doing what he'd decided he didn't want to do, the SOB.

"Al," I asked, "please download a translation program to me for whatever amount of Berrillian language we know."

"It's mostly what these barbarians spoke a million years ago," he replied, "but it's done."

Without checking with me further, after twenty seconds, we materialized in what looked to be a passageway. Outstanding. I stepped out into the corridor and closed the portal behind me. If I was captured or killed, I didn't want these bozos to have access to the vortex. I tiptoed in one direction a few meters, when I heard someone coming from around the next corner. Simultaneously, a very high-pitched alarm sounded. It was like fingernails on a chalkboard blasted through rock and roll stadium speakers. Ouch. An artificial voice said something harsh that sounded like "intruder alert," which made sense.

233

I raised my hands in defense. Around the corner came the scariest-looking thing I'd ever seen or dreamed of in my wildest nightmares. It was a four-or five-hundred-pound tiger, with red fur accented with yellow lightning bolt stripes. And he walked on two feet. His head was enormous. His fangs were extra-enormous. The teeth he then bared in anger were beyond enormous. Gargantuan only began to capture their essence. He sprang at me with a blood-curdling roar, his moon-size paws raised with eight-inch claws uncovered.

I seized him with my probe wires and, to his surprise and my relief, held him suspended in midair. When he realized he was helpless, he roared even louder and swiped at me with his impressive paws. In my head, I said, *Who are you?*

My mind raced with alien knowledge. Tamark, male, Clan Duniritad, fifth aide to pack. Thirty-five years old, carnivorous, never mated, second killed before bonding. Berrill was a forest, no, a jungle world. And I felt his pain, his humiliation, and his rage. Killing the Deavoriath was the only thing that mattered in this universe. He wanted to rip me to pieces. His language flowed into my head. It had morphed a lot over time.

I ascertained where the bridge was and who the commander was—a cat named Havibibo. I slammed Tamark against the nearest wall as hard as I could. He collapsed in a limp, bleeding pile when I released his body and raced toward the ladder leading to the bridge. I didn't encounter anyone else along the way, thank goodness.

When I got there, I charged directly onto the bridge. Man, did I get everybody's full attention quickly. Yeah, a giant mouse just stepped in the midst of a dozen angry felines. A huge male not a meter to my left sprang at me like he was fired from a cannon. He was on me before I could ready my probes or finger laser. The dude was fast.

He slammed into my chest, fangs first, and wrapped his arms around me. A normal human or Kaljaxian would have been driven to the floor, and likely split in half by those jaws. With my augmented strength, I was able to flip him judo-style over my head and push my arms open to break his grasp. He took a goodly chunk of my clothes with him, but my polymer surface remained intact. I needed to shake Toño's hand, yet again, for his unbelievable work, if and when I had the chance.

As two other Berrillians rushed toward me the initial assailant rolled over seamlessly and sprang at me again. That time I caught him with the probe and smashed him into his two crew mates. All three tumbled awkwardly into a corner and didn't get back up.

I identified the one I figured had to be Havibibo. Commanders had a universal look about them. They knew they were in change, and everyone else was their bitch. I threw my hands up and shouted, "Havibibo, call off your boys. I want to speak with you. We don't need to do this."

A slightly smaller figure at his side, presumably a female, put her arm in front of him and charged me. "The night-demon speaks as one of us. I will eat his lungs and breathe his blood."

Wow, corny line. I caught her with my probe before she really got going. She squirmed even more than the others had. She kicked, howled, and went through a litany of colorful swear words.

"Havibibo," I repeated, "I don't want to hurt any more of your people. Please, talk to me."

He held his massive paw in the air and said, "No one attacks him."

Immediately, everyone but the she-devil I held restrained stood frozen. She continued her suspended rampage. I pointed to her with my right hand, kind of a what-do-I-do-with-this implied question.

"Kelldrek," he shouted, "be still."

Slowly, reluctantly, she relaxed. I set her down but kept the probes right in front of her. She looked at Havibibo, started to move in my direction, then literally sat her butt down on the floor, panting mightily.

"You are here," said Havibibo, "and we are listening, Deavoriath scum. Speak."

"Nice to meet you, too," I replied.

"There is nothing *nice* about this meeting. Hold your tongue in your mouth, or I will hold it in my hand."

Okay, I'd lighten up in the interest of interspecies harmony.

"I'm Jon Ryan. I'm human, not Deavoriath."

"I don't know of humans. Where are you from?"

"A place called Earth, but it was destroyed."

"Good. It will save me the trouble. I can see you're not Deavoriath slime. You stand on two legs, not their three."

"Then you see, we have no bad blood between us. There's no reason for us to kill one another."

He smiled. If ever I'd seen an insincere mocking smile, that was it. "Ah, but you see, there is. You possess a Deavoriath machine. That alone is reason to kill you. Plus, once we dispense with your three-legged friends, you humans will be our next target." He addressed the female he'd called Kelldrek. "A new meat to tantalize our pallets. Life just gets better and better, does it not, second?"

She growled and rolled her head. I guess that meant yes.

"I don't want to destroy you, but I will gladly do it if you force me to," I said as coolly as I could.

"Interesting species you humans. You don't *want* to kill? How very odd. How very weak." He waved his paw at me. "Let me make it clear. We *do* wish to kill you. All of you. The galaxy is large enough for but one ruling race, and that race is ours." He swung a dismissive paw in my direction. "The rest of you exist only to amuse and feed us."

"Or," I replied, "to *exterminate* you. I'm beginning to see why the Deavoriath made it a point to try to do that."

"Your Deavoriath friends will soon pay the highest price for their actions, I can assure you." He looked to his bridge crew. "I'm sorry, Jon Ryan, but this conversation is now boring my stripes off." He passed a directing hand from the crew toward me as if to say *have at him, boys and girls.*

In the blink of an eye I sliced everyone in half with my laser, all but Havibibo and his mate. I grabbed her with the probe and held her near the ceiling. "I spare you, commander, so you can consider my words of peace. I take this one as a hostage to demonstrate to you that I can. Know that you are up against a will and a technology you cannot defeat."

With that, I turned and ran toward the cube. Kelldrek, suspended above, made an unbelievable racket. What a bitch. Overhead, Havibibo's voice thundered. "Kill the intruder. He is heading to Deck 8, Section 161. He has my second. She must not be taken alive." Did he mean they should stop me from absconding with her, or that they should kill both of us on sight? Not a very sentimental second to Kelldrek, was he?

I arrived at the cube before anyone else. I opened a portal, dashed in, and shut the wall behind me just as several cats slammed into the hull. They clawed impressively at the exterior but did no damage.

"*Wrath*, fire a series of laser blasts toward the engines to disable the ship. Then take us home. And don't wait for them to drop into real space before we split."

"By your command."

What an annoying acknowledgement. Gotta reprogram that guy.

TWENTY-SEVEN

I returned to the main village. Sapale and the key leaders were all there. I gave them the bad news. Around five hundred ships would be there in half an hour. They looked at me like I'd just killed their puppies with my bare hands. Then they looked at the enraged Berrillian female I held behind me, and their mood slipped another few notches. Yeah, that's what they were up against.

I wanted to return to orbit and take out a few more ships, but Tao pointed out that it really didn't matter. "Five hundred and three ships in orbit, as opposed to four hundred ninety-nine, will not turn the battle."

Crap, I hated it when other people were right. I wanted to be doing something, not just sitting and waiting for an ass kicking. Toño button-holed me and said the AI simulations on the gravity waves looked worse than he'd thought possible. All the while, he stared at Kelldrek, an expression of aghast disbelief on his face. His assessment was that the gravity waves crushed and fractured solid materials quite easily. The frequency of the waves he'd seen used against the cube were centered on the range most likely to damage wide areas of land. He concluded that the gravity weapons were designed as planet killers. That was more bad news than I really needed.

"Doc," I said, "there's always another way, an alternative. Don't tell me those *assholes* are going to swing into orbit and smash Azsuram to pieces. Tell me a solution, even a crazy Jon Ryan–type solution."

He shook his head as if it weighed a ton. "No, my friend, there *is* none. It's too late to evacuate more than a handful." He pointed upward. "Though come to think of it, that's probably the best use for the vortex right now."

I turned to Sapale. "He may be right. Put all the children into the cube. They'll all fit, right?"

She looked at me like never before. There was a tragic disappointment in her eyes. Her magic man had just run out of miracles. I'd never felt so wretched in all my days.

Finally at barely a whisper she said, "Yes, I think so. I'll pass the word."

"You be there, too," I said. I knew she never would. She'd stand in defense of her dream until well past her last ounce of strength. "Someone's got to mind all those urchins. I'm not the nurturing type."

She forced a sad laugh. "I'll see to it that Dolirca is there. Those two Toe cubs of hers will keep them all smiling."

"Where will you be?" I asked her as I stroked her cheek.

"Central Command, with JJ and Tao. We're coordinating the defense from there."

"I'll be with the cube, *obviously*," I said slapping the side of my head. "At least I can keep firing from the ground. *Wrath's* power supply is unlimited."

"After the battle I'll meet you," she said cupping my hand to her face.

"Cool," I replied. "Where?"

"Davdiad's lush gardens, where she never again wears her veils." The Kaljaxian version of heaven. Oh, boy. She was serious.

"Or maybe the canteen for a big ol' bowl of calrf." I rubbed my tummy. "Mmm, mmm good."

She smiled ever so sadly. "Or for a bowl of calrf." She kissed me, then left in a rush.

Back at the vortex, I asked for an update. "How many ships, when?"

"Five hundred twenty-eight are flying in warp space. They should be here in five or six minutes."

"Open fire with everything we've got when they're in range."

"By your—"

"Manly," I said with frustration, "could you be like everybody else and just say, aye, aye, or yes—yowzer—anything but that?"

"Yowzer, Form."

"Oh, and please form a sealed compartment for this thing," I held up Kelldrek. I set her in the corner, and Manly threw walls up to surround her. I could still hear her putting up a terrible racket, but she was secure. I had no idea what I'd do with her, or even why I took her captive. If, or rather *when*, I was killed, she'd die in her little prison. At least there was one upside in that. Thinking of her suffocating made me feel all warm and fuzzy.

The next five minutes were a blur. I helped Dolirca herd kids as far away from me as possible. I couldn't have them getting underfoot and didn't want them distracting me with questions and crying. I also kept checking both my internal chronometer and my handheld's clock. I checked and rechecked weapons status. In short, I was a nervous wreck.

Finally, the call I'd dreaded for weeks came. Al

announced the fleet was dropping into real space and configuring itself overhead. They were a hundred kilometers high. As they assumed their positions, the radar screen looked like a snowstorm. Thousands of landing craft were launched and began descending. That's when the gravity waves began to hit. It was like a battleship of old firing on the beach the Marines were about to land on. They were softening us up.

Right from the first impact, the tremendous effectiveness of the waves became evident. The ground shook, buildings swayed like tree branches in a hurricane, and things started falling everywhere. Within a few seconds, I could see huge fissures opening up in the surface. Buildings and rocks outside the membrane wall crashed to the ground or fell into the newly formed abysses. The inside of the membrane wall was more stable, due to the membrane's inherent strength, but significant damage occurred very quickly, nonetheless. Worst of all, I could see the ground under the membranes beginning to give way.

After a minute the first of our big structures collapsed. It was the unoccupied theater. On the other side of the complex, a shielded building fell onto its side, membrane intact. Things were looking very bad. Our cannons were firing at maximum, and hundreds of the landing craft exploded spectacularly. Al estimated around one hundred would survive long enough to land. That meant several thousand vicious tigers were about to attack us on foot. Then, out of nowhere, Al announced *the miracle*.

"Captain, the warships in orbit are being destroyed."

"What? How ... who?" I stammered.

"Unknown. The ships are rupturing in a straight line, one to the next."

"*Wrath*," I called out, "what's going on up there?"

"A craft of unknown origin and design is piercing the

warships at extreme speed. The last of the enemy fleet is ... there. All enemy warships destroyed."

The gravity bombardment stopped immediately.

"The craft is heading toward the cluster of landing craft," Manly went on. "First impact. Now the ship's firing a laser at the ships it isn't ramming."

"Between her action and our ground defenses how many enemy shuttles will land?"

"A few. Possibly less than ten."

The tide had definitely turned, but there were still maybe a thousand foot soldiers about to land. A thousand maybe we could handle.

"Al, hail the vessel lending assistance."

After a few seconds, he reported, "No response, Captain."

"ETA on the assault force."

"Three craft have landed, two more ... one more about to touch down."

"Can you confirm deployment of foot soldiers?"

"Yes," replied Al. "Several hundred are running in this direction."

I exited the cube but left it open. If I was killed, there'd be no way to get the children out if I didn't leave an opening. Dolirca and a couple of adults stood guard with rail rifles. It was the best we could do.

I ran toward the control center. Our rail guns were now directing fire in the direction of the ground force. Individual aiming was not possible. As a consequence the forest around the village exploded and ripped into flames, like it was raining hell.

Before I was half way to Central Ops the first of the Berrillian foot soldiers burst into the clearing. AI guided guns targeted them immediately. Their losses were horrific but they never slowed their charge. Most ran on two feet, but some came on all four. They carried rifles slung over their backs. That way, they could run on all fours and not drop their guns. I could hear their war cries, as well as their screams of agony. They were the perfect warriors. Too bad they were on the other side.

A few tigers made it to the membrane wall. They ran at full tilt and slammed into it in a manner that would have been comical, if they weren't so damn scary. Faces crushed and blood sprayed against the invisible barrier. The cats behind them stopped before impact, noticing also that their shots were being deflected at the shield wall.

Then an attacker found an opening. Where a building had been toppled to its side there was a break in the membrane. Several cats poured through in a blur— dozens. It was hand-to-hand time. Fragile Kaljaxians versus five-hundred-pound killing machines.

A group of our soldiers formed a line and commenced firing. Many tigers were torn apart as they flew toward the line. Other Berrillians crouched and returned fire. It looked like they used phase-plasma rifles. Whatever they fired, they were extremely effective. Our soldiers fell quickly.

Maybe ten big cats hit the squad and it exploded like billiard balls. Berrillians seized Kaljaxians and ripped into them. Comrades tried to stab or beat off the beasts that were mauling their friends, but they had little effect and soon became the next victims. I fired from a short distance away, and was able to pick the Berrillians off gradually. By the time the ten cats were dead, forty Kaljaxians were in pieces, mutilated beyond recognition.

A second wave of tigers entered the clearing and charged at the membrane. They were quickly directed to the breach. I ran to cover the opening. By the time I made it there and began shooting, five cats had already burst through. They split up into two squads and charged in different directions. Our forces were swarming in my direction, so the group of three Berrillians were quickly surrounded. Our troops were able to take cover and fire on the Berrillians. Two cats returned fire. The other charged on all fours with a deafening war cry. He was lost in bloodlust. He was the first of the intruders to die and didn't take anyone with him. The remaining two lay prone and kept firing for a few minutes before they, too, were killed. Man, were they tough. Fortunately they weren't such great marksmen. They wounded several soldiers, but none too seriously.

The other group was heading toward ... the command center. I couldn't leave my post until I was certain no more tigers were coming. There was still a steady stream of enraged cats rushing at the breach. I used the membrane as a shield. I could fire a few shots, then pull back behind it. Even though they must have known the shield was there, they continued to shoot at me when I was fully covered. I was too inviting a target to ignore.

I held my rail gun in my left hand so I could also use my laser finger. It was a lot more satisfying to fry the bastards.

Several of our soldiers charged after the two Berrillians, though they were considerably slower than the bounding cats. Between assaults on my position, I scanned the ops center. I could see defensive firing. Good. I hoped the tigers would never make it there. They did. I saw one disappear into a door while the other burst into a bloody ball, the victim of several simultaneous rail shots. I closed my eyes briefly and said a prayer.

Then another group of Berrillians charged me and I was back in action. Plasma shots rained into the membrane making a hateful sound. A group of twenty pulled together tightly and rushed toward the breach. They continued to fire on my position, trying to pin me back as they advanced. I curved my laser finger around the edge of the membrane and kept them under constant fire.

When the lead cats died, the ones behind held up their bodies as a shield. That slowed their progress, but the corpses made excellent shields. As the ball of Berrillians reached my position, those left alive hurled the bodies at me. Some rushed under the gruesome projectiles, while others vaulted over them. Once they were in the clear, I shot with both hands and fragmented their assault. Three lived to hit the breach. One slammed into the membrane and flew backward falling in a bloody heap.

One grabbed the rifle with a mighty paw and tried to rip it from my hands. The other rounded the opening and slammed into my chest. A human would have lost the gun and been crushed to the ground. I wasn't a human. I took advantage of the one cat's ferocious bite on the rifle to throw him into the membrane's edge. It sliced him in two.

The cat trying to drive me down ignored his comrade's fate. He pounded the dirt with his hind legs and pulled me toward his teeth with a powerful bear hug. I plowed the butt of my hand into his neck and was able to hold him inches away from my head. He snapped and snarled with abandon. Saliva and hot breath spewed into my face. His fury allowed him to slowly inch over me, but my strength just held. In his language, I snapped, "You're the ugliest kitten I've ever seen."

That broke his focus infinitesimally. My kick to his groin hefted him overhead. He landed hard on his back but snapped back up instantly. He lunged at me insane with rage. I snatched his head with both hands and crushed down on his thin mane. That brought howls of protest, and he swiped at me with one paw. He ripped my shirt to shreds in one pass, then raised his paw and aimed deeper. Before he could strike, I pushed his head down and my knee up. I landed my blow first. His body went limp in my hands and I dropped him.

I quickly confirmed no more Berrillians were heading to the breach. I signaled to a group of approaching soldiers to hold my position as I sprinted toward Command Central. I heard screams and rifle shots that got louder as I approached. Then it was suddenly silent. I hit the doorway and scanned the room. Toño was hunched over someone on the floor. JJ and Tao brandished rifles at the cat crumpled on its side nearby. The Berrillian wasn't moving. I arrived at Toño's side and pushed him away to see who he was tending to.

It was Sapale, or rather what was left of her. The Berrillian had nearly decapitated her, and she was missing a leg. My heart stopped beating and my lungs stopped breathing. I couldn't move, speak, or feel. In that moment, my passion for life flickered out, and an unquenchable rage ignited in my soul. I shoved Toño to the floor and lifted my brood's-mate in my arms. I supported her head so it didn't flop backward as I pressed her to my chest. Toño said something. I have no idea what. It didn't matter. JJ tugged at my shoulder. I don't know why. It didn't matter. I held Sapale, my eternal love, and I began to cry.

Doc told me years ago that robots were incapable of tears, that there was no pathway for tears to flow. He claimed he'd never written a subroutine for crying, that it didn't exist. He was wrong. Androids could cry. A mindless vengeful evil had travelled generations to come to this planet and take from me that which I cared for the most. It was as painful as it was impossible. But it was more real than anything I'd ever experienced, and I could not make it right.

I don't know how long I stood there crying with

Sapale in my arms. Maybe a few minutes, maybe a few days. The next memory I had was that of a stern, dispassionate Tao forcing Sapale's body from my grip, while admonishing me to behave like a soldier in combat. If I'd had any strength left in my body I'd have killed him with my bare hands. But I didn't. Instead, I crumpled to the floor and covered my face with my bloody hands.

Days after the attack, JJ visited me in the vortex. I had been sitting in front of the view screen staring at nothing. It was turned off. He said it was time to bury his mother. He held a hand out to me and guided me out of the portal. As we walked, he said he knew his mother had loved me with an endless passion. He missed her, too. He always would. But he reminded me that his mother was tough— tougher than tough. She would demand of us all that we force ourselves to move forward. She'd be disappointed if we faltered, even for a moment's grief. He was right, of course.

The burial traditions of Kaljax were complex. I'd never paid much attention to them before, and I didn't then. I stood numbly by my family and endured whatever they were doing. We buried my Sapale in the center of the village. A mighty monument would in time be erected on the site. Her final resting place would eventually become the center of a proud, just empire. Over the centuries, Kaljax would be all but forgotten. *Azsuram* would be the new home of its people, its culture, and its collective memory. It would all live because of my Sapale. The legacy of my pure love's vision and force of will.

Sapale's life meant so much to so many. The countless songs and tales of her worth never began to do her life's work justice. She would become in the fullness of time god-like in her legend. But to me, she would always remain my irascible, beautiful, love-rich wife. I've always felt, secretly in my heart, that she was more than I deserved. But that she cherished me as much as I did her reassured me eternally that getting more than I deserved was all right. It was a compliment I would take with grace and humility, and one I would never release from my memories.

TWENTY-EIGHT

I was lost in a dense fog the next week or so. I interacted with no one. The work of digging out and beginning the repairs on the colony had begun. My attention was not required, so I was left to myself. Bone-numbing grief, it turns out, is extra hard on an android. It wasn't eased by the need for sleep, food, or drink. I was cursed with many more hours a day to pine away and to seethe. I hadn't the slightest idea where the Berrillian home world was. But during that abysmal period, an obsession was born in my heart. I needed to find and destroy it. I replayed a dozen different methods I would use to exterminate them as a species. But mostly I mourned the loss of the most important person I'd ever had in my life.

Finally, Toño came to me one day to see how I was doing. He brought a pot of coffee, two mugs, and a sympathetic ear. I told him several times I didn't want to, need to, or intend to talk with him, but he just sat there sipping his drink and waiting until I was ready to open up. Occasionally he'd mention some trivial aspect of the rebuild or pass along greetings from someone, but mostly he waited for me to speak.

"I could have done more," came as an unannounced whisper from my lips.

Toño continued to stare into his mug. "You did more than anyone, and you did your best. You could not have done more." His tone was kind and loving and it blessedly carried no judgment.

"She died. If I'd done more maybe she wouldn't have."

"She died defending her people. Helping them was what she lived for. It was all-out war and we were very lucky to have suffered so few losses."

"You saw what that animal did to her." I stopped momentarily unable to continue. "She didn't deserve to die like that."

"Do you know what happened there at the end?"

I shrugged.

"The Berrillian rushed into the room and pounced on a junior officer unfortunate enough to be standing near the door. They rolled a few times on the floor, then the cat pinned him to the ground and began mauling him. Sapale grabbed a chair and charged over without hesitation. She splintered the metal chair on its back, knocking him off his victim. It took a second to recover, and then he rose up on two feet and grabbed her. She jammed the back of the chair into his throat, but in the end he was too powerful. The beast swatted the chair away, just as Tao got off his first shot.

"He hit him in the arm, causing the Berrillian to arch backward. Instead of returning fire or jumping for cover, the damn cat drove down toward Sapale. He bit her leg and swung her around in the air like a rag doll. Tao hit it twice in the chest and he dropped her. She was lying on the floor underneath the tiger, losing blood rapidly. What do you think she did? She grabbed its throat and tried to choke it to death." Toño shook his head slowly, marveling.

"Just before JJ shot it in the head, the creature raked his big paw across her face and neck. Then it roared and fell to the ground. Tao and JJ rushed over and filled it with rail balls, but it was too late. That's when you came in."

"Really, she tried to choke a five-hundred-pound animal with a neck the size of a tree trunk?"

He nodded and smiled in response.

"Yeah, that would be my girl. Bet she surprised the hell out of the Berrillian." We both chuckled at that. It was good to laugh, if only a little.

"So you see," Toño said, "she sacrificed herself to save that other fellow. And you know what?"

I shook my head.

"The man survived. He's missing an ear and several fingers and has required two operations so far, but he'll be fairly normal before all's said and done." He patted my shoulder. "She gave her life to save his. You should be proud, not sad. You know she'd have wanted you to."

"I know," was all I could manage, just then. Finally I was able to say, "I miss her, Doc. I'm going to miss her forever."

"Me, too, my friend. It's not going to be easy for either of us, this immortality thing. Perhaps we'll get used to it, perhaps not."

I raised my mug. "Here's to never getting used to it."

He clinked his mug to mine. "To never losing our *humanity*."

We sat there in silence for a few moments. "So," I could finally ask, "who the *hell* was our guardian angel?"

He shook his head. "No idea whatsoever. He never responded to any of our hails. After he'd taken out the last landing craft, he went straight for the flagship you disabled, and he destroyed it." He shrugged. "Then he was gone. Puff."

"Could he have been Deavoriath? Did he fold space?"

"*Wrath* is certain he wasn't Deavoriath. No, he didn't fold space or form a warp bubble. He simply accelerated away and disappeared. Like I said," he threw his closed fists open in my direction, "puff."

"Why bother to save our bacon and not even take credit? Who'd do that?"

"Someone who wishes to remain anonymous."

"But why? It makes *no* sense. He either hated the Berrillians or intended to help us. Either way, you'd think he'd have at least said, *hi*. If he's our good Samaritan, he must like us. Why leave someone you like with unanswered questions?"

Toño shrugged.

"If he was out to get the Berrillians, why not enlist our future help? We'd be serving a common cause."

"I can't say. I agree with your reasoning, but that doesn't alter the fact that he clearly wants to remain shrouded in mystery."

"Like I need another mystery," I said.

"At least you're alive to worry. If that ship hadn't intervened, there's no way a single one of us would have survived. We were outnumbered and outclassed."

"Damn mystery," I mumbled. "So how bad were our losses?"

He angled his head. "Bad," he tilted his head to the other side, "but we'll recover. We lost thirty-eight soldiers and about a hundred were wounded. The ground is so unstable, we'll have to rebuild a lot of structures pretty far away from where they stood. But, power, water, and sewage are all functional. Everyone I've spoken with is remarkably upbeat. I think that in six months, we'll be mostly recovered."

"How about my family?"

"Aside from Sapale none were injured. The kids are

pretty shaken, but they're Kaljaxian. They'll be okay. They're a tough lot, as you know."

I rolled my eyes. "Tell me about it."

We laughed again. It felt good.

"There's a council meeting tomorrow, if you're up for it," Toño said. "If not, everyone will understand."

"No," I replied, "I'll be there. If I slack too much, Sapale will rise from the dead just to kick my butt."

"I don't doubt it," he said with a guffaw. "Well, I must be going. I need to check on the wounded and start repairing the equipment that was damaged." He looked at me intently. "Will you be okay?"

I rapped him on the shoulder. "I'm going to be fine. I'll stop by later. Maybe we can walk the area, see what we're looking at in terms of damage."

"Sounds good. Stop by anytime." He slugged back the last of his coffee and set the mug down. He reached over and shook my hand. "If you need anything, I'll be insulted if you don't ask. Oh, at some point you'll need to release Kelldrek. No hurry. The more fatigued she is the easier it'll be to handle her. Let me know when you're up for it. I'll set up some form of cage for her." He waved as he turned to leave.

"I'll keep you posted, my old friend."

After he left, I had Al pull up whatever data we had on our mystery savior. Wow. I mean, I say *wow* a lot, I guess, but wow! What a ship, what an attack. The vessel was a flying pencil, as if built specifically for that type of assault. It was fifteen meters long and three meters across. There wasn't room enough for more than one crewman, assuming she had a crew. But she must have had a crew, because the targeting was so precise. Then again, there was a whole hell of a lot more in the universe I didn't know than I did know.

It was nearly impossible to tell if a ship had a shield

membrane. One had to know specifically what they were looking for to find it. That said, I didn't detect one. It almost had to have one, given how and what it did. The vortexes had unbelievably tough hulls, but even those might have yielded under the type of force involved in ultra-high-speed ramming, and the resultant massive explosion. Not to get too technical, but a membrane also absorbed the momentum in collisions. A ship's hull could be as hard as you'd like, but the momentum of the impact could scramble the occupants of the ship really well. The argument against a membrane being used was that, at least up until then, we couldn't figure out how to maneuver a shielded craft that precisely. To withstand the force, the membrane had to be completely covering the ship. If it was, the engines wouldn't be able to steer the craft. I was left not understanding how the person pulled it off.

But I was the only one who seemed to have the technology to generate membranes. Well, Uto, the guy who gave me the know-how did. Wait, Uto—

No. He gave me the membrane tech. He could just as well have done the same with the person who defended us. It didn't have to be him, up there. Or was it? He sort of had to meet me to hand over the membrane instructions. But he didn't *need* to take a long hot shower with me to blow my enemies out of the sky. Crap, more riddles and loose ends. Them I didn't need.

It still could have been the Deavoriath helping us. I knew they voted not to, but that Kymee fellow seemed pretty sympathetic toward us. He was their science genius, so he could have devised some radical new toys and been dying to use them. Maybe he sped away and *then* folded space? Pretty convoluted reasoning involved in that explanation.

A race like the Berrillians had to have a string of

archenemies from one end of the galaxy to the other. Any one of a long list of civilizations could have been really pissed that the cats were back. They could have intervened to terminate the threat. They owed *us* no explanation and required no thank yous from us, either, because they were simply acting in their own interest. Maybe.

Still, why would they wait until the last minute to attack? This theoretical civilization could have attacked the Berrillians at any juncture. Why wait? Why would anyone wait, actually? Even Uto? If he *was* our champion, why had he waited until we were badly hurt to eliminate the Berrillians? Made no sense. He should have cut them to pieces when they first appeared on our sensors. Why wait? Did he *want* us to suffer?

My train of thought was getting me nowhere. I filed away as many facts as I could about the flying pencil, and put it to rest. There were a million things I needed to do, not the least of which was to begin planning my vengeance against the Berrillians. Oh, yes, soon they would beg me for mercy, and none would come. Before I rested, they would know me as the Rain of Death, the Dark Storm Risen. I would become all of their nightmares churned together with the hatred I held inside. I would dump that fetid concoction on their blighted existence, and they would die in despair, in agony, and in terror.

But, for the present I had a colony to rebuild. It was Sapale's dream that Azsuram become the home of a great civilization. By the blood of the Berrillians, I'd see her dream became reality. The council meeting was grim. Lists were read of the dead, the wounded, and the massive amounts of destruction. Testimonials were spoken, prayers offered, and sorrows shared. Then the business of planning, budgeting, and delegating for the reconstruction began. We were there until nearly dawn.

In the end, I liked the results. In a democracy, no one got everything they wanted or thinks they need. But the initial direction was good, and I could support it.

The hardest part for me came at the very end. Before we adjourned a motion was made to select Sapale's replacement as head of the council. JJ was chosen unanimously. But as he picked up the silly gavel I'd made for her to conclude the meeting, I felt a burning pain deep in my soul. She was dead, buried, and now she was replaced.

I began to wonder over the next few weeks what my role was to be in the design of Azsuram. Sapale was gone. My extended family was there. But, as children did, they grew up and had their own lives that didn't require me. I'm sure they, like all young families before them, wanted their autonomy and separation from the parental units. So, as time passed, I would become a holiday centerpiece, a banquet speaker, and a hallowed patriarch. What I wouldn't become was necessary. I promised my brood's-mate I'd watch over Azsuram as long as I lived, ensuring that it remained safe and true to her vision. But I didn't need to sit in a rocking chair in the center of town to perform that task.

I decided what I wanted to do first was to confront the Deavoriath. I would know if it was they who saved Azsuram. If it wasn't, I wanted them to know the cost of their indifference toward us. I would either thank them or curse them to know what horror they owned. Azsuram lived on in spite of them. I would want them to know that an immortal knew about their sin of omission and would be witness to it until the end of time.

As soon as I'd decided to go, I went to Toño. I asked if he wanted to join me. He did not. I asked why. He told me there was no upside to visiting the Deavoriath. I stated my desire to bless or curse them. He repeated that he saw no upside in going—either of us going. I said honor was at stake. He said honor was internal, not external. It was stored in the heart, not won by shouting while pounding on a table. I said I disagreed. He said he was busy and asked me to leave. I said I had no intention of remaining and stormed out. In the wake of Sapale's death, I would not permit disloyalty to add to my grief.

I sent a message to JJ informing him of my destination and I ordered *Wrath* to take me to Oowaoa. I was there before I knew it. I stepped out into what I'd come to know as a typical Oowaoan day. Gray skies, musty air, and a lifeless feeling all around. After waiting thirty minutes to see if anyone came to meet me I headed toward Kymee's lab. He would know for certain if his people had come to our aid. Plus, I was far too angry to face the sternness of Yibitriander. I may have been a man on a mission, but I knew better than to try and beat trouble out of the bushes with a stick.

Kymee was sitting at a desk in his lab. He was clearly waiting for me. He gestured to a stool across from him indicating I should sit. I did, though stiffly.

"May I get you some refreshment, Jon Ryan?" he asked in a neutral tone.

"No thank you. I haven't come for refreshments."

"I assumed not," he replied, "I assume you've come for blood."

That surprised me. Of all the bitter things I did want, their blood was not one of them. "No. Never. I have come for answers, nothing more."

"So," he said, "a man looking for answers must have burning questions. What burns inside you, Jon Ryan?"

"I assume you know the result of the Berrillian attack on my home."

"*Wrath* is nothing if not a gossip and a chatterbox.

Yes, I know the *numeric* results of the conflict." He leaned back. "I will soon learn, I assume, of the *emotional* costs."

"Does it surprise you that I'd come here for reasons as insubstantial as emotions?"

He shook his head. "Not in the slightest. Remember, we are cerebral creatures, but that does not mean we are without emotions." He thought a moment. "I would say we strive to *master* our emotions, not dissect them out and remove them from our essence."

"Be that as it may. I would know if the craft that destroyed almost the entire Berrillian fleet was yours."

"You would know? And how is it you would? If you knew, why would you come all this way to ask for an answer you already possessed?"

"Don't mock me, Kymee. You're better than that. Please keep in mind my grief and your superior nature."

"You are probably right, at least on some counts. Please don't lower yourself, Jon Ryan, to threats and demands."

"Point taken. My apologies."

"None needed. As friends, let us speak truth and regret nothing said."

"Did you help us by sending that ship?"

"No. It was not our vessel, *or* our doing."

"Do you know whose ship it was, and why they might have come to our aid?"

He shook his long white hair. "No, we do not."

"And would you tell me if you knew?"

"*I* would, Jon Ryan."

I was rapidly approaching a dead end. "Can you offer any insights? What powered the ship? Did it have a shield membrane?"

He shrugged. "No idea."

"And, again, you'd tell me if you knew?"

"I would. Others," he wiggled his flattened hand between us, "possibly, not so much."

"One last question. Where is the Berrillian home world?"

He eyed me suspiciously. "I do not know," he said flatly. "I know where it *was*. We destroyed it. Then we chased them until we grew bored of the pursuit."

"Why do I get the feeling there's a *but* or a *however* missing from that response?"

"Because there were both, my friend. Take this advice from someone who has not just *known* blood-vengeance, but from someone who lusted for it. Avoid it. Do *not* do it. Be a better person, a better form of life. Because in the end, vengeance only begets more vengeance. Your retribution will not go unpunished, so you must give in to your destructive inclination once again. Vengeance is not a word or a concept. It is a demon—a *living, breathing* demon from the darkest of the nether worlds. It cannot be fulfilled, only encouraged. It will *never* release those who succumb to it. Once the malevolent spirit owns you, you are not worthy of the death you deserve and will come to passionately desire. Hear me, young Jon Ryan."

"Ah, okay. Wow, Kymee, thanks for your advice. Please know it has been heard, loud and clear."

"*But,*" he spat back. "Now *you* are the one with the *but,* and it says you have heard nothing."

"I promise you, my friend, I have heard you. I can't help thinking about what you've said. Give me time, please."

"Time," he scoffed. "We've had millions of years and the demon *still* won't release us. Were we to die as a people, we would not be free of the monster's grasp." He tapped the side of his nose with a finger. "Be very cautious. More cautious than we were. More cautious than imaginable."

I needed to change the subject. Kymee was beginning to creep me out. "So back to before. With all your knowledge, all of your experience, you recognize *nothing* about that craft?"

"Mysteries are wonderful things, aren't they? I have not been confronted with one in *ages*." He trembled with excitement. "It's marvelous."

"You'll forgive me if my concerns are more practical and pragmatic. I want only to know who helped us and why."

"It is not enough to know someone *did*?"

"No."

"Perhaps it was an angel of the god your people worship." He spoke resolutely. "Yes. That is it. I'm certain of it now. It was an angel of God. The hand of God saved you." He waited a second then asked, "There, do you feel better now? Fulfilled? Ready to leave?" He wagged his caterpillar eyebrows up and down.

"No I feel patronized and lied to." I couldn't hold back a smile. "Your people, they understand the concept of bullshit, I see."

"Understand? No, my child. We *invented* it."

"Za-*zing*," I said pointing at him. "Good one. I knew right off the bat you were a good egg, Kymee."

"One strives to be a proper calcium carbonate–encased embryo."

"If I wanted to find the person who piloted the ship, would you have any suggestions?"

"Yes," he said, "let it go."

"No, I meant any suggestions how to go about locating them."

"I know what you meant. I chose to answer the question as best I could. If the originators of your salvation wanted to be known to you, they would be. The fact that they are not indicates that pursuing their identity is wrong on two critical counts. One, you insult their wishes by going against them. These people saved your collective butts. The thanks you give them is to defy their wish for anonymity?"

"I'm afraid to ask, but what's the second count?"

"You are correct to be afraid. You risk finding out how far these people are willing to go to remain unknown and unfettered." He gave me an if-looks-could-kill stare. "Some races might be more jealous of their privacy than even the Deavoriath. At least, more than the Deavoriath *claim* to be." He harrumphed after that.

"Are you saying you're sad to see me? What, I haven't grown on you yet?" I smiled real big.

"You seem to have. But as a scientist, I'm confident I'll discover a cure."

"Well, then I'm screwed, poo-pooed, and unshrewd."

"That can't be good. I'm not entirely certain what you just said, but it doesn't sound positive."

"Toño thinks I should give up the search. You think I should, too. The fact that I'm unwilling means I'm either an innovative thinker or an unrepentant ass-meister."

He rolled his head gently in contemplation. "Give me a moment to decide on my vote."

Back to serious, I asked, "Can I count on you in the future for help?"

"You have not forgotten the decision of the Deavoriath. It is unlikely to change in the foreseeable future. Trust me on that."

"No. I mean *you*, Kymee. Will *you* help me?"

"Help you what?"

"Kymee, I'm a little lamb in a forest of wolves I don't even know are there. You have ruled the galaxy. You've got chops. Can you help me when I need it, even if I don't know I do?"

"I'll assume, for argument's sake, the chops I have are

not lamb chops." His ancient eyes twinkled. "I have no problem helping you in a limited, personal manner." He sliced a hand toward me. "I will *not*, however, do so in defiance of the will of my people, as the collective that we are. Should you ask something of me we do not approve of, I will not do it."

"Then I'll be real modest in my requests, won't I?"

"Based on what I know of you to date, Jon Ryan, modesty is not a quality you possess."

"Then I'll simply have to welcome you into the world of Ryan modesty and discretion that exists just below my rugged exterior."

"Not handsome and rugged? Ruggedly handsome?"

I tented my fingers on my chest. "Hardly. I'm much too modest to say such things."

"You know, I'm beginning to think you may have a leg up on us when it comes to bullshitting, Ryan."

To such high praise I could only beam him a smile.

TWENTY-NINE

I had one last task to perform. After that, I'd be free to decide what it was I was going to do with myself. I had yet to inform the worldship fleet—and Amanda in particular —about the destruction of the Berrillian armada. They had to have been sitting on pins and needles. In the days following Sapale's death, I just couldn't muster the strength needed to make the trip. But it was time.

I materialized in my dedicated hangar. Like my last visit, the activity my appearance generated was similar to a bomb going off. Techs ran this way and that, lights flashed, and everybody was shouting to someone on their handheld. It was like one of those old Japanese movies when Godzilla turned the corner and crushed his way down a major city street. Chaos ensued. After exiting the cube, I leaned back against it, and folded my arms. I knew everybody who was anybody would rush to me on the double.

Heath was the first to sprint in, followed closely by De La Frontera. A very pregnant Amanda came in last place, but she definitely had a good reason to be the slowest. I greeted them one by one. While they all caught their breath, I asked where we could go to talk. Amanda raised her hand, indicating her office, as she continued to pant heavily. A golf-cart shuttle picked us up and drove us to our destination. In the few minutes it took to get there, everyone was composed and smiling nervously. We sat across from Amanda in the Noval Office, and she asked if anyone wanted coffee.

"So," she said to me, "don't keep us in suspense. What happened? The fact you're alive to tell the tale suggests things went better than you predicted."

I balled my hands together on my lap and stared at them. "A whole lot better. The Berrillian fleet has been completely destroyed."

"All of them?" asked a stunned Heath. "There were hundreds of ships."

"Every lovin' one—gone."

"So," said Carlos, "*Wrath* performed much better than expected? How marvelous."

"Not exactly," I replied. "*Wrath* did okay. He took out about a hundred warships, but he can't claim the victory."

They looked at each other puzzled. "But—" began Amanda.

"Some mystery spaceship showed up and blew them out of the sky." I mimed an explosion with my expanding hands. I filled them in on the details of the battle.

"And you've no idea," Amanda repeated, "who your benefactor was?" She shook her head. "That makes no sense, but never look a gift horse in the mouth."

A very serious Heath finally asked, "And what of your losses?" Boy nice double entendre there, Heath.

I gave them the numeric totals of dead, wounded, and property damage. I left out the personal part.

"Those gravity waves were certainly deadly weapons when directed at solid planetary targets."

"Tell me about it," I huffed back.

"Were you able to capture any of their craft or personal equipment so we might study their tech?" asked Carlos.

I angled my head. "Not much but a little. All but one of the landing craft self-destructed. The one we captured must have malfunctioned. Toño is tearing it apart as we speak."

"Perhaps you could take me back with you so I might help him?" Carlos asked.

"No problem. I'm sure he'd like that. We also captured a lot of handguns, personal effects, and those sorts of things, stripping their dead."

"Pity we couldn't get our mitts on one of those gravity wave generators," responded Amanda.

"Yeah. Toño's hoping the data banks in the shuttle contain the plans." I shrugged. "We'll see."

"In any case," said Heath with a big smile, "at least you've eliminated the Berrillian threat. That's a true blessing."

My hackle went up. "No. We ended *this* Berrillian incursion," I corrected him. "There'll be more, probably bigger, and definitely better prepared waves to come."

"When might we expect them?" asked Heath.

"Hope for the best and plan for the worst," was my terse reply.

"You don't seem as happy as I might have expected," said Amanda, "from someone who's just won a major victory." She studied my face a while. "How's Sapale?"

I looked away. "Sapale was killed."

"What," exclaimed Carlos. "This is *terrible*, my friend. You should have mentioned it earlier. Here we're asking you all these technical questions, when you have suffered such a personal tragedy."

I shrugged one shoulder.

"My deepest condolences. Please let me know if there

is anything I can do to help." He sat there in disbelief a moment. "She was such a spectacular woman, so full of life."

Heath expressed his sympathies also. It was Amanda's turn. Man was this going to be awkward. Here she's just expressed her secret feelings toward me and now the avenue to pursue them had been tragically opened. I knew neither of the others present knew that little tidbit.

"I ... I can't begin to say how sorry I am for you, Jon. She was one of a kind, a real treasure. If I can ... if *we* can help in any capacity, don't hesitate in asking." She sipped some water. "Are you holding up okay? Your children?"

"They're still in shock. But they're too busy to dwell on it much. I know they have powerful emotions, but in their culture it's frowned upon to show them much." I shook my head softly. "I'm sure in time they'll be fine. They know how passionate Sapale was about the colony. They can demonstrate their love by working that much harder. That's sort of their way, too."

"Gentlemen," Amanda said to the others, "if you don't have any other questions, might I speak alone with General Ryan?"

They looked at each other, clearly a bit confused. Both enjoined me to allow them to help in any way, shook my hand, and then they left us. Carlos said he'd pack and that I should let him know when we were leaving.

"Jon," she said after the door had closed, "I *am* truly sorry. I know how it must seem, my words to you."

"Don't stress. It wasn't your fault."

"But ... you might, you—"

"What? Think you jinxed her? You said the words and she died. You *willed* it?" I swiped my hand angrily between us. "Forget it. Superstition and bad omens aside, I don't think you have *that* much influence." I regretted those words the instant they were past my stupid lips.

"Ouch," was her quick response. "But I guess I deserved that, didn't I?"

"No, Mandy, you didn't. I'm an ass. I lashed out because I'm in pain and you were an easy target. Please forgive me."

Coolly she replied, "Consider it done." Her jaw quivered, but she refused to cry. "I do want you to know I meant every word I said. The fact that my timing was so *epically* bad is something I can't change." She sniffed deeply. "God, I need to learn to keep my mouth shut."

"Nah," I said with my best cute-guy grin. "You keep using it. You're just speaking from your heart. The rest of us'll work on putting up with you."

"Thanks, I think. That was a compliment right?"

"Who can say?"

"Are you planning on staying put on Azsuram? Lord knows there's a lot of work that needs to be done there."

"For a spell, yes."

She raised an eyebrow. "For a spell? That sounds limited."

"Maybe it will be. I'm sorting through things in my head."

"I understand. You've been through a horrible experience. It's only natural."

I shifted in my chair but didn't respond verbally.

"What?" she asked. "You're not saying something."

"I need to get my head straight, sure. But I also think there's a thing I need to do."

"A thing? What? Learn to play a musical instrument? Become a master gardener?"

I chuckled. "No. None of the above."

She got a very concerned look on her face. "You're not planning to go after the Berrillians are you?"

I sat quietly a moment. "Nah, don't think so." I was silent a few seconds. "At first, after they killed her, I was crazy with thoughts of revenge. I wanted to slaughter every one of them; men, women, and children. Twice each, if possible."

"But not now?"

"No, not now. I still hate the very thought of their existence, but I'm not going on a vengeful crusade. I spoke with a friend, someone I respect a lot. He told me I would be making a mistake of major proportions."

"Toño?"

"Nah. But he told me the same in so many words. Kymee set me straight."

"So you went back after the fight?"

"Yeah. I wanted to know if it was their ship that helped us out."

"And since you knew beforehand it wasn't, you wanted to rub their noses in something smelly."

"Basically," I tapped my finger on my chest. "Hey, I'm no angel."

"Never suspected you were." She smiled warmly. "So what might you be doing? You know you're always welcome here officially and, you know, unofficially."

"No. I have to find me."

"I believe the expression is *find myself*, not *me*."

"No, Ms. Grammar, I meant what I said. I need to find someone who I think is me."

"Now I'm completely lost."

"I believe he is, too," I said vacantly. "That's why I need to find the man I might have become."

She rested her head in her hands. "*What* are you on about? You sound like an old man bemoaning past choices."

"No, Mandy, I mean it literally. I think there's another version of me out there in this time stream. He's a

269

me that lived a very different life. If I'm right, he's the one who gave us the membrane tech."

"Why do you need to find him, assuming he even exists?"

"Because I think he's carrying more pain than anyone should have to. He's been through hell and not come out the other side yet, as the storybooks predict."

"And you're the man to help him?"

"Who knows? I *am* the man to find him."

"Maybe. It seems to me the other Jon Ryan doesn't want to be found. Maybe you should respect his privacy and leave him be. Hmm?"

"I know how this one thinks. I'm betting he doesn't feel he's *worth* saving."

"That makes no sense."

"Exactly. We *are* talking about me, here. Why should it?"

To Be Continued ...

GLOSSARY OF MAIN
CHARACTERS AND PLACES:

Number in parenthesis after name is the volume the name first appeared in.

Ablo (2): Led Uhoor to attack Azsuram after Tho died.

Almonerca (2): Daughter of Fashallana, twin of Noresmel. Name means *sees tomorrow*.

Alpha Centauri (1): Fourth planetary target on Jon's long solo voyage on *Ark 1*. Three stars in system, AC-A, AC-B, and AC-C (aka Proxima Centauri). AC-B has eight planets, three in habitable zone. AC-B 5 was initially named *Jon*, by Jon Ryan, until he met the falzorn. AC-B 3 is Kaljax. PC has one planet in habitable zone.

Alvin (1): The ship's AI on *Ark 1*. aka Al.

Phil Anderson (1): TV host, sidekick of Jane Geraty.

Azsuram (2): See also Hodor, Groombridge-1618, and Klonsar. BG 3 was discovered by Seamus O'Leary, the pilot of *Ark 4*. Site of Sapale's new Kaljaxian society. Name means *love of others*.

Barnard's Star (1): First planetary target of *Ark 1*. BS 2 and 3 are in habitable zone. BS 3 was Ffffuttoe's home, as well as ancient, extinct race called the Emitonians. See BS 2 below.

The Beast Without Eyes (2): The enemy of Gumnolar, hence, the devil for inhabitants of Listhelon.

Braldone (1): Believed to be the foreseen savior on Kaljax.

Brathos (1): The Kaljaxian version of Hell.

Brood-mate (1): On Kaljax, the male partner in a marriage.

Brood's-mate (1): On Kaljax, the female partner in a marriage.

BS 2 (1): The planet Oowaoa, home of the highly advanced Deavoriath race.

Command prerogatives (2): The Deavoriathian tools installed to allow operation of a vortex. Also used to probe substances. Given to the android Jon Ryan.

Calrf (2): A Kaljaxian stew that Jon particularly disliked.

Faith Clinton (2): Descendent of the currently presidential Clintons. First a senator, later the first president elected in space. Assassinated soon after taking office.

President Charles Clinton (1): US President during part of Jon's voyage on *Ark 1*.

Sherman Collins (1): Secretary of State to President John Marshall when it was discovered Jupiter would destroy the Earth.

Cube (2): See vortex.

Cycle (2): Length of year on Listhelon. Five cycles roughly equal one Earth year.

Davdiad (1): God-figure on Kaljax.

Deavoriath (1): Mighty and ancient race from Oowaoa. Technically the most advanced civilization in the galaxy. Used to rule many galaxies, then withdrew to improve their minds and characters. Three arms and legs. Currently live forever.

Toño DeJesus (1): Chief scientist in both the android and Ark programs. Course of events forced him to reluctantly become an android.

Carlos De La Frontera (2): Brilliant assistant to Toño, became an android to infiltrate Marshall's evil team.

Chuck Thomas (2): Chairman of the Joint Chiefs of Staff, one of The Four Horsemen, and the first military person downloaded to an android by Stuart Marshall's evil team.

Delta-Class vehicles (1): The wondrous new spaceships used in Project Ark. Real fast!

Dolirca (2): Daughter in Fashallana's second set of twins. Took charge of Ffffuttoe's asexual buds. Name means *love all*.

Draldon (2): Son of Sapale. Twin with Vhalisma. Name means *meets the day*.

Matt Duncan (2): Chief of staff for the evil President Stuart Marshall. Became android that was destroyed. Marshall resurrected him in the body of Marilyn Monroe. Matt no likey that!

Enterprise (2): US command worldships.

Epsilon Eridani (1): Fourth target for *Ark 1*. One habitable planet, EE 5. Locally named Cholarazy, the planet is home to several advanced civilizations. The Drell and Foressál are the main rivals. Leaders Boabbor and Gothor are bitter rivals. Humanoids with three digits.

Exeter (2): UN command worldship.

Farmship (2): Cored-out asteroids devoted not to human habitation but to crop and animal production. There are only five, but they allow for sufficient calories for all worldships and a few luxuries.

Devon Flannigan (2): Former baker who was the assassin of Faith Clinton.

Fashallana (2): First daughter of Sapale. Twin to JJ. Name means *blessed one*.

Falzorn (1): Nasty predatory snakes of Alpha Centauri-

B 5. Their name is a curse word among the inhabitants of neighboring Kaljax.

Faxél (3): The Berrillian species name for itself.

Ffffuttoe (1): Gentle-natured flat bear like creature of BS 3. Possesses low-level sentience.

Form (2): Title of someone able to be the operator of vortex using their command prerogatives.

Jodfderal (2): Son in Fashallana's second set of twins. Name means *strength of ten*.

Jane Geraty (1): TV newswoman who had an affair with newly minted android Jon. Gave birth to Jon Ryan II, her only child.

Groombridge-1618 3 (1): Original human name for the planet GB 3 = Azsuram.

Gumnolar (1): Deity of the Listhelons. Very demanding.

Habitable zone (1): Aka the Goldilocks Zone. The region surrounding a star in which orbiting planets can have liquid water on their surface.

Indigo (1): Second and final wife of the original Jon Ryan, not the android. They had five children, including their version of Jon Ryan II.

Infinity-charges (2): Membrane-based bombs that expand, ripping whatever they're in to shreds.

Jon Junior, JJ (2): Son of Sapale. One of her first set of twins. The apple of Jon Ryan's eye.

Secretary Mary Kahl (2): UN Secretary General at the time of the human exodus from Earth.

Klonsar (2): The Uhoor name for Azsuram, which they claim as their hunting grounds.

Kendell Jackson (2): Major general who became head of Project Ark after DeJesus left. Forced to become an android by Stuart Marshall.

Kashiril (2): From Sapale's second set of twins. Name means *answers the wind*.

Lilith, aka Lily (2): Second AI on *Shearwater*. Al no likey!

Bin Li (2): New UN Secretary General after Mary Kahl was killed.

Listhelon (1): Enemy species from third planet orbiting Lacaille 9352. Aquatic, they have huge, overlapping fang-like teeth, a small bumpy head, big, bulging eyes - articulated somewhat like a lizard's. Their eyes bob around in a nauseating manner. Their skin is sleek, with thin scales. They sport gills, with a slit in their thick neck on either side. Maniacally devoted to their God, Gumnolar.

Luhman 16a (1): The second target of *Ark* 1. Eight planets, only one in habitable zone, LH 2. Two fighting species are the *Sarcorit* that are the size and shape of glazed donuts and *Jinicgus* looking like hot dogs. Both are unfriendly by nature.

Manly (2): Jon's pet name for the consciousness of an unclear nature in the vortex, *Wrath*. He refers to himself as the vortex manipulator.

Stuart Marshall (1): Born human on Earth, became president there. Before exodus, he downloaded into an android and became the insane menace of his people.

Noresmel (2): Fashallana's daughter, twin of Almonerca. Name means *kiss of love*.

Seamus O'Leary (2): The pilot of *Ark 4*, discovered Azsuram.

The One That Is All (2): The mentally linked Deavoriath community.

Offlin (2): Son of Otollar. Piloted ship that tried to attack Earth and was captured by Jon.

Otollar (2): Leader, or Warrior One, of Listhelon. Died when he failed to defeat humans.

Owant (2): Second Warrior to Otollar.

Oowaoa (1): See *Deavoriath*.

Senator Bob Patrick (2): One of The Four Horsemen, co-conspirator with Stuart Marshall.

Chief Justice Sam Peterson (2): Member of Stuart Marshall's inner circle, The Four Horsemen.

Plo (2): First Uhoor to attack Azsuram.

Prime (2): Pet name for the android of Carlos De La Frontera.

Heath Ryan (2): Descendant of original Jon Ryan, entered politics reluctantly.

Jon Ryan (1): Both the human template and the android who sailed into legend.

Jon III and his wife, Abree (2): Jon's grandson, via the human Jon Ryan.

Piper Ryan (2): Heath Ryan's wife.

Carl Roger (1): Chief of staff to President John Marshall, before Earth was destroyed.

Sapale (1): Brood's-mate to android Jon Ryan. From Kaljax.

General Saunders (1): Hardscrabble original head of Project Ark.

Shearwater (2): Jon's second starship, sleek, fast and bitchin'.

Captain Simpson (1): Pilot of *Ark* 3. Discovered Listhelon orbiting Lacaille 9352.

Space-time congruity manipulator (1): Hugely helpful force field.

Phillip Szeto (2): Head of CIA under Stuart Marshall.

Tho (2): The head Uhoor, referred to herself as *the mother of the Uhoor*.

Tralmore (1): Heaven in the religion of Kaljax.

Amanda Walker (2): Vice president then president, a distant relative of Jane Geraty. Wife of Faith Clinton.

Uhoor (2): Massive whale-like creatures of immense age. They feed off black holes and propel themselves though space as if it was water.

Uto (1): Alternate time-line android Jon Ryan, possibly ...

Vhalisma (2): From Sapale's third set of twins. Name means *drink love*.

Vortex (2): Deavoriath vessel in cube shape with a mass of 200,000 tons.

Vortex manipulator (2): Sentient computer-like being in vortex.

Wolf 359 (1): Third target for *Ark 1*. Two small planets: WS 3 bad prospect, WS 4 about as bad.

Wolnara (2): Twin in Sapale's second set. Name means *wisdom sees*.

Worldships (1): Cored-out asteroids serve as colony ships for the human exodus.

Yibitriander (1): Three legged Deavoriath, past Form of Jon's vortex and son of Kymee.

Lt. Gen. Cynthia York (1): Head of Project Ark when Jon returns from epic voyage.

SHAMELESS SELF-PROMOTION

(WHO DOESN'T LOVE THAT?)

Thank you for joining me on the Forever Journey! I hope you enjoyed the Ryanverse. All six books in the series are available on Amazon. They are also on Audible thanks to Podium Publishing. The boxed volumes are *The Forever*, Parts 1 2 & 3.

There is a sequel to *The Forever Series,* also. *Galaxy On Fire* begins with *Embers.* Once you finish this series be sure to check out the new one. Trust me, it's even better.

The third series in the Ryanverse begins with *Return of the Ancient Gods.* The first book is *Return of the Ancient Gods.*

Please do leave me a review on Amazon. They're more precious than gold.

My Website: craigrobertsonblog.wordpress.com

Feel free to email me comments or to discuss any part of the series. contact@craigarobertson.com Also, you can ask to be on my email list. I'll send out infrequent alerts concerning new material or some of the extras I'm planning in the near future.

For more about me and my other novels, check out my

Amazon Author's Page: https://www.amazon.com/-/e/
B00522FURO
There you can learn about me and my other books. The
fun will never stop.

Facebook? But of course. https://www.face-
book.com/Craig-A-Robertsons-Authors-Page-
943237189133053/

Wow! That's a whole lot of social media. But, I'm so
worth it, so bear with me.

Don't be a stranger, at least any stranger than you already
are ... craig

www.ingramcontent.com/pod-product-compliance
Lightning Source LLC
Chambersburg PA
CBHW060433030726
47495CB00003B/864